MW00986587

THE GUILD CODEX: WARPED / FOUR

STOLEN SORCERY
& OTHER MISADVENTURES

ANNETTE MARIE
ROB JACOBSEN

Stolen Sorcery & Other Misadventures
The Guild Codex: Warped / Book Four
By Annette Marie & Rob Jacobsen

Copyright © 2023 by Annette Marie
www.annettemarie.ca

All Rights Reserved. No part of this publication may be reproduced,
distributed, or transmitted in any form or by any means, including
photocopying, recording, or other electronic or mechanical methods, without
the prior written permission of the publisher, except in the case of brief
quotations for review purposes.

This is a work of fiction. Any resemblance to actual persons, places, or events
is purely coincidental.

Dark Owl Fantasy Inc.
PO Box 88106, Rabbit Hill Post Office
Edmonton, AB, Canada T6R 0M5
www.darkowlfantasy.com

Cover Copyright © 2023 by Annette Ahner

Editing by Elizabeth Darkley
arrowheadediting.wordpress.com

ISBN 978-1-988153-71-1

MORE BOOKS BY ANNETTE MARIE

STEEL & STONE UNIVERSE

Steel & Stone Series

Chase the Dark
Bind the Soul
Yield the Night
Reap the Shadows
Unleash the Storm
Steel & Stone

Spell Weaver Trilogy

The Night Realm
The Shadow Weave
The Blood Curse

OTHER WORKS

Red Winter Trilogy

Red Winter
Dark Tempest
Immortal Fire

THE GUILD CODEX

CLASSES OF MAGIC

Spiritalis

Psychica

Arcana

Demonica

Elementaria

MYTHIC

A person with magical ability

MPD / MAGIPOL

The organization that regulates mythics and their activities

ROGUE

A mythic living in violation of MPD laws

STOLEN SORCERY
& OTHER MISADVENTURES

1

"SHIT'S ABOUT TO GO DOWN."

Beside me, Vincent Park nodded in terse agreement. It'd been a while since we'd shared a cubicle, but he'd borrowed Lienna's empty chair without even asking first. I hadn't complained. My cubicle offered a better angle for spying on the rest of the bullpen than his did.

"She's not actually going to do it, is she?" Vinny whispered. "No one is that stupid."

I shook my head. "I wouldn't call it stupid. Desperate, maybe. Angry, definitely. But she isn't stupid."

At the front of the bullpen, Agent Clarice Vigneault stood with her arms crossed, tapping her foot against the floor like an electrocuted Michael Flatley. Her tightly curled black hair vibrated in harmony with her spastic foot, and her eyes, normally soft and welcoming, were fixated on one of the bullpen's three entrances with an air of furious expectation.

2 ♠ MARIE & JACOBSEN

Everyone else surreptitiously watched her with the same doomsday outlook as me. The atmosphere in the precinct had been toxically tense since Söze had shown his extra ugly usurper side, and in the wake of recent events, the levels of paranoia, defensiveness, and I-don't-get-paid-enough-for-this-bullshit had climbed so high they were out of orbit.

"I should stop her," I mumbled, sliding away from my hiding spot behind the cubicle wall. "Distract her or something."

Vinny caught my sleeve and tugged me back. "You want to tell a senior agent what to do?"

"I want to make sure a *good* agent doesn't make a career-ending decision because she's rightfully pissed off."

"Don't exaggerate. It won't be career ending," Vinny said with his usual smug confidence, but he couldn't hide the worried crease between his brows. He was concerned for Agent Vigneault too.

Honestly, Vinny wasn't *that* bad. The enemy of my enemy is my friend, and all that. Plus, Vincent Park had proven himself beyond my ability to doubt him—a highly acute ability, I might add. When it had really counted, he'd fought on the side of justice, and that made his know-it-all, ass-kissing swagger a little more bearable.

I still didn't *like* him. That was impossible. Like liver-flavored ice cream. Who could ever like that? But I could tolerate him.

Caught between the urge to divert Agent Vigneault and Vinny's insistent pull on my sleeve, I hesitated for a minute too long. The bullpen door swung open, and the bane of the precinct's existence walked through.

Agent Söze, Internal Affairs. I didn't know his first name. I didn't care to learn it. All I needed to know was that he was the slimiest blend of evil and insidious, he was totally cool with all means of villainy as long as he could disguise it as MPD-approved justice, and he had totalitarian control of the precinct and all its agents.

If it seems like I'm exaggerating his winning qualities, may I present Case Study A: Around one week ago, he resurrected an ancient MPD provision to sanction the annihilation of an entire guild. He failed—barely—but the fact that he was fine with the mass murder of innocents is indisputable. That, and he has it out for the Crow and Hammer for reasons unknown.

Following him into the bullpen was one of his interchangeable cronies that he'd called in to support his hostile takeover of our precinct. Today's IA goon was Agent Kade, a strong-and-silent type in his early forties with a linebacker's shoulders, perpetual stubble, and Bruce Willis's haircut. He'd been introduced to us as a sorcerer, but he looked like he relied on his fists as much as his magic.

Agent Vigneault swooped toward Söze the moment he appeared. "Agent Söze! I demand an explanation!"

I winced at her aggressive tone. This definitely wouldn't go well for her.

"What is the problem, Agent?" Söze asked neutrally. He didn't lower his voice for the same reason he'd shown up in the bullpen instead of meeting with Agent Vigneault in private: he intended to make this a public display.

Did Agent Vigneault realize that, or was she too angry to care?

"You destroyed a six-month-long investigation!" she half shouted. "My team and I were *weeks* away from bringing down an entire chain of criminal activity!"

The usual ruckus of the bullpen dropped dramatically as every agent pretended not to watch the blooming spectacle. We all knew about the underground network of criminals running illegal bounties in Vancouver that she'd been slowly but surely unraveling—until Söze had pulled the plug earlier this morning.

"The whole illegal bounty system has a single lynchpin—one individual acting as bank and broker," Agent Vigneault seethed. "We know from our informant that the lynchpin keeps records on *every single user*, both clients and assassins. Taking him down will net us evidence for dozens, or even hundreds, of crimes."

Söze gazed at her like she was a particularly dumb-looking dog drooling on his carpet. "Your aspirations are quite grand for a case based entirely on the baseless claims of an untrustworthy informant. You've not only wasted six months of your own time but also monopolized an entire team on this wild goose chase."

"Wild goose—" She broke off into furious splutters. It was strange to see Agent Vigneault, who generally had the temperament of a kindergarten teacher on Xanax, lose her head like this. Söze did that to people.

"I took control of this precinct with one clear mandate," he said, a sneer creeping into his dead voice. "To root out inefficiency, incompetence, and corruption among the agents here. My subordinates are in the process of determining which of those sins applies to your investigation, Agent Vigneault."

"Are—are you kidding me?" Vigneault's hands clenched into fists. "This is crazy! You're deliberately blocking my investigation, aren't you? Why?"

Söze's dark eyes narrowed. "Are you questioning my integrity, Agent Vigneault?"

"You're damn right I am," she shot back, stepping within inches of his face, her voice dropping into a growl. "I'm questioning your integrity, I'm questioning your ethics, and I'm questioning your sanity!"

"Oh, shit," Vinny muttered.

"That sounds an awful lot like insubordination," Söze observed. He looked over his shoulder at his bald-headed goon. "Agent Kade, take Agent Vigneault into custody."

Vigneault recoiled, anger instantly replaced by shock. "Are you arresting me?"

Söze's lips curled into a faint, slimy smile. "Are you resisting arrest?"

Agent Kade produced a pair of handcuffs and slapped them on Vigneault's wrists. She didn't resist, too stunned to do anything about it. The bullpen was so quiet that the metal clicks of the cuffs ratcheting shut rang through the space.

Ever since Söze had taken control of our precinct, every agent had been a wee bit high-strung. Even the agents who supported Söze—not that anyone talked openly about that kind of thing—hadn't been particularly chill. But at this moment, everyone's blood pressure was hitting a new level of intensity. Which, I suspected, had been Söze's plan.

"I'll give you time in holding to reconsider your stance on your terminated investigation." Though ostensibly speaking to Vigneault, Söze was addressing all of us. "If we can't reach an understanding, I will personally dissect every case you have ever touched. I will dismantle your job history, your personal history, and your family's history, until every mistake, every defect, and every sin are laid bare. Do you understand me?"

Holy.

Totalitarian.

Shit.

Vigneault didn't respond, her jaw clenched tight.

Söze nodded curtly to Kade, who guided the cuffed agent toward the door leading to the elevator—and from there, the holding cells. As they left, I spotted Captain Blythe leaning against the wall beside the lobby doors, her arms crossed in all her sterntastic glory.

She'd witnessed the whole spectacle, but like us, she was helpless to do anything about it.

Söze surveyed the bullpen like a ruling lord observing his cowering, subservient vassals, nodded in a satisfied way, and disappeared as ominously as he'd arrived. A low, wary buzz of conversation spread through the bullpen in his absence.

I slumped back in my chair, exhausted by yet another moral defeat.

Vinny puffed out an unsteady breath. Though the ordeal was over, he didn't vacate my partner's chair.

"What's going to happen?" he asked in an undertone.

I shook my head. I didn't know any better than he did. The future of our precinct was about as clear as muddy waters churned up by a piranha feeding frenzy.

"I suppose we should get to work before Söze decides that slacking is a capital crime." Reluctantly sitting up again, I glanced at Vinny. "What are you working on these days?"

He shrugged, avoiding my gaze. "Odds and ends, mostly."

Not a very Vinny-ish response. Normally, he'd have bragged about the high-profile cases he was tackling alongside experienced senior agent, Brennan Harris. Vinny had started at the MPD around the same time as me, and at that point, he'd worn cargo shorts to work every single day. However, ever since he'd partnered up with his idol, his wardrobe had taken a hard shift toward the formal black-and-whites that senior agents like Harris favored.

Some would say going from cargo shorts to a suit is an upgrade. I consider it a lateral move.

Fashion evolution aside, Vinny should've been following Harris around like a mohawked Labrador puppy. But Agent Vigneault wasn't the only one who'd run afoul of Söze. The IA asshole had paired Harris with one of his own lackeys to punish Vinny, leaving the rookie agent high, dry, and partnerless.

I actually felt bad for him. Shocking, I know, but the anti-Söze team needed to stick together.

Vincent tapped a finger restlessly on Lienna's desk, then leaned toward me. "I talked to Agent Harris earlier this morning. Söze assigned him to investigate the death of a GM."

My eyebrows shot up. Guild Masters were hotshots in the mythic community, and a sudden death among their ranks was something the MPD always took seriously.

"Did Harris say which GM?" I asked.

"Georgia Johannsen of Arcana Historia."

I swore under my breath. I'd visited that guild a few times, though I'd never met the GM.

"The librarian found her dead inside the guild this morning," Vinny said. "The thing is, while Agent Harris was talking to me, Agent Söze passed by. When he realized what we were discussing, he snapped at Agent Harris to keep confidential case details to himself."

"Confidential?" I repeated with a frown. "A case involving a GM's death isn't automatically classified."

"Yeah, exactly."

I thought for a moment, then shoved my chair back. "Come on."

Captain Blythe was still loitering around the perimeter of the bullpen—unsurprising since Söze had stripped away most of her duties—and her eyebrows arched questioningly as Vincent and I approached.

"Hey, Cap. Vinny just told me something interesting."

I waved at him to speak. He shifted uncomfortably, puffed out his cheeks, then repeated what he'd told me. Blythe's expression went stonier with each word.

"I hadn't heard a word about this," she said flatly. "Söze must've suppressed the information."

"Definitely," I agreed. "The whole bullpen would know by now otherwise."

The captain's lips thinned as she thought. "Agent Morris, I want you and Agent Shen at Arcana Historia immediately."

"I don't think Söze will appreciate us inviting ourselves to a possible crime scene."

"I don't give a shit what Agent Söze appreciates. He's keeping this quiet for a reason, and I want to know why. Do you understand what I'm saying, Agent Morris?"

I gave a small nod. "Loud and clear."

"What about me?" asked Vinny, staring expectantly at our boss.

Blythe considered his question. "I need you to keep your head down and your lines of communication with Agent Harris open."

Vinny absorbed that with a defeated slump to his shoulders. He didn't like the idea of tapping his idol for information on the enemy, but to my surprise, he responded with a firm, "Yes, ma'am."

The captain scanned the bullpen. "Where is Agent Shen? She's supposed to be on duty."

"I'll find her," I answered, "and whisk her away to the magical land of suspicious GM deaths and douchebag IA agents."

"See that you do."

Vinny and I split as we returned to our respective cubicles. I locked my computer, grabbed my black denim jacket off the back of my chair, and headed straight for the elevator. I didn't need to *find* Agent Lienna Shen; I knew exactly where she was.

She was hiding.

2

"I WASN'T HIDING."

"Oh, please," I said as Lienna and I got off the elevator and stepped into the parking garage. "You literally ducked behind a cardboard box when I walked in."

My partner's casual appearance—hooded jacket and jeans with her trusty satchel slung over one shoulder, beads woven into her long dark hair, and bracelets clacking whimsically with every step—was at odds with her tense demeanor. Her shoulders were stiff, and the subtle, playful glint in her eyes that I loved was notably absent.

"It wasn't even a big box," I teased, hoping to elicit one of her patented eye rolls. "You must have been terrible at hide-and-go-seek as a child."

"I dropped something." She stepped around to the driver's side of our luxurious four-door smart car. "I was picking it up, that's all."

We both got into the micromobile. With its extra pair of doors, it was pretending to be a lot bigger than it was. Lienna and I had seen a couple of our previous two-door models destroyed—one via a bomb and the other thanks to a demon's temper tantrum—and I had little faith that the extra cab space would prevent me from eating my own shinbones in a head-on collision.

"Dropped what?" I inquired as my partner guided the smart car up the parking garage ramp and out into the damp, chilly weather. "Your shift schedule? We were supposed to start working on that Sea Devils report yesterday."

"Are we really gonna do that bullshit report?"

Calling our report on the Sea Devils guild "bullshit" was demeaning to the fecal matter of a bovine male, which was actually useful in certain circumstances. It could be used for fertilizer.

The Sea Devils guild was another item on Söze's "You Offended Me and Now You Will Pay" to-do list. They'd played a role in preventing the outright obliteration of the Crow and Hammer last week, and Söze had really, *really* wanted to obliterate them. Thus, the authoritarian IA asshole had opened an investigation into the legality of every action the guild had ever taken over the course of its extended history.

It was a paper-pushing witch hunt that would take months, and Söze had assigned it to us as a bureaucratic middle finger for our role in saving the Crow and Hammer.

I wasn't thrilled with the idea of screwing over a guild that I would generally consider to be on the "good guy" end of the spectrum, but for the sake of appearances, I'd been fake-working alone at my cubicle for the past three days.

Meanwhile, Lienna had been holed up in the archives, avoiding most forms of human and/or mythic contact.

"No," I answered. "But you could help me *pretend* to do the report."

"For all you know," she said in an attempt at lighthearted indignation, "that's exactly what I'm doing in the archives."

"Or," I countered with a wave of my finger, "could your new avoidance strategy have something to do with the portals Söze and his goon squad stole from your top-secret subterranean lab?"

Her humor melted away. "It's been *days*, Kit."

"And we haven't heard the ittiest-bittiest peep about portals from Söze or any of the IA sycophants who follow him around." I adjusted my legs to avoid a muscle cramp. "Do you think hiding in the archives will make him forget about you?"

Her hands tightened on the steering wheel. "I expected him to turn over the portals as evidence of me practicing illegal magic. The fact that he hasn't worries me."

"That *worries* you? I would've thought the power-tripping lunatic who hates us more than Indiana Jones hates snakes *not* tossing you in the clink would be a relief."

"I don't *want* to be arrested, but if Söze isn't using the portals as evidence, that must mean he wants to keep their existence a secret."

"Because he's going to use them."

She nodded. "But for what?"

Silence enveloped the car's cramped interior as we mulled over all the horrible, likely creepy shit Söze could do with a set of portals in his slimy paws.

"I found something in the archives," she said suddenly. "It's in my bag."

I grabbed her satchel off the center console and opened it up. Inside was the usual menagerie of deadly artifacts—her wooden Rubik's cube, stun marbles, the temperamental wooden knife that could immobilize anyone the user targeted or the user themselves—as well as a thin manila folder.

I pulled it out. "This?"

"Yeah."

I flipped the folder open, fully expecting something that would either illuminate or complicate our current set of insurmountable problems. Instead, I found myself frowning at a photocopied file from … 1927? I scanned the dark, smudged text that had been hammered out on a typewriter before the Second World War.

"'Mythic of Public Note,'" I read aloud. My gaze moved down to the name beneath that title, and my jaw dropped. "*Lon Chaney?*"

Lienna smiled. "Yup."

"This guy's a legend! He was the greatest silent film actor of his time. The man of a thousand faces! He was the Phantom of the Opera, Quasimodo, Fagin in *Oliver Twist*!" I pored over the document. "Why does the MPD have a file on him?"

"Why do you think?"

"No way. He was a *mythic*?"

She nodded. "It doesn't say what type exactly, but—"

"'Mr. Chaney uses his robust magical capabilities to get inside the minds of the tortured characters he portrays.' Sounds like Psychica. That is so cool!" I reluctantly looked up from the document. "Is this part of a case you're working on?"

She shrugged, her eyes on the road. "I just thought you'd find it interesting."

"Damn right." I already had my nose back in the file, curiosity burning through every fiber of my cinephile being. Chaney had been notoriously private, and I was dying to see what the MPD of times past had known about his secretive life.

I only closed the file when Lienna pulled to a stop on the narrow street where Arcana Historia awaited us. The architecture of the building resembled an unimaginative gray brick: rectangular and bland. Lienna parked the smart car out front behind two other MPD vehicles, and we entered through the front door.

Inside was an empty reception desk for a private tutoring service—the guild's public front. We pushed through the frosted glass doors to one side of the small lobby, passed a display case of ancient grimoires, and went through another unlocked door to enter the heart of the guild: an expansive library filled with books on magic, potions, spells, mythic history, and anything else a supernaturally inclined bookworm could hope to lay eyes on.

I expected to find a parade of Söze's handpicked agents and a dead body, but I saw only one person: an elderly lady with a mound of gray curls atop her head, sitting at one of the tables in the middle of the library. Her red-rimmed eyes stared blankly ahead as she sniffled.

Lienna made a beeline for the old woman. "Edith?"

"Agent Shen," she greeted weakly. "Are you here for …?"

Lienna lowered herself into the chair next to Edith. "I'm so sorry. How are you holding up?"

"She seemed completely fine last night. We talked about updating the Spiritalis catalogue." Edith took a shaky breath. "I've worked with Georgia for almost fifteen years, and now she—I can't believe it."

Fresh tears wet her eyes, and Lienna gently took hold of her hand, silently consoling her.

I stood a respectful distance away, leaning against the end of a bookshelf. I'd been to Arcana Historia a few times, but Lienna frequented the library. She must have befriended some of the librarians during her visits, including Edith.

"Has anyone spoken to you yet?" Lienna asked after a quiet moment. "Any of the agents?"

Edith shook her head. "Not after I showed her the—after I took her to Georgia."

"Her?" I asked. Agent Harris was many things, but not likely to be mistaken for a woman.

"An agent. Strong-looking woman in a gray suit."

That sounded like Agent Suarez, one of Söze's lackeys. I'd seen a second MPD vehicle outside, but I'd been hoping it belonged to literally any MPD employee besides a Söze loyalist.

"There's another agent as well," Edith added. "He arrived a few minutes afterward and introduced himself. Agent Harris, he said. He's going to speak with me after he ... examines the scene."

"Where are they now?" Lienna asked.

"In the lazaretto."

I frowned. In the what? That was a word I'd never heard before. It sounded fancy.

Lienna seemed to know exactly what a lazaretto was. "Is that where Georgia is?"

The librarian nodded. "I thought I was the first one here this morning because I usually open the library on Wednesdays. But ..."

"Do you know why Georgia was in the lazaretto?" Lienna asked, still holding Edith's hand.

"She sometimes stayed late to examine the new arrivals," Edith answered. "It wasn't unusual. She preferred to do it after the library closed because of the sensitive nature of the books. More privacy."

My interest in this place spiked. What books of a sensitive nature was Arcana Historia hiding?

"Was Georgia here last night when you left?" At Edith's nod, Lienna looked around the expansive room. "Did you notice anything out of place this morning?"

"No. Everything was normal. I disarmed the security system and made a cup of tea. It was only when I went to see if Georgia had left me any work in the lazaretto … I unlocked the door and … that's when I found her."

Edith broke into quiet sobs. Lienna put an arm around her shoulders, giving her a soft squeeze.

It was strange to see my partner, who'd once threatened to reconfigure my bowels into a rough approximation of Stonehenge, offering such tender comfort. I already knew there were more sides to Lienna Shen than I'd seen, and this reinforced that knowledge.

"Agent Morris and I are going to talk to the other agents," she told Edith. "We'll check in on you soon."

"One more question," I jumped in, pitching my voice to be low and soothing. "Just a quick one. You said you disarmed the security system. Had it been armed all night?"

"Yes." She wiped at her eyes with a crumpled tissue. "It didn't record any activity. It wasn't disarmed by anyone else, none of the exterior doors were unlocked … nothing. Georgia … didn't go home last night."

I nodded. Since Georgia hadn't left, it was unlikely anyone had entered the building either.

Lienna gave the old woman another comforting squeeze, then beckoned me to follow her through the stacks of books.

"The lazaretto?" I whispered as I fell into step beside her. "What is that?"

"A locked room where the library keeps all books that might be too dangerous to be put on the shelves."

"Too dangerous?"

"Books that contain illegal magic, mostly. Usually seized during raids or black-market stings. If the book is deemed safe, it can go out on the shelf. If not, it's either quarantined or destroyed. Georgia Johannsen was one of only a few mythics in the city certified by the MPD to make those decisions."

"Dangerous, illegal books," I reiterated. "Do you think she was murdered over a wildly lethal spell manual or something?"

"We don't even know if she *was* murdered. I didn't want to ask Edith about the manner of death."

Lienna guided me through another row of books into a short hallway and stopped at a door with a *Guild Members Only* plaque. She swung it open.

The interior of the lazaretto was strangely similar to what I'd imagined. Dusty piles of books in various states of disrepair were stacked across a long table pushed up against the wall, and a row of locked cabinets lined the opposite wall. Fluorescent bulbs buzzed above us, casting painfully bright light over the room.

Agent Harris stood near the table, blue latex gloves starkly contrasting with his starched black-and-white attire as he took notes.

Directly in front of him was Georgia Johannsen. She was on her knees, leaning forward at an angle that would have landed her face-first on the floor if it hadn't been for the length of rope wrapped around her neck, the other end tied to the locked cabinet behind her.

Harris looked up, displeased by our unexpected presence. "What are you two doing here?"

Lienna stepped boldly into the room. "We're here to help with the investigation."

Her statement was so matter-of-fact that Agent Harris didn't even question it. He merely frowned and looked back down at his notes. "There isn't much to investigate. As you can see, it appears to be a suicide."

"Where's Agent Suarez?" I asked.

He shrugged. "She was here when I arrived but left shortly after."

I gave Lienna a side-eyed look. She raised her eyebrows. Why would Suarez show up only to leave without participating in the investigation?

Lienna took out her phone and aimed it around the lazaretto, snapping a series of photos, while I got a better look at the body. Sorrow trickled through me. I hadn't known Georgia, but her death would leave a mark on many lives. GMs were integral figures in the lives of their guildeds and local mythic communities. She would be missed.

"There's no sign of a struggle," Harris said in a monotone. "No apparent injuries to the victim other than those associated with hanging. No signs of forced entry into the room."

Lienna made a thoughtful noise, focused on her photo-taking quest. I turned to the assortment of illegal books on the table, most of which were in languages I couldn't read. Georgia had taken great care with them—except for one. It looked like someone had used a live grenade as a bookmark. The pages were crumpled, if not shredded, and the spine was bent in a way that would make a casual perusal of its illicit secrets next to impossible.

Wedged underneath the beat-up book was a familiar clear plastic bag with a zip top—an MPD evidence bag.

"Lienna," I murmured, waving at her to join me.

She peered at the torn book and MPD bag. "Evidence from a case. That's pretty standard. Any unknown books considered suspicious are bagged and sent here for examination."

As she nudged the book aside to get a clear view of the case number on the evidence bag, Agent Harris stepped up beside her. He lifted his much heftier crime scene camera and snapped a photo.

"You should collect that book and the evidence bag," Lienna murmured to him as she aimed her phone camera at said items. "It might not be anything, but—"

"What is this?"

The voice came from the lazaretto's doorway—a voice that sounded like it'd been lubed up with rancid fish oil.

Agent Söze's cold eyes fixed on us, an ugly sneer tugging at his face. Behind him stood Agent Suarez, a woman in her forties who bore a remarkable resemblance to the building we were in— bulkily rectangular, boring, and clad in a drab gray suit.

"What are you doing here, Agent Shen, Agent Morris?" Söze demanded.

"Investigating the death of a respected GM," Lienna retorted, lowering her phone. "As ordered."

"I do not recall giving that order."

"Astute recollection," I said with no small amount of facetiousness. "Our orders came from Captain Blythe."

"You do not answer to her anymore, Agent Morris. You answer to me." He stepped into the small room, shadowed by

Suarez. "And I fail to see how you would find anything of value here to aid in your report on the Sea Devils."

Before Lienna or I could reply, he fired at Harris, "What do you have?"

"My preliminary opinion is death by suicide," he answered dutifully. "Asphyxiation, specifically. I still need to dust for prints and collect—"

"That will not be necessary," Söze interrupted.

Harris bristled. A buttoned-up bootlicker or not, he'd always been an exemplary agent as far as investigative skills and adherence to proper procedure. He was well-known around the precinct for bludgeoning other agents with the rulebook when they weren't performing up to his standards.

But apparently, he wasn't *that* dedicated, because he quickly regained his composure. "Yes, sir."

Lienna had also bristled, but unlike Harris, she failed to recover. "Not necessary? That's standard procedure."

Söze turned slowly to face us, cold eyes narrowing. "Are you questioning my orders, Agent Shen?"

His tone sent a chill through my gut. It echoed his blowup with Agent Vigneault earlier this morning—but Lienna didn't know that. She'd been absent during that debacle, and I'd been too enamored by the Lon Chaney dossier to fill her in.

I put a calming hand on her shoulder, but she shrugged it off.

"I'm just wondering if I missed a memo about new investigative protocols," she replied, disguising her objection with a thin veneer of diplomacy.

Söze took a menacing step forward, an angry vein pulsing in his forehead. "I'm not here to rewrite protocols, Agent Shen. My purpose is to rid your pathetic precinct of all the corruption, inefficiency, and incompetence that runs rampant throughout."

"Incompetence?" she repeated stiffly. "Like failing to dust for fingerprints at a crime scene?"

"Lienna, don't," I hissed.

The vein in Söze's head throbbed harder. "Incompetence like failing to follow simple orders. Incompetence that most of your coworkers share, which is why Agent Suarez will be taking over this case effective immediately."

Suarez stepped through the doorway, bumping me with her square shoulder and extending her thick fingers to take Harris's work out of his hands.

"Hand over your phone, Agent Shen," Söze ordered.

Lienna recoiled. "What?"

"You were taking photos. Those photos are now part of Agent Suarez's investigation."

She gritted her teeth.

Hello, rock. Greetings, hard place. Glad to be between you both this fine Vancouver morning. Were we supposed to lie down and let Söze's corruption coalition do whatever the hell they wanted? Or were we supposed to fight back and incur more of Söze's dangerous wrath?

The frying pan or the fire?

"Now, Agent Shen."

In response, Lienna shoved her phone conspicuously into her satchel.

Söze's eyes bulged like a deep-sea fish that had been brought to the surface by a heartless scientist—but I could only enjoy the sight for a moment. He abruptly calmed again, and a smile that was far more "tiger shark" than "anglerfish" twisted his face with gloating satisfaction.

"Agent Suarez, Agent Harris," he said in an almost singsong croon of malicious joy, "arrest them."

3

WELL, SO MUCH FOR the frying pan. We were leaping straight into the fire.

Since getting arrested wasn't on my agenda today, I dropped a halluci-bomb on the lazaretto and split myself into three. Each Kit wound up and swung at the jaw of an enemy agent. The thing with seeing someone about to slug you in the face—you can't help but get the hell out of the way, even when there's a one-in-three chance you're hallucinating your attacker.

Suarez and Harris reeled backward as my real fist grazed Söze's cheekbone. He'd barely evaded my surprise brawler move, but that was all I'd needed—a clear path out the door.

I grabbed Lienna's arm and hauled her across the threshold.

"Stop them!" Söze barked.

As we sprinted down the short hall, Lienna yanked her cat's eye necklace out of the front of her shirt. "*Ori menti defendo!*"

"*Ori decasus dormias!*"

Harris's shouted incantation rang out on top of Lienna's, and a blast of sizzling ochre magic grazed my left shoulder. My arm went numb.

You know what? I took back every semi-complimentary thing I'd ever uttered about Agent Harris.

With Lienna's mind protected from my warps, I switched hallucinatory tracks and made the two of us explode. A fantastically rainbow-colored detonation of supercharged *Care Bear* proportions roared through the hallway, and when it faded, Lienna and I had vanished.

Though, actually, we were dashing between the tall bookshelves.

Under normal circumstances, I would've felt pretty secure that we were about to make a clean escape, but I'd underestimated Söze before. Last time I went head-to-head with him, he'd been immune to my warps. That was the reason I'd tried to actually punch him instead of using a warp.

Okay, it was one reason. I really would've liked to land that hit.

Three sets of stomping footsteps trailed Lienna and me as we zoomed past Edith, who had turned in her chair to see what all the commotion was. As we ran toward the exit, I modified my halluci-bomb to place a fake door over top of the real one. I shoved it open without breaking stride—with a bit more force than I'd intended. It whipped open and banged loudly against the wall.

"They went through the door!" Harris yelled.

Damn it.

Lienna and I sped down the wide hallway toward the front entrance. I applied the same warp to the glass doors to cover our exit, and Lienna pushed through first. I was right on her heels when a blinding orange explosion shattered the window beside me. Throwing my arms over my head, I stumbled out onto the sidewalk.

Agent Söze stood in a shooter's stance at the far end of the hall, pointing his murderous artifact in my direction.

"What are you doing?" Harris yelled, sliding to a stop beside him. "Anybody on the street could see that!"

Söze's mouth moved with words I couldn't hear.

Whirling around, I leaped at Lienna and tackled her around the middle. We hit the ground as a second orange blast obliterated the double doors and their frame. Glass shards rained down on us.

"Over here," I said breathlessly, tugging Lienna up with me. I pulled her against the wall of the building. Out of Söze's line of fire, I focused on the smart car. A fake Kit and Lienna appeared in the front seats and a fake version of the vehicle peeled away from the curb with smoking tires.

Söze appeared in the now doorless entryway, his dark stare locked on the fleeing smart car. He raised his artifact toward it.

Harris grabbed his arm and yanked it down so his artifact was pointed at the ground.

"Control yourself!" the senior agent hissed. "We're in public!"

Söze's head snapped side to side, taking in the handful of shocked pedestrians peering toward the broken doors and shattered glass. Cars rolled past on the street, the drivers slowing down to rubberneck.

Eyes squinched with concentration, I made the fake smart car turn sharply at an intersection. It earned fake honks from nearby vehicles before vanishing from sight. I had to hand it to myself for the realistic addition of angry Vancouver drivers honking at the smart car.

Suarez, who'd finally joined the other two agents, pulled car keys from her pocket. "Should we follow them?"

Söze shook his head. "We're not prepared for Morris's abilities right now. We'll deal with him later. Both of you, finish up with the suicide and report to me at the precinct later."

"Yes, sir," the other two chimed.

I kept a tight hold on the warp hiding the real smart car as Söze climbed into his black sedan. "Not prepared for Morris's abilities right now," he'd said. In our last encounter, he'd seen through my warps, but today, he'd been fooled. What trick or technique was he using to defeat my abilities?

The sedan pulled into traffic and sped away. Harris and Suarez gave the mess of the doorway displeased looks, then crunched across the broken glass back into the guild.

"Kit?"

Lienna's uncertain, slightly breathless tone startled me—and I realized I was holding her tightly against me, both arms wrapped around her torso. I'd been concentrating so hard on my warps that I hadn't realized I was crushing her to my chest.

I flung my arms out to the sides as though that somehow proved my unasked-for embrace had been unintentional. "Sorry!"

She didn't meet my eyes as she stepped back, her head ducked. "Should we … go?"

"Yeah, let's get out of here."

She headed for the driver's side while I glanced around to make sure no one was looking our way. Seeing zero potential witnesses, I dropped my warp and dove into the passenger seat. I'd barely buckled my seat belt before she stomped on the gas.

"So, the good news is we're still in one piece," I summarized. "The bad news is we're now at the top of Söze's To-Kill list."

Lienna cut off a slow-moving Prius and took a sharp right turn at the next intersection. "Has Söze lost his mind? Does he plan to arrest every agent who doesn't obey his insane orders?"

I kept an eye on the side-view mirror outside my window. No sign of pursuers. "Pretty much. He put Agent Vigneault under lock and key after she called him out in front of the whole bullpen for shutting down her investigation."

"What? When?"

"Earlier today."

"Why didn't you tell me?"

"You distracted me with silent-movie-era paraphernalia." I did one more check through the rear window. "I think our getaway was a success."

When the light at the next intersection turned red, Lienna switched lanes so we could turn right onto Thurlow Street. "Just because I wouldn't give up my phone," she muttered.

"I have a sneaking suspicion there's more to it than that," I said, taking the award for most obvious statement of the day. "Something to do with our recently deceased GM, methinks."

"Söze wouldn't block a suicide investigation for no reason. He's hiding something. We need to figure out what that is."

"And keep Söze from blowing us up in the meantime."

"We can't go back to the precinct." She pulled her gaze off the road to glance at me, a little wide-eyed as though just realizing how many of our options had vanished. "Or our apartments. That's where Söze will look next."

"We can't go anywhere we would normally go."

Lienna yanked her satchel's strap over her head and dumped the bag on my lap. "My cell phone's in there. Call Blythe—her personal number, not her work number."

I fished through her Arcana arsenal until I found her phone. "Have you two been meeting up for secret work sessions? Or is it a girls' night kinda thing? You eat frozen yogurt together and gossip about MagiPol bylaws?"

"Huh?"

"I'm just saying, I don't have Blythe's personal number."

Lienna rolled her eyes. "She gave it to me for emergencies. Like this."

I found the number and dialed. The captain answered after a single ring. "What is it, Agent Shen?"

"Sorry to disappoint, Cap."

"Agent Morris. What's going on?"

"Nothing serious. Söze tried to murder us at Arcana Historia, that's all."

A ruffling sound crackled over the phone, followed by the sound of a door slamming shut. "I'm heading back to my place. Meet me there. I'll text you the door code."

Ending the call, I dropped Lienna's phone back into her satchel. "I suppose you know where the captain lives too."

She smirked. "Where else would we hold girls' nights?"

AS WE DROVE into Olympic Village, Lienna kept a ten-and-two stranglehold on the steering wheel. A permanent furrow was etched between her dark brows, and I wondered if this was a return to her formerly hypertense demeanor or if it was the stress of our new predicament showing.

I wasn't exactly feeling overjoyed at our situation either, but I'd done this before. On the run from the law, on the run from my foster home, on the run from Lienna, even.

For her, though, this was brand-new territory. Oh, sure, she'd faced her fair share of foes—from demon-wielding assassins to a sexy, terrifying rogue druid—but it was different when you didn't have a home base and your allies were running thin.

After doubling back a couple of times and taking more than a few unnecessary turns to make sure Söze and his gang hadn't followed us, Lienna found a parking spot on a side street in front of a row of tall, skinny townhouses packed together like residential, cubist sardines, their homogeneously manicured hedges obscuring their identical front porches.

Even after the smart car had come to a stop and she'd turned off the engine, my partner didn't move. She kept the wheel in a death grip and stared fiercely out the window.

"It gets easier," I told her, breaking the silence.

She didn't move. "What does?"

"Being on the run."

She inhaled slowly, inflating her chest. "That's not—I can handle that."

"Oh?"

Her eyes shifted back and forth as though a scatterplot of words was hovering in front of her, and she was searching for the right ones to direct to her tongue. I waited quietly, ready to listen to whatever she decided to share.

Then she grabbed the door handle and swung it open. "Let's go."

Sighing, I pulled myself out of the car's cramped interior. While frustrating, it was no surprise that Lienna was holding back. That was fairly routine: she kept everything she possibly could private, and I charmingly pestered her until some of it leaked out.

She strode purposefully along the line of townhomes, and I took a few quick steps to catch up, eyeing the cloned dwellings that were only distinguishable by the numbers on the doors.

Well, except for …

"Is that one hers?" I asked, pointing at the second townhome from the end.

Lienna frowned. "How'd you know?"

"I'm very perceptive," I answered with an innocent shrug. "For instance, even when my partner acts stoically unaffected by everything, I can tell when she's actually—"

"No, really," she interrupted. "The captain's address isn't publicly available—for good reason."

"The windows are different." As we approached the townhome in question, the difference became more apparent. "You can see right into all these other houses, but Blythe's windows aren't as transparent … not unlike a certain agent's emotions, which are—"

"That's because they're not glass."

My go-to technique of charming persistence was getting me a whole lot of nowhere. Stuffing my hands into my pockets, I gave up on charm or persistence and asked, "What are they, then? Magic plastic?"

"Bulletproof polymer."

I raised an eyebrow. "That wasn't part of the standard strata package. A little paranoid, isn't it?"

Lienna stepped up to the front door and punched the code Blythe had texted her into the keypad above the knob. "Her position makes her a target. She's not paranoid. She's smart."

The keypad chirped approvingly, and Lienna opened the door to an eerily silent and shadowy main floor. We stepped inside, looking around the open living room—a utilitarian sofa opposite a wall-mounted TV, a single floor lamp in the corner, and a small collection of stark, black-and-white cityscape photography that perfectly reflected the laser-focused lack of bullshit that defined their owner.

The door felt unusually heavy as I shut it behind me. The *thump* of it closing was followed immediately by the *thunk* of the deadbolt engaging, and a beep indicated that it had locked. Had she upgraded the doors and security system too?

I almost missed it in the dimness of the townhome's interior, but on the inside of the front door, a complex circular pattern had been etched into the metal—an Arcana array.

"A protection spell?" I wondered, my voice unintentionally dropping to a whisper. Something about being unsupervised in Blythe's home warranted an indoor voice.

Lienna glanced at it. "An abjuration array."

"Your handiwork?"

"No."

Crossing into the main room, I cautiously explored. Everything was so damn quiet, so perfectly still. The floor didn't creak under my feet, the fridge in the kitchen beyond the living room didn't hum, and light didn't flicker through the windows.

It was spooky.

"I bet the chief of the human police doesn't live in a single-person fortress jacked up with abjuration magic," I whispered to myself as I moved to the staircase that led up to the second level.

"Where are you going?"

I looked down at my foot, which was on the bottom step, then up at my partner, who was hovering in front of the sofa. "Upstairs?"

"We're not here to snoop."

"I'm not snooping," I said, perhaps too defensively. "I'm checking for eavesdroppers and intruders. Don't you find it ominous how freakin' quiet it is in here?"

She rolled her eyes. "Kit, you said it yourself. This place is a fortress. We're perfectly safe."

"Oh." I looked back down at my feet, then hopped up another couple of steps. "Then I guess I'm snooping."

"*Kit.*"

The eerie tingle I felt from the silence and shadows didn't abate at the top of the stairs. To my left, the hallway led to a closed door. To my right, another closed door. And straight ahead? You guessed it, a third closed door.

That was weird, right? Who kept all their doors closed when they weren't home? For all I knew, there was a whole battalion of darkfae and demons hidden in these rooms, lurking out of sight, waiting hungrily for us to get too close.

I opened the closest door, revealing a spacious bathroom with a shower straight ahead of me. My brain flashed to memories of Norman Bates and his butcher knife.

"What are you doing?" Lienna hissed, right on my heels.

"Checking for hidden baddies. Snooping. Whatever you want to call it."

An unfamiliar voice pierced the air. "I don't think you'll find any criminals in my medicine cabinet, Agent Morris."

I'm not proud of it, but I yelped. Just a small yelp, but loud enough that I couldn't play it off as a rogue hiccup.

Fortunately—or unfortunately, depending on your perspective—that voice did not belong to a villainous fae lying in wait to drag me into the ethereal marshes of another realm. Rather, it belonged to Captain Blythe, who was standing at the top of the stairs, arms crossed and scowling at me with effortless, soul-withering annoyance.

"Hey, Cap," I greeted weakly. "Would you believe me if I said I was looking for an antacid? It's been a stressful day and I had leftover pizza for breakfast."

Blythe turned her back on me and headed down the stairs. "We need to talk."

Lienna gave me a particularly dramatic eye roll, then followed our boss back to the first floor. Why did I feel like the odd man out here?

Downstairs in the kitchen, Blythe had turned on the lights and put a kettle on the stove by the time I recovered from my embarrassment and made my descent. As I stepped across the threshold from living room to kitchen, I noticed yet another closed door to my left.

Was it a pantry? A staircase leading down into her secret sex dungeon? A gateway to Narnia? God*damn* these closed doors! My curiosity couldn't handle it.

Lienna was already giving the captain a rundown of our delightful meetup with Söze and Suarez. Blythe leaned against the counter, arms folded across her chest, taking in the tale with restrained intensity.

"I didn't expect it to happen this fast," she murmured when Lienna had finished.

I poked at the plastic fruit in a decorative bowl on the table. "You knew Söze would morph into a comic-book villain and try to incinerate us?"

"I knew things would get worse, and something has pushed Agent Söze to take bolder action." Blythe grabbed a mug and teabag out of the cupboard. "That's one reason I sent you to Arcana Historia."

Lienna's eyebrows arched. "Do you know what Söze is up to?"

"Not exactly." The captain looked at us with narrow-eyed resolve. "We know Söze isn't acting alone. Not only does he have subordinates who obey him unquestioningly, but he also has other allies within the MPD."

"Yeah, whoever let him off after he tried to *Damnatio*-dust the Crow and Hammer," I said tersely.

She nodded. "Someone in the upper ranks of Internal Affairs is backing Söze. But I believe it runs deeper than that. He couldn't act with this level of impunity with only one or two allies in the upper echelons of MPD power to protect him."

"Wait." Abandoning the inedible fruit, I stepped closer to her. "Are you saying there's a *group* of psychos like Söze enabling his crackpot power trip? How many people in the MPD are part of this?"

"That's the question," Blythe replied grimly. "And what we need to learn. To find out how widespread the corruption is, we first need to know Söze's goal. What is he trying to accomplish and why?"

Silence pressed in on us. I dug my fingers into my temples, worsening my sudden headache instead of helping it. Suspecting Söze had a friend or two in high places had been bad, but this? How many MPD bigwigs were backing him? How far did the corruption spread—and what was their goal? What was so special about our precinct?

"Söze will have you arrested or killed the moment he sees you," Blythe said, breaking into my dire musings. "You'll need to keep your heads down and stay off his radar. I have to maintain appearances at the precinct, but I need you to continue your investigation into Georgia Johannsen's death. Look for—"

A sudden thump vibrated through the ceiling, emanating from somewhere upstairs. The three of us looked up, frowning in confusion.

"Uh," I began uncertainly. "You don't happen to have an exceptionally large poodle up there, do you?"

Blythe's lips pressed thin. Turning off the steaming kettle, she strode toward the stairs.

Something small and shiny came flying out of the darkness at the top of the staircase. It arced downward, soaring toward Blythe. She flicked her hand up, and the object halted in mid-air.

It was a small potion vial, its pink and blue contents swirling ominously.

With a quiet *fizz-pop*, the gaseous contents flashed to gray—and the vial exploded into a thick cloud of fog that rushed to fill the townhouse, rendering all of us blind to whatever danger was about to descend the stairs.

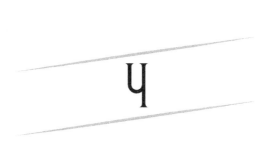

AS EVERYTHING IN SIGHT turned to opaque white mist, I had the brief, chagrined thought that our attacker was either damn lucky or dangerously clever—because with one little smoke bomb, they'd hamstrung my warps *and* Blythe's telekinesis.

That was all I had time to think before the thud of colliding bodies sounded from the spot where I'd last seen the captain. A grunt erupted, followed by the crash of overturned furniture.

"Blythe?" I yelled, taking a couple of uncertain steps forward.

"Kit!" Lienna called from somewhere behind me—but I heard nothing from Blythe.

"Lienna, use your—"

Before I could finish my instruction, a shadow appeared in the fog—a large man dressed in black charging straight for me with a dagger aimed at my chest. I grabbed his wrist, pushing the dagger away from my vitals, but his momentum hurled me backward. I landed on the kitchen table, slid across it, and fell off the other side along with the bowl of plastic fruit.

As I hit the floor, I considered making myself invisible, but the smoke bomb was doing that already. I needed to warp a nice, big distraction for Mr. Knifey, but I couldn't *see* him. I'd have to drop a halluci-bomb on the whole townhouse, which would be warp-style friendly fire for Blythe and Lienna. If Lienna could use her cat's eye spell, I could at least—

Wait, no. She'd used it while we were escaping Söze, Suarez, and Harris. It was out of commission until the spell recharged.

Gritting my teeth, I scooted under the table. If I called out to Lienna and Blythe, I'd give away my position. Lienna must have had the same idea, because she was silent as well. I strained my ears for any sound.

Something clattered loudly, and I shot out from under the table, racing toward the sound. A shadow in the fog—our stabby new friend, hunched over the kitchen counter with his back to me. But he wasn't alone.

Lienna was bent backward under him, clawing at his hands around her throat, her feet kicking helplessly at the cabinets.

Lunging for his back, I wound up to punch him in the lower ribs and break a few bones. He spun around, dragging Lienna by the neck, and threw her into me. I slid into her, catching her middle as she burst into a fit of gasping coughs.

Our attacker pulled another knife from amongst his clothes. A black hat, sunglasses, and a lower-face mask obscured his features, but somehow, I knew he was smirking. His body language screamed smug anticipation.

But the fog was thinning. I could see him—and I could target him.

I hit him with a mean Funhouse warp that flipped the floor and ceiling at rapid, random intervals. He staggered back into the counter, then raised his arm, the dagger glinting. He hurled the knife at my face.

The blunt handle hit my cheekbone so hard it snapped my head backward. Lienna lurched in my arms as she croaked, "*Ori dormias!*"

I felt her arm move as she threw the stun marble, and I heard it clang against the backsplash. I blinked my starry vision back into focus as the knife-wielding bastard rushed out of the kitchen and disappeared into the fading haze.

"He's escaping," I grunted, taking a few steps after him—but the clack of the front bolt interrupted my pursuit. The door slammed open, and a rush of cold air sent the fog swirling.

"Kit, are you okay?" Lienna asked, appearing beside me.

I gingerly probed my throbbing cheekbone. He'd thrown the knife so hard and fast that I hadn't had a chance to dodge, but still caught in my Funhouse warp, he'd messed up his technique. If the knife had hit me blade first, well, let's just say my face would've been a lot less symmetrical.

"I'm okay," I told her. "What about you?"

"Fine." Her voice had acquired a new chain-smoker's rasp, and she had a hand curled around her throat. That cloak-and-dagger douche canoe had been halfway to strangling her to death.

A silent heartbeat passed, and our eyes locked, something unsaid hanging between us. I wasn't sure what. Relief that we weren't hurt? Residual fear at having seen each other in mortal danger? Frustration that our attacker had escaped and I was completely misreading the moment in the desperate hope that Lienna cared about me as more than a partner?

Her eyes suddenly widened and leaped away from mine. "Captain Blythe?"

I snapped back to reality with a curse and spun toward the stairs where I'd last seen the captain. "Blythe?"

The fog had settled to knee height, eddying dramatically in the breeze from the open front door. As it swirled, I glimpsed a blond head down near the floor.

Lienna and I dashed toward her. She was slouched against the wall, a decorative table lying on its side nearby. Her chest rose and fell in shallow, rapid breaths, and she had two hands wrapped around the hilt of the dagger embedded in her inner right thigh.

"Captain!" Lienna dropped to her knees beside Blythe. Blood had soaked her pants around the knife and was starting to pool on the floor.

Blythe cracked her eyes open. "He went for ... femoral artery. Didn't ... let him ... pull it out."

Panic swirled in my brain as I tried to remember the details of my mandatory first aid training. Femoral artery. As in the big artery in the groin area that, if severed, caused the victim to bleed to death in a mere three to five minutes.

That knife stuck in her leg, blocking the wound, was the only reason she was still alive. And the only reason she'd been able to keep hold of said knife while being stabbed with it was her crazy-strong telekinetic skills.

"Good," Lienna said breathlessly. "That's good. Keep holding the knife. Kit, give me your belt."

I whipped it off and handed it to her. She carefully slid it around Blythe's thigh above the knife.

"We can't take her to the precinct," Lienna said to me, her face white. She pulled the belt tight around Blythe's leg. "It isn't safe. Where's the nearest hospital?"

"A healer has a better chance of saving her."

"Lots of guilds have healers, but can we trust—"

I shot to my feet. "The Crow and Hammer! They're a combat guild. They'll have healers. And is there any other guild we know that is one-hundred-percent anti-Söze?"

A grimace rippled across Blythe's face. I couldn't tell if it was from the pain or the very thought of receiving life-saving care in the guild run by her nemesis, Darius King.

"We need to get her into the car," I said. "Should we—"

Blythe grunted, "Keys."

"Huh?"

"Pocket."

Lienna was quicker on the uptake. She pulled Blythe's keys from her pocket, hit the unlock button, then stuffed them in her own pocket. "We'll have to take out the knife before we can move you, Captain."

Blythe nodded.

I darted into the kitchen and returned with a tea towel. Lienna pulled the belt tighter around Blythe's upper thigh, then gently pushed the captain's hands away to take hold of the knife's hilt.

Blythe hissed as Lienna slid the blade out, and I pressed the tea towel to the wound. Blood soaked into it, and my heart raced.

Lienna took over applying pressure as I lifted Blythe into my arms and carried her outside. Her black SUV was parked at the curb directly in front of the house, and Lienna used one hand to open the rear passenger door.

Together, we got the captain into the back seat. I squashed myself into the limited floor space so I could keep pressing on the wound, while Lienna got behind the wheel and punched the accelerator, simultaneously dialing a number on her cell phone.

"Darius," she said. "We're on our way to your guild. Captain Blythe was stabbed. She needs a healer urgently."

I could hear a muffled voice on the other end but couldn't make out any words.

"Okay," Lienna replied. "We'll be there in five."

She dropped her phone back on the passenger seat.

A harrowing five minutes later, she sped past the front of the Crow and Hammer, turned into the alley behind it, and screeched to a stop in the parking lot.

Just outside the guild's rear door, a smartly dressed man with salt-and-pepper hair and a perfectly groomed beard waited: Darius King, GM and silver fox of the Crow and Hammer. Accompanying him was a large, muscular man with an ebony complexion and shaved head who I would have assumed was a combat mythic if he hadn't been holding a brightly colored medic bag in one hand.

As they hurried toward the vehicle, I threw open the door. Blythe grabbed my hand, her lips quivering.

"It's okay, Cap," I said soothingly, trying to ignore how blood-soaked the tea towel had become. "You'll be safe here."

She dug her nails into my skin. "Eggert," she sputtered hoarsely. "Call Eggert."

Before I could process her words, Darius and the healer were at the open door. I scooted out, and the healer leaned inside. After a rapid assessment of Blythe's condition, he and Darius pulled her out of the car. With Darius carrying her and the healer applying wound pressure, the two of them rushed her into the guild.

Lienna and I closed the SUV's doors and followed them. The rear entrance led directly into a narrow kitchen with saloon doors straight ahead. Pushing through them, we found ourselves in the dimly lit pub, sparsely populated by a handful of guild members whose eyes all turned our way. Darius, the healer, and Blythe were nowhere in sight.

A woman with a friendly face and her brunette hair tied up in a messy bun hurried toward us—Clara, Darius's assistant guild master.

"Agents," she said with clear concern, "are either of you hurt?"

We both shook our heads.

"Where's Captain Blythe?" I asked.

"Darius and Miles took her up to the infirmary. Our other healer, Elisabetta, is on her way as well." Clara eyed us, her concern growing. "Why don't you two clean up? I'll get a cold pack for your cheek, Agent Morris."

I abruptly noticed the pain throbbing across the left side of my face.

Clara showed us to the ladies' and men's showers in the basement, where Lienna and I split up to wash our hands and dab at the blood on our clothes as best we could. Lienna's clothes weren't too gory, but I'd ended up looking like a *Carrie* cosplayer, and when Clara brought me a squashy gel ice pack, she also passed over a clean shirt.

With the blessedly cold pack numbing my cheek and a too-tight BC Lions t-shirt straining across my pecs—not my usual style, I promise—I found myself sitting tiredly in Darius's office while Lienna recounted our day so far to the GM. A hell of a day it'd been.

Darius probably knew a good dry cleaner, I thought idly. He'd better, considering the gnarly bloodstains he'd added to his spiffy dress shirt and vest combo.

As usual, the silver fox betrayed none of his thoughts while Lienna spoke. If I was picking up on anything, it was a subtle sense of agitation.

"Just before the attack, Captain Blythe ordered us to continue investigating Georgia's suicide," Lienna told him, wrapping up the tale.

A small crease formed between Darius's eyebrows. "It wasn't a suicide."

"How do you know?" I asked.

Tightness pulled at his features—painful grief he couldn't hide. "I knew Georgia. Her death was not a suicide."

I lowered the ice pack from my face. "Were you close with her?"

"I'm on friendly terms with all the GMs in Vancouver—or at least speaking terms." The tension in his features shifted. "Do you suspect Söze of being involved in Georgia's death?"

"His behavior suggests as much," Lienna said. "We just don't know why or how."

"You're also assuming Söze is behind the attack on Aurelia?"

It always slightly weirded me out when Darius used the captain's first name.

"If the slimy shoe fits …" I slapped the cooling pack against my cheek again. "We couldn't identify the assassin, but he got inside Blythe's house unnoticed, and he was prepared for her with a smoke bomb."

Darius nodded, familiar with the big weakness of telekinetics: they needed to see objects to move them. "The attack was planned."

"Yeah, though I don't think the assassin expected me and Lienna to be there with her."

The GM's gray eyes moved between us. "In your opinion, has Söze escalated to the level of ordering the assassination of the precinct captain?"

"Probably," I answered. "He's been stepping it up ever since he tried to take out your guild. Intimidating people, interfering in cases, targeting other guilds, arresting agents, trying to kill us, using magic in public, stealing Lienna's—"

My partner shot me a warning look and I choked on the word "portals," mentally kicking myself for almost blowing her biggest secret.

"He's lost it," I concluded lamely, adjusting the hem of my overly tight tee, which kept riding up my stomach. "When can we see Blythe?"

Darius arched an eyebrow, aware that I'd aborted the previous topic. "That won't be possible anytime soon."

"We need to talk to her."

"Her recovery is our first priority. She lost a dangerous amount of blood, and there could be further complications."

Lienna and I shared a grim look. We'd called Captain Blythe because we had no options now that Söze wanted us permanently out of the picture, but it didn't sound like she'd be able to help.

"Once it's safe to move her," Darius continued, "I'll take her to a secure location where Elisabetta and Miles can tend to her—and where no one else can find her to finish the job."

"Where's that?" Lienna asked.

"It would be best if you didn't know." He saw our coming protests and raised a quieting hand. "The fewer people who have access to that information, the safer Aurelia will be."

There was a certain protective logic to that.

Lienna apparently agreed, as she sighed and nodded. "Fine."

Darius leaned back in his chair and laced his fingers together. "What's your next move?"

Lienna and I were in a rough spot, and I was only too eager to get help from an experienced, unflappable, well-connected ex-assassin who hated Söze as much as we did, but his guild had a huge Söze-style bullseye on it. He had all his guildeds to worry about, and we couldn't ask for more than he was already doing by saving and protecting Blythe.

"We've got things under control," I said, keeping my tone light. "You take care of Blythe, and we'll take care of Söze."

I couldn't tell if he believed my bravado, but he didn't try to poke holes in it, which I appreciated.

"Let me know if you need anything."

"Yep. Come on, Lienna."

Together, we left his office and traipsed through the guild. Only when we were outside and walking up to Blythe's SUV did she speak.

"Why didn't you ask Darius for help?" she said. "I thought you would."

"We don't need him." I winked at her. "Blythe already told me what we're supposed to do next."

"She did?"

"Yep. She told me to call Eggert."

Lienna's relief faltered. "Eggert?"

"Eggert," I confirmed. "Our favorite mustachioed former security—"

"Kit," she interrupted with a sigh. "Just tell me what Blythe said."

"That's it. That's all she said."

She gave me a confused look, and I couldn't blame her. As much as I liked Trevor Eggert, I didn't see how he could help us. Söze had dismissed him last week for the crime of being human, and we hadn't heard from him since.

Well, only one way to find out what Blythe meant.

Unfortunately, calling him wasn't as simple as pulling out my phone. After arriving at the Crow and Hammer, Lienna and I had powered our devices down to prevent anyone from tracking our whereabouts. We really should have done that *before* driving to the guild, but we'd been focused on saving the captain.

We drove to a nearby mobile store and bought prepaid cell phones. Standing with Lienna in the parking lot beside Blythe's SUV, I removed the SIM card from my original phone, turned it back on, and checked my contacts for Eggsy's number. Adding it into my new device, I hit the call button.

As it rang, I noticed that Lienna's gaze was lingering a lot lower than my face. Maybe I should stop fixing this overly tight shirt and just let it ride up my abs.

That was a good sign, right? That she was attracted to me? Or was her covert staring more like when someone has something stuck in their teeth and you can't stop staring at it while they talk?

A familiar voice filled the phone at my ear. "Hello?"

"Hey, Eggsy," I greeted, getting my brain back on track. "It's Kit. I have a new number."

"I see that. How are you doing these days?"

"Been better. I've got some bad news." I hesitated, scrambling to come up with the right words. "Blythe was attacked this afternoon. She's alive, but she's in rough shape."

"Oh, jeez. Where is she now, then?"

I recalled Darius's warning about revealing her location. "We got her to a healer, and she's in good hands. The last thing she told me was to call you."

"Did she now? Hmm." A sound that could only be Eggert's mustache brushing against the phone's microphone crackled through the speaker. "I guess that means it's time."

"Time for what?"

"Time to show you the Batcave."

5

"YOU LOOK EXCITED," Lienna commented as she guided Blythe's SUV westbound through the cobblestone streets of Gastown. "Did you forget we were almost killed twice today?"

"Small potatoes," I said dismissively. "Eggsy said he's showing us the *Batcave*. I'm trying not to get my hopes up."

She rolled her eyes. "Are you expecting Trevor Eggert to secretly be Batman?"

"God, no. His mustache would clash horribly with the Dark Knight's cowl. I'm expecting him to be my Alfred."

"Oh, so *you're* Batman."

"Duh. I've already got the brooding orphan thing working in my favor."

"Brooding?" Lienna turned onto Cordova and took us into the heart of downtown. "What if I want to be Batman?"

I pondered this, appreciating her willingness to banter. Her tension had diminished marginally since we'd left the Crow and Hammer, but her shoulders still looked like they had the consistency of marble.

"I can see that," I acquiesced. "All the gadgets and the penchant for violence."

"You can be my Robin."

"Uhh …" I scrunched up my nose. "Oh! How about Wonder Woman?"

Lienna turned off Cordova and into the circular driveway of a tall, glass-walled condo complex. "I don't want to be Wonder Woman. I want to be Batman."

"No, *I'll* be Wonder Woman. She's got an invisible jet!"

"That seems appropriate," Lienna agreed, parking in a visitor stall.

"Wait," I said, peering around at the unexpectedly familiar guest parking lot. Leaning sideways to look out the window, I realized this wasn't just any tall, glass-walled condo complex. "What are we doing here?"

She opened her door. "This is it."

"No, no," I replied with a defiant chuckle. "That's a mistake."

Eggert had texted the Batcave's address to both of us, but I'd been too busy adding a handful of key contacts to my new phone—and texting my new digits to a couple of them—to look at it.

She frowned. "Why is it a mistake?"

I gestured emphatically and wordlessly at the ritzy structure. She leaned through her open door to gaze up at it, and realization widened her eyes.

"Oh." She glanced at me. "*Oh.*"

"Are you *sure* this is the place?"

She held her phone toward me. I squinted at the digital characters, still in denial, but the address was correct—including the unit number.

"You have got to be shitting me!" I growled, every iota of excitement over the "Batcave" burning away in a surge of jilted vexation. What the actual hell, Blythe?

Heading inside, we passed through the first set of doors. Before Lienna could reach for the panel to buzz up to Eggert, the security door beeped, and I pulled it open to find the doorman walking around his desk with a big grin.

"Mr. Morris!" He extended his hand. "It's been a while."

I shook his hand, concealing my bad mood. "Hey, Hardy. How have you been?"

"Can't complain. What brings you back here?"

"I'm visiting a friend."

"Oh, that's great!" He gave me another amicable grin. "I didn't realize the new tenant was a friend of yours."

"Yeah," I grumbled.

With Hardy's blessing, Lienna and I boarded the elevator and rode up to the eleventh floor. Moments later, I found myself staring resentfully at the silver numbers on the door: 1106.

Since I was just standing there, mentally berating Blythe, Lienna stepped up beside me and rapped on the door. It swung open to reveal Eggsy, his bushy bristles bending across his grinning top lip.

"Hey there, agents. Welcome to the Batcave."

"I guess that means I *am* Batman," I muttered, stepping inside.

Lienna made a quiet noise in her throat that wasn't quite neutral enough to hide her amusement.

I kicked off my shoes, feeling the slick hardwood under my feet. The familiar open floor plan greeted me with its luxuriously large kitchen, floor-to-ceiling windows overlooking the harbor, and a wide electric fireplace.

The living room, however, had been transformed into a surveillance center. A long, wide desk was crowded by a triple monitor setup, a laptop, and a labyrinthine mess of cables that ran to the multiple computers on the floor underneath. One monitor was split into quadrants, each featuring a security camera angle inside the MPD precinct.

"Some of this here is beyond me," Eggert told us as I gawked at the juxtaposition between my memories of the room and its current state. "But I do my best to keep up with Captain Blythe's requests. Can you tell me what happened to her?"

"An assassin," I answered. "Probably arranged by Söze, but we have no proof—yet. Have you been here since he fired you?"

Eggsy nodded. "The captain contacted me right away, saying she had a new job ready for me. She had this place all set up. I guess she was expecting we'd need a base of operations outside the precinct."

Lienna tapped the monitor with the security cam feeds. "You've been watching us."

"Watching Söze," he corrected. "Mostly, anyways."

"Blythe's extra set of eyes," I murmured.

"What's that now?"

"Lately, the cap seemed to have preternatural knowledge of that shitstain's whereabouts, and she'd only explain it as having an 'extra set of eyes.' That was you."

Eggert gave a bashful smile. "Guilty."

Lienna leaned closer to the trio of screens. "How are you accessing the precinct's security system?"

"You'd have to ask the captain," he said with a headshake as he eased into the desk's rolling chair. "I'm just following her instructions."

"Seems like the captain has all sorts of secrets." I wandered into the kitchen. The windows provided an expansive view of the water, the north shore in the distance, and the seemingly endless sky. "Do you know how long Blythe has had this place?"

"Nice, isn't it?" he replied obliviously. "She told me she snapped it up after she put away the criminal who used to live here. Apparently, it's a good spot for mythics trying to keep a low profile. People don't ask questions."

Groaning, I slid onto a stool at the island and braced my head in my hands.

"Something wrong, Agent Morris?" Eggsy inquired. "You're not injured now, are you?"

"Just emotionally," I grumbled. "Did you know I currently live in a closet-sized room and share a bathroom with three other guys?"

Eggsy's confused silence answered me.

I didn't realize Lienna had come up behind me until she patted my shoulder gently. "Don't take it too hard, Kit. This is a good location for covert activities. That's why criminals like it here, right?"

Raising my head, I gave her a long, hard stare.

"Former criminals," she corrected.

My stare didn't change.

Her lips twitched. "Well, either way, welcome home, Batman."

I groaned. Blythe needed to get back to full health as soon as possible so I could ask her a few pointed questions about her real estate decisions. Had she really taken on this place as her Batcave because she could keep a low profile here?

Or did she find some twisted amusement in owning a condo that used to be *mine*?

MY STOMACH SOUNDED like a hippopotamus gargling hunger-flavored mouthwash. By the time we'd reached Eggert's hideout, it'd been nearing dinnertime, and Lienna and I had skipped lunch thanks to all the "running for our lives" and "making sure our captain didn't die" activities we'd been involved in.

Thus, Eggert had offered to procure supper from a bougie Italian joint down the block that I would occasionally visit back when Coal Harbor had been my home base. Eggsy informed us that Blythe had left him a bit of cash to cover operating costs, which he used primarily to pig out on the upscale dining offerings of the neighborhood. He'd promised to be back "in a jiff" with the best the menu had to offer, leaving my appetite temporarily dampened by the mental image of him slurping spaghetti through his bristly nasal strainer.

Alone with Lienna in my former luxury suite, I glared at the high-end finishes, comfortable furniture, and general cleanliness I'd missed so sorely while living in a craptastic rented room for the past eight months.

Way to remind me how much crime really did pay, Blythe.

"We need a plan," Lienna said. She was sitting in Eggsy's chair, watching the monitor with the camera feeds. Söze was standing outside Blythe's former office, discussing something with his lackey, Agent Barrows, a stocky man with a ponytail and an ever-present tablet that he was always referencing. Guessing by the intensity of Lienna's focus, she was attempting to lip-read.

"Well, we have a goal, if not a plan," I replied from my spot on the sofa. My favorite spot. Where I used to sit and watch movies in my free time. All things considered, I'd had more free time and far fewer near-death encounters as a crook. "Take down Söze. That's the goal. My only concern is the, you know, *how* of it all."

She spun the desk chair around to face me. "The old-fashioned way."

"You'll have to be more specific. In my previous life, 'the old-fashioned way' meant stealing everything someone owned. Or killing them."

"We find proof of what he's been doing and expose him."

I pursed my lips, considering the possibilities. "There was proof that Söze was doing all kinds of shady shit when he tried to wipe out the Crow and Hammer, and he didn't even get a slap on the wrist. Like Blythe said, he's acting with impunity because he knows his buddies in the upper MPD ranks will protect him."

"Then we need proof that can't be swept under the rug." She leaned forward, elbows braced on her knees. "Proof that he murdered a GM and attempted to murder Captain Blythe."

My eyebrows shot up. "Wait, do we know he did those things? The smoke-bomb assassin wasn't Söze, and all we know about Georgia's death is that Söze wants it labeled a suicide and Darius contests that factoid."

Lienna rolled her eyes. "That's why we need to *investigate*, Kit. Captain Blythe told us to keep working on Georgia's death."

"All right," I agreed. "So, what's our theory? She died inside a locked room inside an empty, locked guild. Unless we unwittingly stepped into a mythic adaptation of an Agatha Christie classic, nothing about that scene screams 'murder' to me."

"That's true." She held up a finger. "But there is a pattern."

"Polka dots or plaid?"

Cue another eye roll. "A pattern between Arcana Historia and Blythe's house."

I thought for a second—then it hit me. "Locked! Blythe's place was sealed up like the Pentagon. We've got a double-locked room mystery on our hands."

"You say that like this is an extravagant game of *Clue*."

"I say that," I replied, "like it's a thousand times more interesting than doing a deep dive on the legality of the Sea Devils' entire history."

She huffed. "Can't argue with you there."

"We just need to figure out how Söze did it." I racked my brain for ideas. "In *The Adventure of the Speckled Band*, the villain sends a venomous snake through a hole in the wall to—"

Lienna held up a hand, interrupting me. "Are you giving me the Wikipedia summary of a Sherlock Holmes story?"

I shrugged. "It's a locked room mystery. Seemed relevant."

"I don't think Söze is using snakes."

"What about a fae?" I suggested. "They can go through walls, can't they?"

"Söze isn't Spiritalis," she said, shooting down my unspoken theory about a covert network of fae assassins. "I've got a theory. A *real* theory."

"Fine. Let's hear it."

Lienna stood up from Eggsy's chair, inhaling deeply. "He could be using portals. My portals."

"Holy shit," I whispered, letting the significance of that theory hit me. "Way to bury the lede."

"We know Söze has the portals." She paced the limited floor space. "And it would explain how he got in and out of the lazaretto without alerting the library's security system."

"And how someone got into Blythe's place," I concurred. "But the attacker who stabbed Blythe wasn't Söze."

"So he had one of the other IA agents do it, or he hired an assassin. It doesn't matter."

"But it *does* matter, because we have to prove it."

Sighing, she dropped back into Eggsy's chair. "We need evidence."

I leaned forward on the sofa. "We can't go back to the library or Blythe's place. Söze's goons will be on the lookout for us. Besides, if he is behind all this, they'll have both scenes cleaned up by now."

"I took some photos at Arcana Historia," she said, pulling out her new phone and tapping on the screen, "but Harris had way more time at the scene than we did. If we can access the case file …"

She squinted at her phone, then sighed in frustration. "My access has been revoked."

"Shit, already?" I hastily pulled out my phone and attempted to log in to the MPD archives. A friendly error message popped up, informing me that my account had been disabled. "He doesn't waste any time, does he?"

Without our logins, we couldn't even see the basic information in the archives that all mythics could access, let alone case files.

"I don't suppose you have a secret hobby of stealing your coworkers' passwords, do you?" I asked.

"With your psycho warping, we could get close enough to the precinct to talk to a few agents without being caught, but …"

"We don't know who we can trust," I filled in. "Talking to anyone would be a risk, even the agents we *think* are on our side. There's no guarantee they won't run straight to Söze and stab us in the back."

"And we don't know who the mole is either," she added.

Ugh, the mole. That anonymous, weasely agent who'd been selling insider secrets to an unknown number of rogues.

Blythe had first tipped us off to the existence of an information leak inside the precinct a few weeks ago. Then Zak—otherwise known as the Crystal Druid or the Ghost or the Scary But Ridiculously Handsome Dude Who Has Definitely Killed People But Most Of Them Were Bad So He's Kind Of A Good Guy—had revealed he'd known about, and had been using, our precinct's dedicated mole for years. He'd traded us a USB stick of moley evidence, which should've been a big help, but our investigation had stalled out.

We knew enough to know we weren't anywhere close to catching the sleazeball, and all the while, he was selling off classified MPD information to anyone with a fat enough wallet—

Wait a minute …

"The mole!" I exclaimed, startling Lienna. "We need information. And the mole has information."

My partner sat in silence, finger tapping against the desk in thought. "We decided that was too dangerous."

"The situation's changed. Desperate times, desperate measures."

She shook her head. "Maybe we should look at the transactions again. If we can figure out who the mole is, we'll have the upper hand. We can blackmail them."

"Firstly," I replied, raising a single finger, "I am both shocked and overjoyed to hear you suggest the dark art of blackmail."

There was eye roll number three.

I put up another digit. "Secondly, we've been banging our heads against that wall long enough to cause long-term brain damage. If we keep staring at those transactions and dates and all that shit, concussion scientists will want us to donate our gray matter after we die."

"Concussion scientists?"

"I'm positive that's a real profession."

"Yes, a CTE doctor," she informed me.

"The point is," I said, guiding us back on topic, "we're on the run with only Eggert, his fancy computer setup, and the lovely view outside my ex-windows for resources. Using the mole isn't the best plan, but it's our *only* plan." I frowned. "Which, I guess, makes it our best plan too."

She grimaced. "Where's the USB stick?"

I pulled my keys out from my jacket pocket and jingled them. Dangling from the keychain was one black-and-silver USB stick. Zak had been using the mole for years to obtain information necessary to keep up his secretive rogue existence, and he'd recorded every one of those interactions. Or, rather, those transactions. Lienna and I had enough dates and times to narrow down our suspect pool to senior agents who'd been at the Vancouver precinct for at least six years and who had access to some high-level shit. But it still left us with too many agents to vet thoroughly.

Lienna arched an eyebrow at my keychain. "I thought Blythe told you to keep the USB stick out of the precinct."

"I'd rather have it on me. Safer than my sock drawer, right?"

In truth, I didn't keep much of anything of value in my apartment anymore—not after, during the Zak saga, it'd been broken into by a creeptastic luminamage who'd given me the parting gift of a knife in the leg.

Lienna surrendered the desk chair to me, and I unclipped the USB stick from my keys and plugged it into the leftmost computer. Zak had included instructions on how to contact the mole, but Lienna and I had agreed that trying to trick the mole into revealing themselves wasn't worth the risk. If we screwed it up, the mole could go to ground. Or worse.

But right now, we weren't trying to trick them. We legitimately needed their services.

I accessed a folder on the drive, and it opened to reveal a program we hadn't yet run and a file labeled "Instructions." I opened the latter and blinked at the large, all-caps words right at the top of the plain text file.

```
NO NAMES
NO LOCATIONS
NO STUPIDITY
```

Subtlety was not Zak's forte.

Further instructions told us to launch the program, type in a complex URL, and follow that up with a password consisting of numbers, letters, symbols, Egyptian hieroglyphics, two Rothko paintings, and the lyrics to an Ella Fitzgerald scat.

The program was a Tor browser—an encrypted network that made completely anonymous internet usage possible—and the link took us to a black page with a single blinking, green cursor in the top left corner. It looked like the loading screen for a program in *The Matrix*. Or the Angelina Jolie and Johnny Lee Miller classic, *Hackers*.

Not knowing what else to do, I typed in the convoluted password and hit enter.

A single word flashed in response:

```
>Waiting...
```

And so we waited.

"Are you sure about this?" Lienna asked as we stared at the blinking cursor.

"Nope," I answered truthfully.

She made a noise that fell somewhere between a groan and a sigh, then began to pace nervously between the desk and the window. I was tempted to close my eyes and relax into the padded rolling chair, but I didn't want to take my focus off the screen.

After a couple of minutes of Lienna wearing a groove into the hardwood, a new message appeared:

```
>Capybara has logged in.
```

"They're here!" I said, sitting upright.

She rushed over to the desk and eyed the monitor. "What do we say?"

Before we could figure that out, the mole sent a message:

```
>Capybara: Who is this?
```

"Do we tell them we're the Ghost?" Lienna asked.

I shook my head. "No names."

"I'm not sure that qualifies as a name."

My fingers tapped across the keyboard:

```
>You: I need information on the death of
Georgia Johannsen.

>Capybara: What are you looking for?
```

I looked up at Lienna, who shrugged. "Anything. Everything."

```
>You: Everything. Photos, surveillance
video, reports, etc.

>Capybara: That's a tall order. It'll cost
you.

>You: How much?

>Capybara: 10k.
```

"Holy shit," I mumbled. "The mole business must be booming."

Lienna gritted her teeth. "Talk about greedy."

"I don't suppose you're a trust fund kid with a six-figure inheritance kicking around?"

"I'm a second-generation MPD agent. You're the one who used to work for the big law firm."

"Yeah, well, all my assets were seized, remember?"

"What're we gonna do, then? Barter with them?"

Another message blipped onto the screen:

```
>Capybara: Can you pay or not?
```

The lock on the apartment door clunked open, and Eggert walked in, proudly displaying two enormous paper bags that smelled like heaven's garlic garden.

"I've got four types of pasta," the modern Marlboro Man announced, "plus prosciutto flatbread, a cinnamon ricotta bread thing that tastes better than—"

"Eggsy," I interrupted, my starved brain cells fighting over what was more important—food or the mole. "How much cash did Blythe leave for that operating budget?"

"Oh, I never really counted it all."

"Where is it? Can you grab it? Quick!"

He dropped the paper bags of deliciousness on the kitchen island and hurried down the hallway to my former bedroom.

Another impatient message popped up on the screen:

```
>Capybara: You've got 10 seconds.
```

"Hurry up, Eggsy!" I called.

Between the sounds of him rummaging through the closet, I heard him grumble, "You kids better not be doing that online bidding thing with the captain's money here."

In a panic, I leaned over the keyboard and answered:

```
>You: I have the money.
```

"What are you doing?" Lienna hissed. "We don't know if we can pay yet!"

"Let's hope Blythe stashed some serious cash." I tried to ignore the way my mouth watered at the smell of the scrumptious Italian food wafting into my nostrils. "If not, we'll figure it out."

She raised a skeptical eyebrow. "How?"

"You're the one who suggested blackmail."

A new message appeared:

```
>Capybara: Unmarked bills in a paper bag.
Leave it in the garbage can at the north
corner of the lower level of Robson Square
at 7pm tonight. Log back in after for
further instruction. Call yourself Rose
Petal.

>Capybara has logged out.
```

Closing the browser, I exhaled slowly as Eggert returned to the living room with a silver briefcase in hand. Lienna tugged it away from him, dropped it on the kitchen counter next to the bagged pasta, and popped it open. Stacks of colorful Canadian bills lined the inside, a few of which had been pulled apart, seemingly to pay for Eggert's newfound appetite for pricey cuisine.

I let out a low whistle. "No need for blackmail."

"This much cash …" Lienna uttered quietly. "Captain Blythe must've been planning this for ages."

I picked up a stack of fifties and flipped through it with my thumb. "Let's hope we aren't about to throw ten grand in the trash for nothing."

6

"I'VE GOT A BAD FEELING *about this*," Lienna's voice crackled in my ear.

I adjusted my earbud. "About my wig? I couldn't agree more."

As I walked past a parked car on Howe Street, I caught a glimpse of my reflection in its window. Long black hair did not suit Kit Morris.

"*About making deals with an MPD mole*," Lienna said from the safety of my former condo, presumably sitting behind the desk in the living room.

I pushed my cheap sunglasses up my nose, even though it was almost seven o'clock at night and the sun was disappearing behind the horizon. "I look like Tommy Wiseau."

"*We don't know who the mole is,*" my partner continued. "*This could be a scam or a trap.*"

"Whoever they are, they fed Zak information for years. I think we can trust them to do what they said they would."

"*An endorsement from Zak doesn't comfort me.*"

I crossed the street and stepped into Robson Square, the three-block public plaza at the heart of downtown Vancouver. To my right was the Vancouver Art Gallery and to my left a staircase that led down to the lower level of the square, where a domed ice rink was getting some use despite the mild temperatures.

I headed down the stairs. "I bet Zak never wore a wig and sunglasses around downtown at night."

"*It's a disguise, Kit. I thought you'd be excited to go incognito for a secretive spy mission.*"

"I'd be more excited if I didn't look like a hungover Vincent Vega." At the bottom of the stairs, I paused, gripping the very expensive paper bag in my hand a little tighter and observing the handful of pedestrians strolling through the open square. No one seemed overtly suspicious. "This dollar-store getup really diminishes the fun of playing Jason Bourne."

"*We don't know what kind of mythic the mole is,*" Lienna reminded me. "*Your warps might not be enough to disguise yourself. Now, hurry up. You've only got two minutes.*"

I checked my watch. Sure enough, it was 6:58. Time to find that garbage can.

I turned to the north corner of the lower level, where a nail salon and a lawyer's office met at the edge of the square. A green metal garbage can stood just outside their doors.

As I passed behind a pillar, I unleashed a halluci-bomb that redecorated me as a Matt Damon doppelganger in casual jeans and a gray t-shirt. Seeing as I was about to throw a huge wad of moolah into a garbage bin, it made sense that the mole was somewhere nearby to observe the drop—hence doubling up on my disguises.

Keeping to the square's perimeter, I reached the garbage can just as my watch struck 7:00. With one more glance around, I shoved the paper bag and its contents inside.

"Done," I told Lienna. "Send the message."

The sound of her typing rattled through my earbuds. As I walked away from the bin, I Split-Kit myself, sending fake Matt Damon across the square while the real me, now invisible, slipped into an out-of-the-way nook where I could still see the garbage can.

Just because we legitimately needed the mole's information didn't mean I couldn't get a glimpse of them in the process.

"*Okay,*" Lienna breathed. "*I told them we made the drop. Now we just—*"

Her voice cracked and went silent.

"Just what?"

"*Shit.*" She exhaled sharply. "*The mole says they left a bag for us on a bell cart inside the lobby of Hotel Vancouver—and it won't be long before the staff notice it and take it away.*"

"Goddammit!" I hissed, pulling out my earbuds and shoving my sunglasses up on top of my head. Abandoning my hiding spot, I sprinted across the square, narrowly dodging a gaggle of teenagers exiting the ice rink. Reaching the stairs, I took them three at a time, muscles pumping as hard as I could push them. At the top, I broke left, racing toward the opposite side of the square from which I'd entered.

At the road in front of me, the light was red, but traffic was sparse, so I went full rebel and jaywalked—or jayran—across to the other side, skirting around a taxi that had no idea I was there since I was still invisible.

Slipping into the narrow space between a covered bus stop and a building, I dropped the invisi-warp and kept running.

Just my luck: another red light at the next intersection. The hotel was in view, but traffic was heavier here, so I thumbed the crosswalk button incessantly, watching for a break between the cars. Beside me, a very relaxed middle-aged man in a Whitecaps hoodie was smoking a hand-rolled cigarette that, judging by its smell, contained no tobacco whatsoever. He gazed at me with a wide grin.

"Love your hair, man," he said in a hoarse voice.

"You want it?" I asked.

His eyes widened. "Yeah."

The light turned yellow and a few gung-ho vehicles sped through the intersection while the rest slowed down.

I tore off the wig and tossed it, sunglasses and all, to my new friend. "All yours."

"Woah," he mumbled in hazy awe as I sprinted across the street.

Careening onto the hotel's driveway, I slowed to a speed walk, trying to catch my breath before I pushed my way into the lobby.

The woman behind the front desk gave me a friendly nod, which I returned before sweeping the lobby for the mole's drop. To my right, a young bellhop was inspecting a lone duffle bag on a bell cart in the corner.

I jogged over to him. "Oh, thank goodness. I thought I lost this!"

The bellhop looked up at me. "This is yours?"

"Yup." I reached down and grabbed the bag's handles. "I was on my way to the airport when I realized I left it behind."

The young man smiled politely. "What room number, sir? Just so I can confirm—"

I turned away from him and speed-walked toward the door. "Sorry, flight leaves in an hour!"

Outside, I hurried away from the hotel and rounded the corner, finally stopping in front of a swanky jewelry store a block away. I put my earbuds back in and dialed Lienna.

"*You get it?*" she asked, picking up instantly.

"I think so." I knelt and unzipped the duffle bag. Inside was a stack of manila folders with MPD stamps on them. "Yeah, I got it."

"*Good. Eggert's on his way to pick you up.*"

"Thanks." I leaned back against the window of the jewelry store. "I can't believe that sneaky bastard got the better of us."

"*Well, they wouldn't have lasted this long by taking risks.*"

"Sneaky bastard," I repeated in a grumble. "We should've planned this better. If Eggert had manned the computer, you could have come with me and one of us could've stayed behind to watch for the mole."

"*We couldn't have predicted this. Besides, outing the mole was secondary. We got what we really needed.*"

I glanced down at the duffle bag and its illegally acquired contents. "Let's hope it's enough."

AFTER EGGERT DROPPED me off at the Batcave, he went home for the night, leaving Lienna and me to sort through the evidence we'd acquired from the mole. It didn't take us long to realize that the stack of MPD-stamped manila folders contained, well, not much.

"This is a whole pile of nothing," I groused. "They swept it all under the rug."

Lienna flipped through the few dozen crime scene photographs Agent Harris had taken. "I was afraid of this."

"No autopsy, no toxicology." I tossed one folder onto the coffee table between us. "Edith's statement is only a few sentences, even though she's the one who found the body. Even if this *was* a suicide, that's shoddy work at best."

I reread the single-sheet report filed by Söze's stooge, Agent Suarez. It didn't tell me anything new: death by self-inflicted asphyxiation, locked room, no abnormalities in the security system. Suarez even added a note indicating that "workplace stressors" may have contributed to Johannsen taking her own life.

Pure bullshit, from top to bottom.

"Do you have the evidence catalog?" Lienna asked, fixated on a crime scene photo.

I shuffled through the papers in front of me, then handed it to her. "Did you find something?"

"Maybe." She scanned the sheet, brow furrowed. "That's weird."

"What is?"

She held up the photo, revealing an image of the destroyed book and the evidence bag underneath it. "An official MPD evidence bag, right? A case number and everything on it."

"Okay?"

She handed back the evidence catalog. "What does it say on there?"

I scanned the sheet. "Nothing. Just 'one evidence bag, torn.'"

"No mention of the case number or what that case was. Why leave that off?"

"Laziness?" I suggested. "Incompetence? Söze's orders? He wouldn't let Harris dust for prints either ..."

As I trailed off, her eyebrows lifted pointedly.

"Söze's orders," I repeated grimly. "Did he want the case number on that bag omitted for a reason?"

"Unfortunately, we can't answer that question because we can't access the database."

Grinning, I scooted toward the desk. "We do, however, know someone who can."

"No, Kit," Lienna said, following on my heels. "We're not paying the mole another ten thousand dollars to run a case number!"

"You're right." I plugged Zak's USB key into the computer. "We won't pay them anything."

As Lienna leaned over my shoulder, I loaded up the top-secret Tor browser and entered the password. After a moment, "Chinchilla" entered the chat.

"Chinchilla?" I asked aloud.

"They were 'Muskrat' when I talked to them during the drop."

As before, our mole acquaintance's first question was who we were, and I dutifully told him that I was "Rose Petal," the moniker they'd bestowed upon us prior to the drop.

>Chinchilla: Do you have another request?

>You: Actually, I have an issue with our last one. Something's missing.

>Chinchilla: I gave you everything there was.

```
>You: I believe you. But I've got a crime
scene photo of an evidence bag with a case
number, and no corresponding information on
that case.

>Chinchilla: Take it up with the agent who
filed the report.

>You: You know as well as anyone that the
case number on that bag should be linked in
the evidence catalog. I paid $10,000 for
all the information on the Johannsen
suicide. I expect to get my money's worth.

>Chinchilla: I don't do refunds. Goodbye.
```

Lienna gripped my shoulder and hissed, "Do something."

```
>You: Wait.
```

We stared at the screen silently, waiting for the notification that our mole had logged off. It didn't happen. My fingers returned to the keyboard.

```
>You: Just look up the case for me. 30 sec
of your time to keep me as a customer.
```

No response beyond the blinking cursor.
"Are they still there?" Lienna asked.
"I think so."
Finally, more text appeared.

```
>Chinchilla: What's the case number?
```

Lienna dashed around to the sofa, grabbed the crime scene photo, and slid it to me across the desk. I typed it in and hit enter.

```
>Chinchilla: One minute.
```

Lienna's relieved exhalation tickled my neck as she leaned over my shoulder again. "I thought for sure that they'd refuse."

"Me too." I glanced sideways, found her face inches from mine, and forgot what I'd been planning to say.

A message from the mole turned my attention back to the screen.

```
>Chinchilla: That case number doesn't
exist.
```

"What?" Lienna exclaimed. "That's impossible!"

I agreed, and that's exactly what I typed back.

```
>You: That's impossible.
```

```
>Chinchilla: Did you type it in right?
```

I grabbed the crime scene photo and compared it to the message I'd sent earlier. I could feel Lienna doing the same behind me.

```
>You: Yes, it's correct.
```

```
>Chinchilla: Then I don't know what to tell
you. There's no file in the system with
that case number.
```

```
>Chinchilla has logged out.
```

"Well." I shut down the browser. "That was helpful."

Lienna folded her arms over her chest. "How was that helpful?"

I unplugged the USB key. "Because now we know that someone put a fake case number on that evidence bag—and how much do you want to bet that 'someone' was Söze?"

Lienna paced away from the desk, her eyes narrowed in thought. "Why? For what purpose?"

"That," I said, moving back to the sofa and slumping onto the cushions, "is a fantastic question."

My partner continued to pace. "Georgia received potentially illegal books in evidence bags all the time. It was part of her job. Was there something special about the book?"

I picked up the stack of crime scene photos and listlessly sorted through them again. "Could it have been dangerous? Maybe it had a spell in it or something."

"I doubt it. It was too badly damaged for any spell inside to still work."

"What if it wasn't damaged when she received it?"

Lienna frowned, then shook her head. "Georgia knew how to check for dangerous Arcana. An assassin could have slipped a poison powder between the pages, but a poison would kill her, not make her hang herself."

She was right. No matter what that book had been, it hadn't made her hang herself, nor could a book stage a suicide if something else had killed her.

"What else do we know about Georgia?" I wondered aloud, focusing on the photo in my hand, which showed the GM's keychain, complete with a plastic corgi. "Apparently, she liked dogs."

"She was at Arcana Historia for almost twenty years," Lienna said. "She wasn't married, no kids, but she did have two corgis at home."

"And she liked weird-ass coffee," I chimed in, holding up a photo that appeared to show the contents of the lazaretto's trash bin, which included a paper coffee cup with the order scrawled on the side. "Dark roast with a bag of mint tea."

"That *is* weird-ass coffee."

I squinted at the image of the coffee cup, trying to make out the label. "The Molly Roger's Roastery. I've been there. It's a few blocks west of here, right on the waterfront."

Lienna pivoted mid-step to face me, her lips quirked down. "That's a long way from Arcana Historia. Why would she go all the way over there for a coffee run?"

"Good question. If that cup is recent, maybe we can find out." I glanced at my watch. It was nearing eleven at night and well past java time. "In the morning."

Hands clenching and unclenching with pent-up frustration, Lienna looked ready to argue, but she seemed to realize the futility. "I guess so. There isn't much else we can do right now. We should get some sleep.

As much as I shared her frustration, it'd been a hella long day. I headed to the bathroom to wash my face and steal some of the resident mouthwash, reminding myself to grab a toothbrush at some point tomorrow. When I came back out to the living room, I found Lienna seated on the sofa, staring into the distance, tension etched into her face.

"You can have the bed," I told her.

She blinked a few times, brain returning to the present. "Sorry?"

"I can take the sofa. The bed is all yours."

"Oh." She sounded marginally surprised by the offer. "I can sleep here. It's your bed."

I shook my head. "It's Blythe's now, and using a bed owned by *El Capitan* kind of freaks me out. I've crashed on that sofa too many times to count anyway. I'll sleep just fine."

She smiled thinly. "Thanks."

Pushing off the sofa, she walked past me toward the master bedroom, tension ratcheting through her body.

"Lienna," I murmured. "Are you okay?"

She paused in the bedroom doorway but didn't look back at me. "Just tired. Been a long day."

"We'll figure this whole mess out," I said to her back, attempting a soothing tone. "I know it's only a coffee cup, but at least we've got a lead. We've done more with—"

"Kit," she interrupted firmly, still speaking to the doorframe. "I'm fine."

With that, she disappeared into what used to be my bedroom. There had been a time when I would have been thrilled at the prospect of the mysterious and beautiful Agent Shen slipping beneath the covers of my bed. I maybe even would've flirted playfully about sharing the bed before offering it to her.

Moving woodenly, I dropped onto the soft cushions of the sofa. Lienna's emotional doors were locked and barred, no visitors welcome. Par for the course, right? So why did her every rebuff sting like this?

And why did I keep trying?

7

I MAY HAVE OVERSTATED my ability to sleep on this sofa.

Yeah, I'd fallen asleep in this very spot dozens of times, usually while partway through a movie with an empty can of Dr. Pepper and a bowl with a few kernels of uneaten popcorn on the coffee table. But those times, I hadn't been aching, bruised, overtired, and stressed from multiple near-death experiences.

I tossed and turned for almost an hour before finally throwing off the light blanket Lienna had found in the bedroom somewhere. It was soft and fluffy and smelled vaguely reminiscent of Captain Blythe—same laundry detergent? Not only were *eau de Blythe* and relaxation deeply antithetical concepts, but so were soft, fluffy, and Blythe. Double the brain discomfort.

Sitting up, I peered blurrily at the tech desk, then stood and stretched. The multiple computers were pumping out heat like happy little space heaters, and I'd stripped down to my boxers to compensate for the extra tropical temperature in the room.

I padded barefoot across the hardwood, heading for the bathroom. Maybe a cool shower would help me relax. The bathroom was directly across the short hall from the master suite, and I paused in front of the closed door, wondering if Lienna was asleep. Would the sound of the shower wake her?

"Hey."

I started at her muffled voice. It sounded like she was right on the other side of the door. I opened my mouth to apologize when she spoke again.

"Yeah, it's me. Sorry for calling so late."

I blinked at the closed door.

"How is …"

Her voice grew more distant. She'd walked away from the door. I didn't move, feeling equally guilty and confused. Guilty for eavesdropping and confused about who she was calling when she thought I was asleep, while we were on the run, when contacting anyone was a risk.

"… know that." Her voice grew clearer again as she moved closer. "I'm in the middle of a case. I can't …"

I lost track of her words again. She must be pacing back and forth.

"Are you sure?" A pause. "Okay. Just … don't contact me unless … yeah. I'll call you." Another, longer pause. "Yeah."

My hands curled, fingers clenching and releasing. Stepping away from her door, I entered the bathroom and locked myself in, then started up the shower.

We'd been through a lot together, Lienna and me. From our tumultuous first few weeks, her the prodigy rookie with something to prove and me the lifelong conman with nothing to care about, to partners who worked together every day, risking our lives for each other, protecting each other.

We were so close, yet not close at all. At least, not close enough for anything close to the anxious, heartfelt vulnerability she'd expressed in that one quiet "yeah." Whatever she and the mystery caller had been discussing, I was betting Lienna's recent tension was related.

But when I asked her about it, she was "fine."

How could Lienna trust me with her life but nothing else? Was it her fear of my abilities? Was it because she didn't reciprocate my feelings and didn't want to lead me on, having made it abundantly clear that dating was off the table?

Maybe I was being arrogant, but I was pretty sure she *like*-liked me. I'd kissed her twice, and both times she'd kissed me back in a way that only a person who was enjoying said kiss would do. That said, I wasn't asking her to confess her undying love or get in bed with me. I just wanted her friendship.

But she wouldn't give me even that much. It wasn't just that she wouldn't open up to me about this secret stressor or that she'd tried to hide that phone call from me. She had every right to privacy, especially when it was personal. The problem was that she was intensely private about *everything* personal, and I didn't know what to do anymore. Did I give up and treat her like a co-worker? I tried to imagine that, but I couldn't do it any more than I could stop worrying about who'd she called, why she wouldn't tell me, or what was really going on.

Instead of helping me relax, showering merely gave me more uninterrupted time alone with my thoughts. I wrapped it up after a ten-minute scrub and soak, using only a plain bar of soap, because the shampoo also smelled like Blythe and I wasn't going there. I towelled dry, pulled my boxers back on, and peeked into the hall.

The bedroom door was still shut tight, no light shining under it, and I crept back into the living room. Sitting on the sofa, I turned on the TV, scrolled through a selection of Netflix titles, and tried to find something slow and quiet to lull me to sleep. I was in luck: *Lost in Translation* popped up in the "Meditative Drama" category. That seemed like the perfect lonely film for a sleepless night.

I turned the volume down so low it was a bare murmur. Slumping back in the cushions, I watched Bill Murray's cab ride through Tokyo, culminating in his awkward welcome to a luxury hotel.

Midway through, the two leads were getting ready for their night on the town, when the bedroom door clattered. I fumbled for the remote and hit the pause button.

Lienna appeared, venturing into the room with small steps. I opened my mouth to apologize, but my voice dried up. She'd wrapped a fuzzy throw blanket—similar to the one I'd discarded earlier—around her shoulders, leaving her legs visible from mid-thigh down. Her smooth, toned, bare legs.

Half my brain locked on that sight, fully prepared to trace and retrace every curve, from thighs to knees to calves to narrow ankles, while the other half skipped straight to wondering what she was—or wasn't—wearing under the blanket.

After an embarrassingly long moment of slack-jawed gawking, I gave myself a mental slap and focused on her face. Her cheeks were noticeably flushed.

I cleared my throat and gave her an apologetic smile. "Sorry. Did the movie wake you up? I shouldn't have …"

I trailed off as she crossed the room and sank down on the sofa beside me. Not *right* beside me, but not on the far cushion either. Kind of halfway between the two. She was still blushing, and I could feel a little heat on my cheeks as well—and it wasn't from the computer-generated temperature. I was practically nude here, and Lienna wasn't exactly fully clothed herself. I considered pulling my blanket over my lap, but it was too late; she'd sat on it.

"I couldn't sleep," she mumbled. "Is this *Lost in Translation?*"

Her hair was out of its usual ponytail, a rare sight. The shiny raven locks fell almost to her elbows, mussed like she'd been tossing and turning in bed before this.

Or mussed like someone had been running their hands through it. Which I really wanted to do. I wanted to—

Her eyes caught mine, dark and tired and oddly questioning.

Wait, she'd asked me a question.

I looked away before I said something stupid. "Uh … yeah. *Lost in Translation.*"

She leaned back, getting more comfortable. Was she staying to watch it with me?

"Should I … restart it?"

"It's okay. I've seen it before."

That surprised me. She didn't watch a lot of movies, at least compared to me. Unsure what to think, I hit the play button.

The movie resumed, but I wasn't paying much attention. Lienna kept her eyes on the TV, not glancing my way, her face still flushed. She shifted, adjusting her blanket. A few minutes passed, and she shifted again, stretching out her legs. With Herculean effort, I kept my eyes on the screen.

"It's warm in here," she muttered.

I nodded. "I'm not half naked for the fun of it."

Even though my gaze was firmly fixed on the movie, I could sense her giving me a curious side-eye. Real smooth, Kit Morris.

"Doesn't this place have air conditioning?" she asked.

I stared blankly at her for a moment. Maybe it was the lack of sleep or a heat-induced brain melt, but somehow it'd completely slipped my mind that this condo—*my* old condo—came with the built-in, modern comfort of AC.

"It sure does," I answered, annoyed with myself.

I hopped up and strode across the room to the thermostat near the bathroom and fiddled with the touch screen. The quiet hum of the incoming cold air made itself known.

I turned around—and caught Lienna swiftly looking away from my naked back.

Slowly returning to the sofa, I sank onto the cushion next to her. If I was going to make a move, this was the opportune moment. Would I ever get a better chance than this? She'd joined me, while I was mostly undressed, in a state of semi-undress herself, in a dark room, while we were all alone.

The breeze from the AC vent overhead washed over my bare skin, cooling my body and my thoughts. Lienna had made her stance on our relationship clear. No flirting. No romance. No dating.

Definitely no Netflix and chill.

I glanced at her profile, her attention on the TV, then wordlessly tugged the free corner of my blanket over my legs and settled back. Until she indicated otherwise, I would assume she was here with me for my company and nothing else. That wasn't a terrible thing. I wanted to spend more time with her.

I just wished I was worth more than wordless company, and that the next time I asked if she was okay, she would admit she was not "fine" at all.

———————

THE MOLLY ROGER'S ROASTERY was blurry.

Or it seemed blurry to my sleep-deprived brain. Despite the brisk ten-minute walk along the harbor between the Batcave and the coffee shop, I was still having trouble escaping the sandman's grip. Foolishly, I'd forgone the mud-like brew Eggert kept on hand in the condo in favor of grabbing some joe at the Molly Roger.

Last night, Lienna and I had ended up watching the whole movie. Only after the credits rolled had she mumbled a good night and returned to the bedroom. I'd fallen into a fitful sleep and woken up feeling exhausted, frustrated, guilty, and generally just baffled.

At just past seven a.m., we entered the coffee shop and found ourselves at the back of a line of bright-eyed and bushy-tailed business folk ready to shock their systems with pirate-themed java before the workday began.

"I'll grab the coffee," Lienna said. "Why don't you talk to the baristas and see if anyone remembers Georgia?"

I nodded blearily and stepped out of the line, making my way to the barista station, where I homed in on a curly-haired twenty-something who looked like Justin Timberlake's grouchy cousin.

"Hey," I said, trying to put as much early morning pep into my voice as possible. "I've got a few questions for you."

"Line's over there," he replied without looking up from the cappuccino machine. A burst of steamed milk obscured his face momentarily.

"I'm not looking for the line," I told him. "I'm looking for answers."

The barista, who was most certainly not bringing sexy back, glanced up at me with a scowl, only to come face-to-face with my MPD badge—which, thanks to a trusty warp, looked like a very official Vancouver police badge.

He didn't look impressed as his scowl deepened. "Did I get your order wrong, officer?"

Something told me this dude wasn't a member of the VPD fan club.

I held up my phone, displaying an image of Georgia Johannsen. "Do you recognize this woman? We think she was in here between two and four days ago."

"Nope," he said after a cursory once-over of the photo. He finished off the drink he was making with a sprinkle of cinnamon and set it down on the counter. "Cinnamon Landlubber Latte!"

A well-dressed woman in stilettos pushed past me to grab the ultra-sweetened pseudo-coffee.

"She would've had an unusual order," I pressed. "Dark roast coffee with a mint teabag in it."

The barista screwed up his nose. "Oh, I remember that. Are you gonna arrest her? Because that drink is a crime against both coffee and tea."

I wanted to agree, but I was trying to present a "professional law enforcement officer" vibe. "When was she here?"

"Yesterday—no, two days ago, about lunchtime." He filled a new cup with almond milk and threw it under the steamer. "She was with one of our regulars and some other guy."

Lienna rounded the corner of the counter and handed me a wonderfully large, steaming cup of coffee.

"The Sleepy Kit Special," she murmured too quietly for the barista to hear.

I blinked. "What's that?"

"Large medium roast with a double shot of espresso."

Bang on. That was my go-to form of caffeination when my energy tank was empty.

"We call that the Double Pegleg Eye Patch," the grouchy barista corrected, his hearing better than I'd expected.

I removed the lid from my drink and blew across the dark surface, desperate for it to cool enough to drink. It smelled so good, but I'd endured enough burnt tongues in my life to hold off on drinking the bean-flavored lava.

"Tell her what you told me," I instructed the barista.

He filled the cup with drip coffee and reached for a lid. "That you should arrest that woman for her repulsive taste in coffee?"

"No, that—"

"Captain's Au Lait!" he called out, setting the cup on the counter. "The lady with no tastebuds was here two days ago at lunchtime with two other guys. One of them is a regular. His name is Anson."

Lienna sipped her own drink, apparently immune to the scalding temperature. "Do you know his last name?"

The barista snorted. "Of course not."

Lienna and I stared at him silently, unwilling to take that utter lack of information for an answer.

He sighed. "He works somewhere around here. An editor or something. Comes in every day and orders a white mocha with soy milk and a sesame bagel with cream cheese. He wasn't in yesterday, though."

Lienna was already on her phone, digging through the internet for someone named Anson who was an "editor or something."

"Thanks for your help, Oscar," I said.

"My name isn't Oscar."

"Really? You seem like an Oscar."

Barista the Grouch gave me another scowl and returned to his duties.

I swivelled back to Lienna, who grinned and held up her phone, showing a photo of a solemn middle-aged man. "Anson Goodman, editor-in-chief of Vancouver's top mythic news outlet."

"And he's close?" I asked.

She nodded. "Right next door."

8

"'PACIFIC SCIENCE FICTION AND FANTASY,'" I read, staring at the brass plate affixed near the elevator. "'Established 2004. Suite 611.'"

Lienna's thumbs were zooming across her phone screen as she wrote out a text. "Eggert says Söze arrived at the precinct and went straight to his office."

"And his goons?"

"Markovich, Suarez, and Kade are all at the precinct as well. Eggert can't see the other two on the cameras, but we're probably safe."

The elevator dinged and we stepped inside the mirrored box.

"I remember seeing the signs for this place," I said as the doors closed. "I used to come to this building regularly when I lived in my condo, but I had no idea it housed a mythic newspaper."

"Why'd you come here?" Lienna pointed at a poster affixed to the wall of the elevator. "For the hot yoga?"

She knew I did yoga—for its great many health benefits—but she still sounded uncertain, like I might laugh.

"I usually took the Vinyasa class," I replied with a grin, "but yeah."

She made a thoughtful noise, her eyes going oddly distant. I was about to ask her what was wrong when I realized her cheeks had flushed slightly pink. What the hell was she imagining right now?

The elevator doors slid open, pulling Lienna back to the real world, and we stepped out into a hallway with sleek gray carpeting and deep blue walls. Taking a left, we headed toward suite 611, where Pacific Science Fiction and Fantasy awaited us.

PSFF was a guild unlike any other in the city. Its front was that of a magazine, primarily publishing speculative fiction and the odd interview or article. But the guild's true nature was as the only mythic news outlet in Vancouver. Since its inception, it'd existed exclusively online as a password-protected website, accessible only to those with valid MID numbers.

Lienna opened the door, and we were immediately met by a woman in her thirties with blue-streaked hair. She sat behind the front desk, munching on a breakfast sandwich. Behind her were three offices, all with the doors shut and blinds closed.

Surprise flickered over her face. She probably wasn't used to random walk-ins. "Uh, do you have an appointment?"

"Are you Jasmine Ray?" Lienna asked. I also recognized the woman from the "Our Team" page on the PSFF website. It had listed half a dozen employees, including Anson Goodman, whom we were pretty certain was the GM.

"Yes, but—"

Almost in unison, Lienna and I flashed our badges.

Jasmine frowned at them, then looked us up and down. "*You're* MPD? Seriously? This guild is older than you two."

"This guild is only fifteen years old," I muttered.

"We need to speak with Anson Goodman," Lienna told her. "Is he here?"

The woman sighed. "I don't know. I think so."

"You don't know?" I waved at the three office doors. "Do we need to play a round of *Let's Make a Deal* to find out?"

Irritation tensed her lips. "He was in his office last night, and his door has been closed and locked since this morning. I don't know if he's still in there. He didn't respond when I knocked."

"Uh … does he often lock himself in his office all night?"

"No. He's been acting weird since yesterday afternoon," she added reluctantly.

"What kind of weird?"

"Paranoid, I guess." She peered worriedly at the third office in the row. "He canceled all his meetings and barricaded himself inside. He only opened the door long enough for me to hand him food before I left last night."

Lienna shot me a quick look. This random coffee cup lead was getting more interesting by the second.

"That's his office?" I confirmed, pointing.

At Jasmine's nod, Lienna and I approached the last door. The blinds were closed and the lights were off. If he was hiding in there, wouldn't the lights be on?

"Did something happen yesterday?" Lienna asked Jasmine, who'd followed us. "Something to trigger his paranoia?"

"I'm not really sure. I transferred a call to him just before he went into lockdown, but I don't know if it was related."

Lienna pursed her lips. "A phone call from who?"

"No idea. It was a blocked number. A male voice, though."

I rapped my knuckles sharply on the door. "Mr. Goodman? MPD. We need to speak with you."

Silence.

I jiggled the knob, but it was locked. I looked at Jasmine. "Do you have a key?"

She shook her head. "Anson has the only key."

Lienna reached into her satchel, but her solution would likely involve melting the handle—or blasting the door down.

"Do you have a couple of bobby pins?" I asked her.

She paused her search for something magicky. Arching an eyebrow, she dug into her bag again before producing two black bobby pins. I spent a few seconds bending them into the shapes I needed, then leaned over the handle and inserted them into the lock.

"Standard MPD training," Lienna murmured to Jasmine, who I imagined was giving my back a suspicious stare.

Lying to a civilian? Tsk, tsk, Lienna. My lock-picking skills originated wholly from a shitty childhood. I could warp whatever I wanted, but warps didn't open the door when your asshole foster parents locked you out of the house on a cold winter night.

With a prod of a pin, the lock gave way and the handle turned. I pushed the door open, and it smacked into something hard.

Jasmine hadn't been kidding when she'd said Anson had barricaded himself inside his office. Through the inch-wide gap, I could see a tall piece of wooden furniture—probably the back of a bookshelf. Together, Lienna and I put our shoulders against the door, slowly shoving the bookshelf out of the way until there was enough room for us to squeeze through.

Other than the bookshelf, the office was surprisingly tidy.

Minus the dead body slumped over the desk.

"Anson!" Jasmine cried out, having shimmied through the gap behind us.

She tried to run past us, but I caught her arm and calmly stepped in front of her, blocking her view of her GM. "Leave this to us, okay?"

Lienna carefully stepped toward Anson and touched his neck with her fingers, checking for a pulse. She raised her head, her eyes soft with sympathy. "I'm sorry, Jasmine."

"Oh my god," the reporter whispered, tears spilling down her cheeks.

Gently, I took her hand. "Why don't you step outside for a minute?"

She blinked through her tears and nodded.

"Do you have someone you can call?" I asked. "One of us can stay with you."

"No, it's okay," she said through a sniffle. "I'll be okay."

"Let us know if you need anything." I pulled the bookshelf farther from the entrance so Jasmine could get out easier, then closed the door behind her. Turning back around, I saw Lienna, hands on her hips, staring at Anson's body.

"This can't be a coincidence, right?" I said bleakly. "Two dead GMs in two locked rooms?"

"This one isn't staged like a suicide," she observed.

I walked around the desk, observing the objects around Anson's slumped frame. "No pills, no noose, no gun, no obvious injuries. How do you think Söze is going to write off this one?"

It had to be Söze. There was no doubt in my mind. That slimy bastard was whacking GMs and using his power within the precinct to keep "homicide" off the paperwork and squash any investigation into their deaths.

"Two suicides would be suspicious," Lienna mused darkly as she prowled the small room for clues. "I'm betting this one will be labeled as natural causes. Heart attack, maybe. He was cold to the touch, so he's been dead for a few hours."

"Other than the indisputable fact that Söze is the living embodiment of a festering foot sore with powerful friends, and as nauseatingly nefarious as he is, why is he killing GMs? What's his motive?"

"We might not know motive," Lienna said, bending down beside the desk, "but we know the method."

Straightening, she held up a small black disk slightly larger than a coaster, with faintly visible runes etched into its surface.

"Holy shit," I whispered. "A portal."

That stiff tension in her shoulders was back in full force, and she didn't look pleased to have her theory confirmed. "The killer used this to escape after killing Anson. He activated it, jumped through, and came out at the exit portal somewhere outside the building."

I nodded slowly. "He couldn't take his escape portal with him. That means there should have been one in the lazaretto at Arcana Historia too."

"Suarez was first on the scene, according to Agent Harris."

I swore under my breath. "She was off doing something when we arrived. I bet she was smuggling it out of the building. Harris might not have seen it."

We split up again, quickly and quietly scouring the office for more clues. We both had our phones out, snapping pictures of anything that seemed remotely relevant, but there wasn't much. Anson had been a fastidious man, his surroundings clean and organized. The only sign of anything not in spic-and-span shape was a large envelope on his desk that was torn apart so badly it looked like it had insulted Anson's mother and he'd beaten it to a pulp.

"I'll check on Jasmine," I told Lienna after taking a photo of the pitiful paper scraps.

I found her behind the desk near the front door, staring off into space. Between her blue-streaked hair and smeared mascara, she gave off a distinct "Sk8er Boi"-era Avril Lavigne vibe.

"Were you able to talk to someone?" I asked softly.

She nodded. "I called the hotline."

It took me a moment to understand which hotline she meant. Horror flashed through me. "The *MPD* hotline? Why? We're already here."

"I know," she mumbled, barely looking at me, hazy with shock and grief. "I just thought … they could send someone more … experienced."

Note to self: donning a boring black suit to a crime scene wasn't such a bad idea. Witnesses wouldn't think I needed my hand held by a senior agent.

"When did you call?" I asked, trying not to sound panicked.

"As soon as I came out here. They said they would send somebody right away."

I forced a fake smile onto my face. "Good work. I'll be right back."

I hurried to Anson's office as fast as my double-espressoed legs would carry me, shutting the door firmly behind me.

"Söze's on his way," I told Lienna, who was taking photos of the body. "He'll be here any minute."

"Shit." She shoved the portal into her satchel. "Let's get out of here."

We moved around the bookshelf and were about to open the door when the clatter of PSFF's front entrance froze us in our tracks.

"Where is the body?" a loathsomely familiar voice asked Jasmine. "And the two other agents? Are they still here?"

I gritted my teeth at Söze's sleazy, eager tone. He was drooling over the chance to catch us.

Her voice muffled by Anson's office door, Jasmine confirmed our position. Footsteps thumped toward the threshold, then the door whipped open. It banged against the wall, revealing Söze and Agent Yao, an IA lackey with a classic Beatles haircut and a wispy circle beard. Their gazes flashed around the room, searching for a sign of us.

A sign they wouldn't find, because Lienna and I were hunkered down in a corner behind the desk, under the safety of my invisi-warp.

"I don't see them," Yao said. He strode into the room, barely noticing Anson's body as he scanned the floor. "I don't see the artifact either."

Söze's jaw clenched, and a vein in his cheek pulsed. "Check the other rooms. And be careful. You know what he's capable of."

Aw, how sweet. Söze thought my magic was scary.

Yao hesitated. "Do you have any more of that mental fortitude potion?"

"If I had more, I'd be using it," Söze snapped. "Now *get searching*."

Yao speed-walked out of the office. A sneer distorted Söze's ugly mug as he scrutinized the room. He'd already drawn a narrow silver artifact, holding it out in front of him, ready to blast anything that moved into a gazillion fiery pieces.

My teeth ground together, luckily too quiet for him to hear. A mental fortitude potion. That was how he'd made himself temporarily immune to my warps.

How fortunate for me that his supply had run out.

"I know you two brats are probably in here," he hissed. "I will give you five seconds to show yourselves and return the artifact before I set this whole place on fire. Five, four, three—"

His countdown was cut off by an audio hallucination I layered into my invisi-warp. A knocking sound rattled the window behind Anson's desk. Söze's eyes snapped toward the noise. A Fake Kit clung to the outside of the thick glass, wearing those high-tech gloves Tom Cruise used in that *Mission: Impossible* movie where he climbs the Burj Khalifa.

Söze froze, momentarily stunned by the scene. Fake Kit peeled one hand off the window, flipped him the middle finger, and jumped into the emptiness, vanishing from view.

By the time Söze pressed his nose against the glass to observe my dance with gravity, Lienna and I had snuck past him, slipped out of the office, and dashed toward the front door.

In under a minute, we were back on the street, lives and freedom intact, one entrance portal richer, and with the added confusion of another murdered GM launched like an artillery shell into the chaos of our investigation.

9

AFTER TAKING A CIRCUITOUS ROUTE back to the condo to ensure
no one had followed us, we checked in with Eggsy and stashed
the portal artifact from Anson's office in a specialty abjuration
safe Blythe had added to the master bedroom.

Then we grabbed some grub.

Because the drizzly Vancouver weather gods had decided to
take a break that day, Lienna and I carried our Japanese takeout
to a nearby park across from the harbor, leaving Eggert to man
the computers and keep an eye on the IA Shit-Squad. Other
than the odd jogger, we were alone.

I shoveled a chopstick full of yakisoba into my famished
maw while my partner sat with her untouched salmon nigiri
on her lap, staring blankly into the distance.

"Wishing we'd gone for burgers instead?" I guessed,
digging my chopsticks back in for another bite. "Don't get me

wrong. This is delicious. But when stress and starvation gang up on me, there's nothing quite like a juicy burger with extra—"

"Extra bacon, extra cheese, and crispy onions."

I blinked. "I didn't realize we have the same burger preferences."

She rolled her eyes. "*I* prefer a slice of grilled pineapple on my burgers."

I blinked again. "Grilled pineapple is delicious. But also, how do you know my favorite burger toppings?"

Not answering, she selected a piece of her raw fish and popped it in her mouth. "This is a lot."

"It's eight pieces of sushi. That barely qualifies as a snack."

"I meant our investigation."

Still lingering on thoughts of burgers, I hummed an agreement. "It's like a gruesome fast-food combo: two homicides, one attempted murder, with a conspiracy at the MPD's highest levels on the side."

"Yeah." Her voice sounded thin and strained.

"Did anything in Anson's guild fall into place for you?" I asked, downing more noodles. "A piece of this shitty puzzle we're trying to put together? We confirmed that Söze's using portals, but I didn't see anything in there to help us move forward."

Lienna poked at her nigiri. "The portals are a problem."

I waited a moment for her to continue. "Of course they're a problem. They're helping Söze murder people."

"But they don't make sense."

Again, I waited, and again, she didn't add anything. Suppressing my frustration, I said evenly, "Well, I'm not an abjuration expert, so you'll have to walk me through this. From what I understand, Söze or his minions portal into a locked room, off the victim, arrange the scene to cover up the murder, then portal out. When the call comes in, he makes sure one of his lackeys is first on the scene to grab the leftover entrance portal. Am I missing something?"

She swallowed her mouthful. "Two things. First, they need to get an exit artifact into the locked room ahead of time so one of them can portal inside."

"Right." I scraped together the last of the noodles in my box. "Do you have a theory about that?"

She made a thoughtful noise as she prodded her food with her chopsticks. "It's not like they could slide it under the door. It would need to be hidden, but not inside something solid, like a drawer or a cabinet; otherwise, the assassin would snap his own neck as he came out of the portal."

The mental image of Söze launching out of a portal, only to be crushed inside an old wooden desk drawer, brought me an unexpected moment of joy. I must have been smiling because Lienna raised a curious eyebrow.

"You just pictured that, didn't you?"

My grin widened. "Didn't you?"

She rolled her eyes again. "The point is that he would've needed a safer way to sneak the exit portal inside. Like an empty cardboard box, or ..."

"A book!" I jumped in. "Such as a shady grimoire inside an evidence bag."

Her eyes narrowed as she considered my theory. "That might work."

"It'd explain why the mole couldn't find that case number. The evidence bag was a fake. The grimoire was probably fake evidence too. Its only purpose was to get the portal inside the lazaretto." I thought back to the inside of Anson's office. "The envelope on

Anson's desk. It was ripped apart like the book. They were shredded by a whole-ass human bursting through them."

"So, Söze slips a portal inside the book and sends it to Arcana Historia, then mails another one to Anson." Lienna tapped her fingernails against the side of her takeout container. "How'd he get one inside Blythe's house?"

I shrugged. "Hid it in one of her file folders? Dropped it in her purse? Wait, does Blythe carry a purse?"

"There'd be ways for him to do it," Lienna agreed. "But there would still be issues. How did he know the victims would be in the room at that time? How did he know Georgia and Anson were alone?"

"Surveillance?"

"How do you put surveillance on the inside of a locked library in the middle of the night?"

She had a point.

"Is that the second problem you mentioned?" I asked. "Surveillance?"

She shook her head. "No. These were my portals. I created them, so …"

Her eyes went distant as she followed a silent thought, and her lips quirked down.

"Do you feel guilty?" I blurted, the thought popping into my head so suddenly I couldn't stop the question. Her magic might have been the tool used to assassinate two guild masters and damn near kill our captain.

She frowned. "What?"

"It's not your fault," I said softly. "If Söze killed them, he would've done it with or without your portals."

Her large brown eyes blinked at me, but I wasn't sure if she was surprised or confused.

"I know that, Kit. I'm not beating myself up because Söze stole my magic for his own purposes."

Her gaze darted away from mine for a second, a brief but telling slip in eye contact. She might not be beating herself up, but she wasn't unaffected. She felt some degree of responsibility.

"Okay," I agreed carefully. "Is there something else bothering you? You've been tense, and I know it's not just the crazy carousel of fugitive life we've found ourselves riding. You were on edge before any of this began."

The phone call I'd overheard last night replayed in my mind as I waited for her answer—only for disappointment to sting me as soon as she spoke.

"I'm fine."

I really hated that word.

"You don't seem fine to me. What's really bothering you?" I leaned forward. "We've been through a shitload of stress since we began working together, but nothing has tensed you up like this."

She broke eye contact with me again, as though she couldn't hold my probing stare for more than a few seconds at a time. "It's nothing you need to worry about."

"But—"

"Let it go, Kit. I'm fine."

There it was again, the word lacquered in finality: Fine.

I slumped back against the bench in defeat. "Sure, okay. What's the second problem with the portals, then?"

"Recharge time." She set her half-eaten nigiri aside and crossed her arms. "I know how long the portals take to recharge, and the timeline doesn't fit."

"How many sets do you think he has?"

"Two or three." Her lips pressed into a thin line. "I grabbed the other partially completed portals right away, but I forgot

I'd left some loaded in the laser-etching machine for the final step. Obviously, Söze figured out how to finish them. It wouldn't have been that hard. I'd done all the difficult parts already," she added bitterly.

"Each teleportation requires a portal set, and each murder requires two teleportations—one in and one out." I considered the three portal attacks. "Except for Blythe's place. Whoever came at us there only used one to get in, then ran away. How long do the portals take to recharge?"

"Over forty hours," she answered. "There wasn't enough time between Georgia's murder and Anson's to fully recharge two sets, never mind use them at Blythe's house."

"Söze stole everything from your lab. Could he have created more—"

"Not a chance. Even if he could figure out the whole process—which I highly doubt since he isn't an abjuration sorcerer—the minimum timeframe for creating a portal set is three weeks. There are several charging phases that can't be skipped."

I draped an arm over the bench and leaned back, closing my eyes. "How the hell is he pulling this off?"

"I have no idea."

"Maybe he got help," I mused, eyes still closed. "An all-star team of the best abjuration geniuses he can coerce, bully, or bribe into employment."

"As far as I know, there isn't a single other person in the city—or the province—who knows the first thing about portals. Unless …"

My eyes popped open at the warily considering note in her voice. "Unless what?"

She bit her lip uncertainly, then turned her gaze to me. "Do you remember Robin Page?"

10

ROBIN PAGE WAS TERRIFYING.

Allegedly.

Demon contractors were, in my opinion, at least partially unhinged to jump headfirst into the bloodthirsty pool of eternal damnation in exchange for controlling a nightmare-fueling hellbeast. And by my estimation, Robin Page's sanity was even more questionable. Not because she came across as bat-shit bonkers, but because she seemed *completely normal.*

It was downright unsettling.

In the realm of demon puppeteering, she was an undisputed black belt—she'd once opened a classic cola can of whoop-ass on half a dozen substantially more experienced contractors without breaking a sweat—but she also had to get up on her tippy toes to get over the five-foot mark. She looked like a "librarians gone mild" poster child and had the disposition of a frightened church mouse. When I'd pretended to arrest her, she'd almost burst into tears.

She was a walking contradiction. Combine that with the pair of semi-portal-related encounters we'd had with her, and that made her extraordinarily intriguing.

"What do you think the chances are that Robin is under Söze's thumb?" I asked Lienna as we rode the elevator up to the sixth floor of Robin's apartment building. We'd visited her at home once before, but she'd moved since then. I'd had to call up Clara, the Crow and Hammer's assistant GM, to find out where the contractor's new haunt was.

"Slim," my partner answered.

"We should still have a combat plan, in case this little chat goes south and we need to do the danger-dance with her demon."

Lienna shrugged. "Same as always. You distract her, and I'll handle the demon."

We'd used that strategy in the past, and it had worked like a charm on legally contracted demons. Contractors needed to concentrate to control their demons' actions, and if there was one thing my psycho warping was good for, it was screwing up the concentration of others.

"You don't want to have a contingency?" I pressed. "Robin isn't your standard contractor."

"Assuming her champion isn't around, I think we'll be fine."

The elevator doors slid open, giving us a view of the long hallway. And look at that—halfway down the hall, Robin stood in front of an apartment door, her keys in one hand while she peered at her phone in the other. She wasn't alone, but her companion didn't look like a contractor's champion.

He had a reusable grocery bag in each hand and a Vancouver Grizzlies ball cap pulled down low on his head. His bright red, long-sleeved shirt clung to his lean frame in a way that suggested he was one-hundred-percent hard muscle under his clothes. Even odder, he was wearing sunglasses despite the hallway's dim lighting … and he was barefoot.

His head had already been turned toward us as the elevator doors opened, and he didn't look away as we stepped into the corridor. On second thought, maybe he was her champion? One with an aversion to footwear.

"Miss Page," Lienna called out as we headed their way.

Robin glanced up from her phone, and her expression was neither surprised nor pleased. "Agent Shen, Agent Morris … I was just reading Clara's message that you'd be stopping by. You got here fast."

"Call me Kit," I told her, hoping a friendly attitude might offset her disapproval of our visit on short notice. "We have some questions about an investigation. Can you spare a few minutes?"

She darted a shifty glance at her companion. "I'm a little busy right now."

He remained statue still, grocery bags dangling from his grip. With Robin's nervous demeanor and the way Mr. No Shoes lurked behind her, a pang of concern shot through me. Was she in danger? Was she his hostage?

I reminded myself that Robin Page was a world-class contractor; if her buddy in the ball cap was a threat, she could use her demon to turn him from shredded into shreds. Maybe they were on a date and she was worried we'd ruin it?

"We just want to pick your brain about something," Lienna assured her. "It'll only take a few minutes."

Robin glanced again at her boyfriend and/or kidnapper, who didn't appear to offer much of a reaction, then nodded. "All right."

She unlocked her apartment door and stepped inside, the man following right behind her. Lienna and I ventured in with a bit more caution.

The space had that boxy setup of buildings constructed a few decades ago, but it'd been remodeled with updated appliances and flooring. Right off the entranceway was a kitchen, spacious enough but hemmed in by a peninsula counter. On the other side was the living room, which held only a gray sofa and a collection of moving boxes.

Robin headed straight into the kitchen, and still in sunglasses mode, the guy dumped the grocery bags on the counter. He then leaned against the wall at the entrance to the kitchen, either to block Robin from exiting it or to keep us out.

"So you just moved in, huh?" I asked, trying to cut through the silent tension with some amicable chitchat as Lienna and I positioned ourselves across the counter from her.

"Yeah." Robin started emptying the grocery bags, seemingly out of a need to keep her hands busy. "There was a fire at my old building."

"That sucks." I peered at the large bag of flour she'd unloaded. The grocery bag hadn't looked that heavy while her buddy had been holding it. "Baking something?"

"Just cookies," she mumbled. "So, what can I help you with?"

I helped myself to a barstool and plopped down, while Lienna chose to remain standing. Since Robin hadn't asked her friend to leave the room, he must have been a mythic she knew well enough that she didn't mind having this conversation in front of him.

"We have an unusual case," my partner said, understating the unmitigated shitshow we were neck-deep in. "With some unusual magic involved."

Robin had finished unloading the groceries. She peeked at her male companion, then pulled out a large mixing bowl. "What kind of unusual magic?"

"Portals," I told her.

"Portals?"

Her hand floated toward the infernus hanging around her neck. Infernuses were the key to a contractor's control of their demon, and I didn't like that she was reaching for it at the first mention of portals.

Lienna's hand dropped surreptitiously to her satchel, ready to draw one of her many artifacts should Robin whoosh her demon out for some blood and havoc. On the other side of the counter, Robin couldn't see Lienna's movement, but the kitchen sentry noticed. Even with his gaze hidden behind sunglasses, I could tell his attention was locked on my partner.

"I don't know anything about portals," Robin said flatly. She grabbed a bag of brown sugar instead of her infernus.

"You met with me a few weeks ago to ask about a spell array that contained Arcana Fenestra elements," Lienna reminded her, easing her hand away from her satchel.

I eyed Mr. Sunglasses. "For those of us in the room who don't dabble in dead languages, that's Latin for 'portal magic,' right?"

"More or less."

"Unless you *do* dabble in dead languages," I said to the guy. "I don't think I got your name."

His head swiveled to me. "Z."

"Z?" I echoed. "Like the letter?"

"Yes."

He'd only spoken two syllables thus far, but for some reason I couldn't pinpoint, they'd come across as undeniably menacing.

His lounging posture against the wall was supposed to look casual, but there was nothing chill about him. And the sunglasses couldn't hide the way he was watching us with unbreaking focus.

"What is that short for?" I asked. "Zander? Zeppelin? Zorro?"

"No. Just Z."

I nodded. "I once considered going by K until I realized people would think I was agreeing with them all the time."

"The array you asked me about," Lienna interjected firmly, rerouting the conversation. "What did you learn about it?"

"Nothing really." Robin turned away from the counter to poke at the oven. It beeped, then hummed loudly as it began to preheat. "It was a research project I was doing in my spare time."

"What about that little incident with the giant monster and busted helipad?" I asked. "We found a portal there, too. A big one."

Robin kept her back to us, still studying the oven's display. "I told you I had nothing to do with that array. It was … someone else."

I shrugged. "We're just following a pattern. Portals for research, portals on a helipad, and now some more portals. Right now, you're a connection in two out of three."

Robin turned back around, her eyebrows pinched together and a spark of anger in her eyes. "You said you just wanted to pick my brain, but now you're accusing me of being involved in a portal conspiracy?"

I held up my hands. "I didn't mean it like that."

"Besides," she snapped, "weren't you the ones who told me to leave that portal out of my report to the MPD?"

She wasn't wrong. A month and a half ago, Lienna and I had agreed it would be wise to keep all portal chatter away from suspicious eyes—particularly Söze's. We hadn't wanted an investigation into the existence of portals in Vancouver springing to life and endangering Lienna, so we'd suggested to Robin and her cousin that they omit that little detail from the reports they'd filed with the precinct.

"We did," Lienna confirmed.

"But now the MPD is investigating portals?" Robin whipped toward the fridge, motions sharp with temper, and I squinted at her back, trying to reconcile this version with the timid girl who'd almost cried when I'd pranked her.

Lienna stifled a frustrated sigh. "This situation is different."

Robin returned to the counter with a container of eggs and cracked two into the mixing bowl. "How?"

"We're tracking an assassin," I answered.

It wasn't an entirely accurate statement, but it was shocking enough to get Robin to look up from her mixing bowl. She glanced again at her silent pal. "An assassin … using portals?"

"Looks like it," Lienna confirmed.

"How?"

"They're using portals to get at the victims, then escape the crime scene undetected."

"I don't even know how …" Robin trailed off, looking back and forth between Lienna and me. "You don't think … I'm not a killer."

"You say that, but you give off some real creepy murder vibes," I said. "Like Sweeney Todd, but with icing sugar instead of meat pies."

She gripped the mixing bowl, her knuckles going white. "What?"

Her barefooted bodyguard tensed like a compressed spring ready to burst open. Lienna, on the other hand, targeted me with an eye roll.

"Kit," she warned.

I grinned. "I'm kidding. We know it's not you."

Robin relaxed somewhat, then turned to the fridge again. She replaced the eggs and came back with a new ingredient. "I honestly don't know much about—"

"Woah, hold up," I interrupted. "Is that sour cream?"

She paused in the midst of dumping the container's contents into her batter. "Uh, yes."

I quirked a curious eyebrow, but before I could delve into the details of sour-cream cookies, Lienna took over again.

"Do you know who Agent Söze is?"

Robin nodded as she added vanilla to the mixing bowl. What in the name of Julia Child was she making?

"What do you know about him?" Lienna pressed.

"Only what I've heard from my guildmates at the Crow and Hammer."

"So nothing good," I said with a humorless snort. "What about you, Z? Any run-ins with Söze?"

"No," he answered in what sounded less like a straightforward answer and more like a straightforward threat.

I tried not to stare at him. Something was off about this dude. The way he spoke, his menacing presence, and the absurd outfit—it all reeked of someone hiding something. Something dangerous. Lienna was too focused on grilling Robin to notice, but I'd been watching him the whole time, my suspicion growing by the second.

While Robin repeated the warnings Darius had given his guild about Söze, I created a Split Kit warp that covered the entire apartment. Leaving fake-Kit on the barstool, my invisible real self stood up and walked around the counter, closer to the mysterious stranger.

The hue of his skin was unusual. A sort of medium brown, but with a reddish undertone. And not in a "cute blush" way. It was unlike any skin tone I'd ever seen before, and the closer I got to him, the stranger it seemed.

I stopped almost toe to toe with him. He was a few inches shorter than me, but that didn't lessen his intimidation factor. This close, the subtle feeling that'd been itching across my senses since first approaching him and Robin in the hallway was strong enough to set my pulse thudding: the instinctive feeling of being hunted. My lizard brain was convinced I was no longer the apex predator in the room, and it was pumping adrenaline into my bloodstream in preparation for fight or flight.

I tried to peer through the reflective lenses of his sunglasses. The need to uncover what was really going on with this guy was buzzing through me more urgently, as though the danger increased with each passing second. Knowing it would blow my cover, I reached up slowly, inching my fingers to the side of his glasses.

I was millimeters away from pinching the frame when a vise clamped around my wrist—Z's hand.

I froze, momentarily stunned by his light-speed movement and the raw power in his fingers—fingers tipped with dark, pointed nails that looked a hell of a lot like claws.

"What are you doing?" he whispered, casually choking the life out of my wrist.

How the shit could this guy see me?

I wrenched my arm free—or I tried to. Not only did his grip not break, but his arm didn't so much as wobble. I was taller and heavier than him, but he might as well have been made of stone for all I could shift him.

My flight instinct hit hard, and I yanked my arm again, simultaneously releasing my useless warp. Lienna and Robin jumped at my sudden teleportation from the barstool to being Z's hostage. They went rigid, grasping the situation immediately.

"Let me go," I bit out through clenched teeth.

To my surprise, Z released my arm—then he grabbed me by the throat, lifted me off the floor, and threw me backward with inhuman strength.

II

I HIT THE COUNTER on my back, slid across it with limbs flailing, and pitched off the other side, my stunned brain still catching up to my sudden, violent relocation.

At the same time my back slammed hard into the carpet beside Lienna's feet, Z landed on the counter in a ready crouch, sunglasses pointed at me and Lienna, claws tipping his curled fingers, and a long, thin tail uncoiling behind him, its barbed end lashing.

On my back on the floor, I had half a second to act—so I hit Z with my meanest Funhouse warp. His perception split into a dozen fragmented inversions, and unlike my invisi-warp, this one affected him—he swayed on the counter, his tail snapping more violently as though to recover his faltering balance.

But my hope snuffed out as fast as it had sparked when he steadied himself an instant later. He launched off the counter, catching Lienna in the chest. She crashed down on her back beside me, her Rubik's cube flying from her grasp. Z landed between us, a hand around our throats. His fingers tightened like iron bands, restricting my airway.

Walking out of the kitchen, Robin appeared in my line of vision. She stopped beside me and looked down at the two helpless MPD agents on her living room floor.

"Did you come here to investigate me?"

Her question was as stony as the hostility in her blue eyes. Holy hell, this girl had toughened up since our last encounter.

I wheezed, and Z loosened his crushing grip enough for me to get a lungful of air.

"We're investigating portals," I said with sincerity—and a good dose of desperation. "We thought you might know something."

She squinted at me with an odd, vaguely distracted expression, then demanded, "Why did you go after Zylas?"

Zylas. So the "Z" did stand for something.

My gaze darted to formerly-Z-now-Zylas. He still wore sunglasses, but I now knew what they hid—the telltale glow of his demonic red eyes. Robin's companion was her demon in disguise. A walking, talking, human-imitating demon that she'd taken grocery shopping.

"I wasn't going after him," I said innocently, trying not to hyperventilate with my limited airflow. "His glasses were on crooked. I was just going to fix them for him … in secret, so he wouldn't be embarrass—"

My voice cut off as Zylas squeezed my vocal cords like a stress ball.

Robin sank down to sit on her heels. "I'll tell you a little-known fact about demons. They can tell when someone is lying."

Oh shit.

"Why did you go after him?" she asked again.

Zylas loosened his grip again, and I gulped. My panic was increasing with each second he had me pinned. He might be on the "short and slim" side for a demon, but the evidence so far suggested he was just as lethal as his beefier cousins.

"He seemed suspicious," I told them, opting for honesty this time. "I wanted to get a closer look to see what he was hiding. It was just curiosity!"

Frowning, Robin glanced at Zylas again. He stayed focused on his victims, but his head tilted slightly toward her. The silence stretched like an elastic band about to snap, and I wished I could see Lienna—to make sure Zylas hadn't choked her unconscious.

"*Ch*," the demon grunted, the sound rife with irritation.

Robin pursed her lips, then gave a slight shake of her head. "You and Agent Shen helped Darius, Ezra, and Tori. I don't want you to get hurt. If Zylas lets you up, will you listen to what I have to say?"

"We'll listen," I blurted, grabbing this chance to avert what was otherwise looking like imminent death.

"Agent Shen?" Robin asked.

"Yes," Lienna croaked. "I'll listen too."

The bruising grip on my jugular disappeared, and Zylas rose to his full height with fluid grace. I scooted backward and scrambled up, Lienna mirroring me before I had a chance to offer her my hand. Side by side, we faced the contractor and demon pair.

This close, Zylas could disembowel us both before Lienna could speed-chant a spell, and my warps had done nothing more than annoy him. We were helpless against his physical strength and speed, and on top of that, I was highly concerned that he might be fully unbound—as in, he had control of his explosive demonic magic.

Anticipatory silence hung between us, but before any of us could break it, a loud *meow* sounded somewhere around ankle level. Another predator with claws and a tail and a carnivore's lust for blood had entered our standoff, but it wasn't a demon.

It was a cat. A super cute black cat with white paws that leisurely walked over to Zylas and batted at his leg.

Zylas ignored the white-footed feline, his menacing focus centered on us. But as the universal law of felines states, cats who want attention cannot be ignored. With another plaintive meow, it jumped up onto his thigh and clawed its way up his jeans and shirt, coming to rest on the back of his neck, splayed out across his shoulders, purring loudly.

Cats must be magical. It was the only explanation for why, despite the very real danger to my life, I wanted to pet it. Desperately. But there wasn't an ant's chance under a magnifying glass that I was moving any closer to Zylas.

Stupid demon. Let me pet your cat.

Robin cleared her throat. "So, I know how this looks, but Zylas and I have a contract."

"*Suuuure* you do."

The sarcastic response was out of my mouth before I could consider how dumb antagonizing the contractor and her demon was. I winced at my obvious death wish, my heart hammering frantically.

"No, we really do have a contract." Robin tapped her infernus. "It's just, uh, a lot looser than normal. But he's not a bloodthirsty monster like other demons."

"Sometimes," Zylas corrected. "I make exceptions."

His voice was suddenly different—a strange shift in the way he enunciated his words. An unfamiliar, inhuman accent roughened each syllable, enhancing the malice in his tone.

"You will make an exception too," he continued, pushing his sunglasses up and pulling his ball cap off with the same motion. "You will pretend I am a fully contracted demon, and I will pretend to be a fully contracted demon, and no one will die."

Robin winced slightly at his blunt threat, but I barely noticed, too fixated on the glowing red eyes boring into my skull. Undeniable intelligence gleamed in his stare, and it was the most terrifying moment of this encounter so far.

"No one will die?" Lienna repeated quietly. "With such an illegal contract …" She glanced at Robin. "Can you control him at all?"

"I don't need to. He controls himself." Robin laced her fingers together in front of her. "We've gone this long without him going on a killing spree—and he's saved a lot of lives."

My mind spun back through every case and incident where Robin Page's name had come up, and many of my questions suddenly had answers.

"You know what?" I said abruptly. "I think we got off on the wrong foot. Or claw. Or whatever. We're not even here to investigate your demon. We really just need your help."

Zylas's crimson eyes narrowed slightly, and Lienna muttered something under her breath that definitely included my name in an exasperated tone. So maybe I was jumping the gun on a truce, but what else were we supposed to do? We couldn't lie since demons could detect lies—super handy power, that—and we couldn't just waltz out of the apartment.

Besides that, curiosity was strongly challenging my sense of self-preservation. How and why had Robin tamed a demon into dressing like a human, carrying her groceries, and befriending a kitten? The cat was still curled over his shoulders and purring in that insistent, "feed me, minion" way.

"The assassin we're investigating is Agent Söze and his lackeys," I went on, pretending my nerves weren't still lit up with the need to flee from the demonic danger a few feet away. "Seeing as Söze tried to eradicate your guild, that means the four of us can safely be in cahoots."

Zylas frowned. "That does not mean we can be … *cahoots*."

"*In* cahoots," I corrected automatically. "And I think it does. Söze is our common enemy. We can't bring him down if we're fighting each other."

Or more accurately, if Zylas killed us first, because I didn't see any way to best a demon from three feet away when my warps had little to no effect on him.

"So you'll keep our secret?" Robin prompted.

"Yeah," I agreed firmly.

Robin looked expectantly at Lienna. My partner shifted her weight, hesitating with her wary gaze on the demon, then heaved a sigh. "Yes, we'll keep your secret."

Zylas gave a short nod, presumably confirming our truthfulness with his mysterious, built-in lie detector. That was enough for Robin. With a relieved smile, she scooted back around the kitchen counter to her abandoned cookie batter as though her demon hadn't just attacked and almost murdered two MPD agents in her living room.

The rest of us weren't quite so ready to relax. Despite our promises to keep his secret, Zylas's ominous scrutiny hadn't lessened. His attention remained on us as he scooped the cat off his shoulders and tossed it onto the sofa—very gently, I noted.

His tail snapping just like the annoyed feline on the sofa, Zylas backed into the kitchen after Robin, stopping at the far end of the peninsula where he could protect her and attack us with equal ease. I surveyed his position, and feigning a calm confidence I didn't feel, I moved to stand at the counter across from him. My throat still throbbed from his iron grip, reminding me of the danger.

"So," Robin said, vigorously mixing her cookie batter, "how can I help with Söze and the portals?"

Moving cautiously closer to the counter, Lienna gave Robin a full rundown of what Söze had been up to: the stolen portals, the two murdered GMs, the attack on Blythe, the recharge times, and the fact that the only conclusion we could come up with was that someone with abjuration knowledge had to be helping Söze.

"Which is why we wanted to talk to you," my partner explained. "You're the only other person I could think of who knows anything about portals."

"I'm not an expert—not even close—but some arrays can be optimized to shorten the recharge period. Would that be possible for a portal?"

While Lienna and Robin delved into a brainstorming session involving every bit of magic they'd ever read about, I kept my eye on the flesh-and-blood demon standing nearby. In shedding his Grizzlies hat and sunglasses, Zylas had revealed a set of short horns protruding through his messy jet-black hair, not to mention those eyes that burned like red-hot charcoal. They gazed sharply at me as I stared at him, unable to help myself.

"I have to ask," I said in a voice quiet enough not to interrupt the much more important conversation happening beside us. "What's it like?"

"What is what like?"

"Hell. Like, are we talking more *Constantine*? You know, that classic ultra-red landscape? Deserts and lava and anguished spirits being tormented for all eternity by bloody, grotesque abominations with pitchforks and fire-breath? Or more *What Dreams May Come*? Empty and surreal enough to make your soul shudder?"

He responded with a low growl.

"You don't watch a ton of movies, do you?" I asked.

"I do not watch *screens*," he answered.

"Why not? Do they look different to you? Is it some kind of demon eyeball thing? Can you see colors humans can't too? What about x-ray vision?"

"You talk too much."

"A blessing and a curse. I'm actually surprised you talk at all. I assumed you guys did all your talking with your fists, if you know what I mean."

His lips curved up, revealing flawless white teeth with predatory points. "I use my claws for that."

An uneasy shiver ran along my spine. "Uh, so, yeah, on the topic of talking, do demons have their own language? Your English is really good, by the way, but you have an accent, so I'm assuming you have a mother tongue."

He grumbled irritably. "*Zh'últis.*"

"Yeah, like that. What does it mean?"

"Stupid," he translated, a mean glint in his glowing eyes.

"I'm totally going to use that," I said, unbothered by his insult. "Can you teach me to swear? Demons have swear words, right?"

Another nonverbal growl was all I got back.

"What about speeding up the recharge without altering the array?" I heard Robin suggest.

Lienna leaned forward. "How? With a secondary spell?"

"Maybe," Robin murmured as she spooned batter onto a cookie sheet. "I read about a charging array in a book on astral Arcana."

"But the charging spell would also need to recharge," Lienna countered. "I don't know if that would help Söze."

Sounded like spell-ception to me. Charging within charging. Arrays within arrays. The type of sorcery that a lowly Psychica mythic like me knew nothing about, so I turned my attention back to Zylas.

"If I give you a phrase in English," I said, "could you translate it into demonic for me?"

"No."

"No, you can't? Or no, you won't?"

His upper lip curled derisively. Definitely the latter. I could work with that.

"We could make a trade," I offered. "You teach me something in your language, and I'll give you a badass English line in return. There are some Samuel L. Jackson quotes I think would suit you magnificently."

"No," he repeated.

"Come on, dude. I know you'll probably never run into a snake on a plane, but I still think it—"

"What about a nexus?" Robin asked with sudden excitement, accidentally mashing a ball of cookie dough into a pancake on the baking sheet. "Agent Söze could be using one to recharge the portals!"

Lienna frowned. "Would that speed the process up?"

"I think so." Robin hastily reformed the squashed cookie ball. "I read about them. There are dozens in the Vancouver area, some stronger than others."

"Are any of them strong enough to triple or quadruple an artifact's recharge speed?"

"I don't know. I'm only familiar with the theory of nexus charging."

"Uh," I interjected, "for the less knowledgeable in the room, what's a nexus?"

"A sorcery construct for amplifying power," Lienna answered quickly. Seeing my blank look, she added, "They're set up in locations where the natural energies of the earth are concentrated and can be used to enhance certain types of Arcana spells. Most cities with mythics have at least a few. If Söze is using one, we could catch him in the act."

Robin's lips quirked down. "If you don't know which one he's using or when, it might be a long shot."

Lienna and I shared a look, unable to argue with Robin's assessment. She carried her cookie sheet over to the oven and stuck it into the heated interior. As she returned to the counter and started cleaning up, I rubbed a hand over my face.

"It's a decent lead," I said, "but with just the two of us, we'll have a hell of a time covering more than a couple of nexuses. And if we take too long, he'll have plenty of opportunity to kill again. At this rate, Vancouver's GMs will be extinct within the month."

Worry pinched Robin's brow. "Can't you get other agents to help you?"

Lienna shook her head. "We can't trust anyone. We don't know who's in Söze's pocket."

We were also fugitives who couldn't return to our precinct, but we didn't need to mention that part.

"I see." Robin gazed down at the sink full of dirty dishes, then turned to Zylas. They exchanged a silent look before she refocused on me and Lienna. "I could help with the nexuses."

"How?" my partner asked.

"Well, not just me," Robin clarified. "My guildmates will know more about Vancouver's nexuses than I do, and I can ask for help staking them out."

The aroma of baking cookies filled the kitchen, and I had to swallow a mouthful of anticipatory saliva before I could speak. "Are you sure they'll do that for us?"

Robin nodded. "No one hates Agent Söze more than the Crow and Hammer."

"That would be great," I said. "But you two should stay away from the nexuses or anywhere else Söze might show up. He's a loose cannon. You don't want to find yourselves in his crosshairs, especially given your ... unique situation."

Robin's mouth flattened. "We'll be careful."

"Where's the nearest powerful nexus?" Lienna asked. "Kit and I can get a head start on checking them out."

"Uh ..." Robin's eyes drifted up and to the left as she rifled through her memory bank. "I only remember the locations of a few. There's one at UBC in the Nitobe Memorial Garden, but I don't know how strong it is."

"We can start there. Let us know how it goes with your guildmates and if they can help." Lienna hitched her satchel up her shoulder. "Let's get going, Kit."

I held up my hand. "Not so fast. I have two pieces of unfinished business here. First, I'm not leaving until I get to try a cookie. And second, Zylas and I aren't done with our discussion."

Glowing red eyes narrowed at me. "No."

"Don't provoke him," Lienna hissed.

"I just want to make a simple trade."

An exasperated snarl crawled out of the demon's throat. "Do you ever stop?"

"Rarely," I replied with a smirk. "It's just a couple of demon words swapped for a couple lines from my internal compendium of film quotes. What do you say, Z?"

"If you stop talking to me," he growled, "I will teach you *one* thing."

My smirk widened into a genuine grin. "Excellent."

12

"ESHANA HH'AINUN MAILESHTA," I growled in my best demon voice.

Lienna rolled her eyes as she started the car. "How many times do you need to repeat that?"

"As many times as necessary to ensure I never forget it," I told her, buckling myself in. "I'm the one person in the entire world who can quote John McClane in demonic, and it would be a crime against *Die Hard* fans everywhere if I messed it up."

She cast me a sideways look as she accelerated away from the apartment building and turned right onto 4th Ave—a straight shot to the university. The gray sky was growing noticeably dim as the unseen sun began to set, making the city gloomier than it usually was in the winter months.

"I don't think it means what you think," she informed me.

"How would you know?" I squinted at her. "You don't speak demonic, do you?"

I was fairly confident that Hellbeast Languages 101 wasn't a standard abjuration course. But I was just a lowly psycho warper, so what did I know?

"No," she admitted. "But the syntax doesn't match. And think about it. Most of it is a meaningless interjection. How would he translate it?"

I frowned.

She took a hand off the wheel to hold up a finger. "Also, he said he would teach you 'one thing.' Not necessarily the thing you asked for."

"*Eshanā hh'ainun mailēshta*," I whispered to myself, mulling over each syllable. Then I weighed it against its alleged English counterpart: "Yippee-ki-yay, m—"

An angry Vancouver driver blared his horn outside my window, unduly censoring my translation.

"Anyway," Lienna said as the irascible driver passed us at Mach 5, apparently furious that we were driving in our lane at the posted speed limit. "We have a lead, which is good."

"Right, the nexus thingy." I abandoned my questionable demonic quote to dig through my memory banks for anything I could recall about them. "What are we looking for exactly? Will we recognize it when we see it?"

"An artifact will mark the spot, but it won't be obvious. I'll be able to recognize it, though. Then we just have to wait and see if Söze shows up."

I gave a disappointed *humph*. "I thought we'd need to do something, I dunno, cooler—more magical—than that."

"Afraid not. Just back-to-the-basics detective work."

I slouched in my seat, relishing the legroom of the SUV, but a buzz from my jeans pocket interrupted my vehicular luxury. I pulled my phone out and checked the screen: a text message from Vera, who had yet to respond to my message about having a temporary new number.

Being a smuggler on the shady side of the law, the tall, tattooed seer was one of my stranger allies. After I'd joined the ranks of the MPD, she'd kept her distance more often than not. I hadn't actually expected her to reply to me.

I unlocked my phone and was immediately taken aback by the all-caps sentence she'd fired my way:

```
DO YOU EVEN REALIZE HOW MUCH SHIT YOU'RE IN
RIGHT NOW?
```

I re-read the message, making sure I hadn't missed something because, yeah, I had a pretty good idea of the quantity of shit I was in.

But how the hell did Vera know about that?

"What's going on?" Lienna asked, glancing sideways at my confused expression.

"I'm not sure." I sent a single question mark back to Vera. Within seconds, she fired me another text.

```
Life or death situation, idiot. Yours,
specifically.

And Lienna's!
```

Well, that wasn't comforting. I typed out a reply:

```
What are you talking about?
```

Her answer was quick but not very helpful.

```
Meet me ASAP if u dont want to die
```

Was it just me, or were her messages losing grammatical integrity? My phone chimed again as she sent a dropped pin on a map—a spot behind an out-of-commission brewery on the east end of Kitsilano.

"Vera seems to think we're in danger," I told Lienna.

My partner snorted. "Didn't need her to tell us that."

"This might be something different," I said. "She wants to meet."

"Now? What about the nexus?"

I wanted to follow our lead too, but Vera wouldn't contact me like this if it wasn't important. "We should see her first."

My partner glanced at me, lips pursed. "You still trust her?"

Lienna and Vera didn't exactly get along. It was your classic case of people on opposite sides of the law butting heads—and one innocent Kit regularly caught between them. While the two of them had been forced to partner up in the past, their cooperation had yet to foster any warm, fuzzy feelings.

"She's never given us a reason not to." I jerked my thumb over my shoulder, pointing behind us. "We need to go that way."

Lienna sighed, shoulder checked, found a gap in the traffic, and pulled a hasty U-turn, rocketing the SUV back in the direction we'd come from.

I sent off a quick message letting Vera know we were on the way. As Lienna drove, nerves prickled down my spine. I found myself checking the mirrors and peering out of the SUV's windows. Nothing looked suspicious, but I also didn't know what I should be looking for.

In less than ten minutes, we'd pulled off the main drag and onto a pockmarked gravel road that approached the old brewery's parking lot from the south. A barbwire-topped chain-link fence cordoned off the north and east sides of the lot, while the dilapidated concrete building provided a formidable barricade to the west.

As the SUV's suspension labored across the multitudinous potholes, a brash revving rose up behind us. In the mirrors, I saw a motorcycle with a rider clad in black leather speed into view, zigzagging around the worst of the pavement perils.

"That's her," I said.

Vera lifted one hand off the handlebars and waved it frantically. Lienna slowed the SUV to a stop in the middle of the parking lot. As I opened my door, Vera hopped off her bike, barely getting the kickstand down in her haste. She sprinted toward us, still gesturing wildly. She was yelling something, but the words were muffled by her helmet.

"What?" I demanded, adrenaline firing through me as I caught her contagious urgency.

She yanked her helmet off, revealing her short blond pompadour hairstyle. "*Get out of the car!*"

I'm not normally a "blindly follow orders" type of guy, but when someone shouts a command in *that* tone of voice, I obey first and ask questions later. I threw myself out of the SUV, stumbling on the gravel before whipping around to make sure Lienna was doing the same. She'd mirrored me, half a second behind.

A buzzing noise overhead grabbed my attention. I craned my neck upward as a small white object thirty feet in the air zoomed toward us—a drone.

"Kit!" Vera yelled urgently.

The moment the drone was lined up above the SUV, blue light lit its underbelly. A splash of faintly glowing liquid spilled down in weird globs and splattered across the SUV's metal roof with heavy *thunks*.

For a split second, nothing happened. Just the obnoxious buzzing of the drone's propellers—then the goop exploded.

Blinding cerulean light consumed the SUV and a blast wave knocked me on my ass. I rolled onto my knees, senses reeling from the impact and from the *cold*. Instead of a fiery, searing pain, I was damn near frozen. An arctic chill had hit me along with the concussive force, plunging my body temperature so sharply that my teeth were chattering and my exposed skin had gone numb.

I dragged my head up, and my eyes widened at the sight of Blythe's SUV, which had been simultaneously ripped apart and frozen into a giant, jagged blue icicle.

My frantic gaze swept across the scene. "Lienna?"

Vera appeared beside me, grabbing my jacket to haul me away from the SUV and the buzzing drone thirty feet above. "We have to get away—"

"Lienna!" I yelled again as I threw off Vera's hand. I sprinted around the vehicle, passing too close to the sub-zero cloud of cold radiating off the ice. The bitter chill sank into my bones, making my muscles tremble. But then I was past it—and I spotted Lienna.

She was crawling away from the ice on quivering arms, her whole body shaking violently.

"Lienna!" I skidded to her side and seized her left arm. Vera was there an instant later, pulling on Lienna's right arm. We got her up, but before we could move, Vera went rigid.

I didn't need to know what future vision her seer gift was showing her, because the drone was zooming toward us and the coming danger was obvious. Now that we'd so considerately grouped up, it was going to goop us all in one hit.

What sick genius had come up with the idea of exploding people with alchemic ice using a *drone*?

"Run!" I roared, not waiting for Vera to finish her vision.

We bolted away from the drone, and it flew after us, bobbing and weaving as its unseen controller tried to line it up just right. It seemed the operator didn't want to waste their murder-ice alchemy on a missed strike, giving us a slight advantage. *Very* slight.

The abandoned brewery loomed ahead, and we raced for it as fast as our hypothermic legs could carry us. But the operator had figured out where we were headed, and the drone dove to hover barely five feet above our heads, matching our frantic pace.

A blue glow lit its underbelly.

"Watch out!" I cried.

Hauling Lienna with me, I swung left and Vera swerved right. A single glob of blue fluid splatted on the ground where we'd been. Ice expanded in a rush as fast as a dynamite blast, and for a second time, I was hurled off my feet by the arctic force.

Lienna and I landed hard, my arms wrapped around her protectively. Cold more brutally intense than that genius time I'd fallen into the Pacific Ocean in the middle of winter pierced my skin. The instinct to curl into a ball gripped my muscles, but I forced myself to stagger up, dragging Lienna with me.

"This way!" Waving at us to follow her, Vera shot ahead toward a heavy steel door in the nearest wall of the brewery. She pulled something out of her jacket pocket and held it straight in front of her. "*Ori impello maxime!*"

A nearly invisible ripple of force launched out of her fist and torpedoed the brewery's door, wrenching it off its hinges and sending it crashing down somewhere inside the threshold.

But Lienna and I were still too far from safety.

The drone dive-bombed toward us. My warps were useless against its navigation camera and I had no weapons. I couldn't do a damn thing but stagger away as it closed in again.

Lienna pulled away from my arms and cocked her hand back. For a wild second, I thought she was about to throw a stun marble, but instead, she hurled a fistful of muddy gravel at the incoming drone with all her strength. Pebbles ricocheted off its lightweight body and pinged off one of its four propellers, making it bob drunkenly in the air.

I seized her other hand, and we sprinted through the open doorway into the brewery's dark interior and careened to one side of the threshold. My back hit the wall, Lienna's back against my chest as we sheltered just inside. We were shivering violently, and I clenched my jaw against the uncontrollable chattering of my teeth.

Vera was positioned on the other side of the doorway, mirroring my position against the wall. The whine of the drone came closer and closer to the open door. I nudged Lienna aside as I readied myself.

My eyes met Vera's, and I knew she had the same plan as me: smash that homicidal drone into the floor the moment it flew through the doorway and pray to Jack Frost that we didn't get iced in the process.

The whirring grew louder. Then suddenly, the noise retreated. Silence fell.

I let out a rushing exhalation. "Now what?"

Vera's expression was grim. "The assassin won't give up that easily. The moment you go back out there, the drone will try again."

"I'm sorry, but"—I cocked my head like I might've gotten ice in my ears—"did you say *assassin?*"

"I told you that you were in deep shit." She jerked her head toward the brewery's dark interior. "Come on."

Without thinking, I caught Lienna's hand as I stepped forward, drawing her with me. Her arm stretched out, limb rigid, and a slash of rejection cut into me—but before I could release her, her fingers clamped around mine and she rushed to my side, keeping pace with me.

I tightened my hold on her hand, my chest aching, but I had no time to cross-examine my feelings.

Our footsteps, harsh breaths, and occasional bursts of teeth chattering echoed through the cavernous space. Otherwise, it was dead quiet. Through the darkness, I could barely make out the silhouettes of the massive machinery that had been employed in the production of whatever cheap beer they'd churned out here. The whole place reeked of stale hops and mildew.

Vera guided us to a set of metal stairs that jutted upward into the middle of the room and led onto a catwalk that hung about fifteen feet above the floor in a grid-like pattern.

"Where are we going?" I whispered, rubbing my free hand over my opposite arm for warmth.

"As high as we can," Vera answered cryptically.

I realized she was expecting to go Round Two with the drone, and I peered around us again, seeing little more than varying shades of black and gray. "You think it'll follow us in here?"

She put a finger to her lips.

I stopped and listened. Back in the direction of the destroyed door, a familiar buzzing noise that I was feeling increasingly spiteful toward grew louder.

Well, shit.

13

TAKING CARE TO TREAD LIGHTLY, the three of us wove through the catwalk until we found another staircase that took us to the upper level, which was so close to the ceiling that Vera and I had to crouch slightly to avoid conking our noggins on the various beams that ran overhead.

The drone's whine doubled in volume, a new echoey reverberation adding to its noise. It was inside.

"Time's up," Vera said. "Got a plan?"

"Me?" I shook my head. "Unless the operator is hiding in here, they're probably beyond my range. Either way, I'd have no way to tell if I was affecting them."

Lienna tugged her hand from mine, leaving my chilled palm even colder. She dug into her satchel and pulled out her Rubik's cube. She looked it over for a few precious seconds as the drone's noisy blades grew louder, then gripped one side, twisting it slowly before turning it and twisting again. She repeated the twists half a dozen times until one face of the cube had lined up in a compact circular array.

"Is this some new horror you've concocted recently?" I whispered warily.

She shook her head. "I just tweaked the dome shield to make it stronger against water-based elements."

"Not ice elements?"

"Ice is made of water, Kit."

I opened my mouth, then closed it. Hypothermic Kit was a little slower than properly heated Kit, okay?

"Can it stop the drone's attack?" Vera asked.

"It should," Lienna answered, failing to imbue me with any confidence.

"Good. I have a plan." Her eyes glazed with a vision of the future. "As soon as the drone—"

With a loud whine, the drone rose through the open areas between the catwalk less than twenty feet in front of us. It swiveled in place and a small blinking red light rotated into view.

The camera.

Pointing straight at us.

"The shield!" Vera yelled.

The drone tilted forward and accelerated, closing the gap like it intended to bludgeon us to death. Five feet away, it pulled up short and tilted backward to show its underside. That blue glow flared again.

"*Ori te formo cupolam!*" Lienna cried, thrusting the wooden cube toward the drone.

Instead of spilling goop for gravity to pull to the ground, the propellered robot fired a gob at us like a deadly spitball.

Lienna's watery shield shimmered around us an instant before the goop splattered against it.

Ice exploded across the shield. It was a testament to Lienna's abjuration skill that the rippling barrier held against the concussive force.

Unfortunately, the catwalk wasn't nearly as tough.

Metal screeched, blown apart by the ice, and the elevated pathway heaved as it tore away from its anchor points. The next thing I knew, there was nothing solid beneath my feet. The catwalk had split down the middle and the section where I stood dropped like a trapdoor.

I plunged downward with a shout. Through more desperation than agility, I grabbed the railing on my way past. My weight wrenched painfully on my arm, and I clung to it like my life depended on it—which it did.

Ice crashed to the floor twenty-five feet below my dangling shoes, forming a nice, jagged landing platform for when I inevitably lost my grip.

"Kit!"

Panic laced Lienna's voice, and I craned my neck to look up. She clung to the railing on a section of catwalk that was hanging at a forty-five-degree angle. Her Rubik's cube and its shield were nowhere in sight; she must've dropped it when the catwalk had given way.

"Kit, hold on!" she called, bracing her feet as though to move closer to my broken section. "I'll—"

"No!" I stretched up my other arm to get a second hand on the railing, but the shift in my weight caused the railing to groan. "Don't come any closer, Lienna."

Her face was bleached of color, a white oval in the darkness. "But Kit—"

Over the diminishing racket of falling metal and ice, a terrifying buzz rose in volume. The drone sped out of the darkness and picked a new position—half a dozen feet above my head. Hanging helplessly, I stared up at it, knowing that whether I let go or not, I was done.

"Kit!" Lienna screamed.

Blue light lit the bottom of the drone.

"*Ori impello maxime!*"

Vera's voice rang out in vicious triumph, and I belatedly spotted her clinging to the other side of the broken catwalk, tucked in the shadows with her artifact aimed straight at the drone.

The magical haymaker hit the little flying beast like a boxer punching a teacup. Propellers shattered, pieces shooting everywhere, and the frame was thrown back into a steel pillar.

For one glorious heartbeat, I thought we were safe.

Then the drone exploded.

Every ounce of whatever alchemical super-ice bullshit its operator had equipped it with erupted like an inverse Krakatoa, spewing deadly spears of frosty hate in every direction. The frigid blast wave rammed into me, and as all the heat vanished from my body, I was torn away from my precious handhold.

Caught in the concussive force, I felt like I was floating, held aloft by an icy cloud.

Then I realized the opposite was true: I was plunging through the brewery's beer-scented air like a Kit-shaped popsicle about to shatter against the unforgiving concrete below.

An impact thudded through my numb body, rattling my bones.

Oh god, I was dead. I'd fallen two stories off the top catwalk and splattered against the brewery's floor, and now I was off to meet St. Peter at the pearly gates. I only hoped for three things: unlimited junk food, unlimited movies, and unlimited time with Gillian, because if I got into heaven, she'd definitely be there too.

But instead of an infinite supply of Netflix, candy, and the best foster mom the world had ever seen, I was greeted with freezing temperatures and a throbbing, full-body ache like I'd been punched everywhere at once.

Cracking my eyes open, I saw my breath misting in front of my face. I was lying on what looked like a catwalk—the second level one, I realized. Stifling a groan, I levered myself into a sitting position and peered blearily at the shadowy shapes of heavy-duty machines. Unless the afterlife reeked of malt and mold, I hadn't yet died.

Not only was I down a catwalk level from my previous position, but I was a good twenty feet away from the shattered section of catwalk where I'd been hanging. The explosive force had thrown me, and instead of falling straight down to my death, I'd traveled on a more horizontal trajectory.

I looked at my trembling palms, dotted with scrapes and lacerations. Tossed through the air like a ragdoll, and not only had I landed safely on a catwalk, but I'd instinctively caught myself and prevented a nice, gory head injury.

I should buy a lotto ticket.

"Kit!"

Clanging footfalls accompanied Lienna's sharp voice, and the catwalk vibrated with her steps as she came into view, dashing out of the darkness toward me.

"Lien—"

Before I could get her name out, she'd reached me. She dropped to her knees, threw her arms around me, and buried her face in my shoulder. Jaw hanging open, I sat unmoving, wondering if maybe I had died after all.

I was about to lift my aching arms to wrap around her, but she pulled back. Her red-rimmed eyes searched my face, and then she cleared her throat.

"I thought you'd fallen," she croaked. "Are you okay?"

"Aside from feeling like a crash-test dummy in cold storage, I don't think I'm broken anywhere." I rolled my aching shoulders as shivers built in my muscles. "Are you hurt?"

"I'm fine."

For some odd reason, I didn't trust that word anymore. "And Vera?"

"I'm here." She limped into view, gripping the catwalk railing. "But we can't hang around and chat about the weather. The assassin might not be done yet."

Oh joy.

With Lienna's help, I climbed to my feet, the shivers really taking hold and shaking me from head to toe. The cold only deepened as we hobbled along the catwalk toward the stairs, Lienna's arm around my waist and mine around her narrow shoulders.

"Let's walk and talk," I suggested. "By which I mean, Vera, please explain why someone wanted to Han Solo us."

Both women gave me a confused look.

"Frozen in carbonite at the end of *The Empire Strikes Back*," I clarified. "Not my best reference. I think my gray matter is still iced over—which brings me back to my original point. What the frozen hell was all that?"

"*That* was Daedalus," Vera answered as we descended the stairs back to ground level.

I gripped the railing tightly with my free hand. My muscles felt so sluggish that every step was a chore. "Is that an alias?"

Vera nodded. "I don't know his real name, so don't ask. He's new—him and his drones."

"New to what?"

"Black spots. And you two have been marked. That's what I wanted to warn you about, but Daedalus got to us first."

"Marked with a black spot?" I asked, feeling a strange combination of intrigue and terror. "Like in a pirate story?"

"Pretty much. It's all hush-hush, underground bullshit, but I like to keep myself in the know."

"Or in other words," Lienna muttered, "you like to use it to find clients to smuggle out of the country."

Vera ignored that. "Lucky for you two, I was checking the list today, and I saw your names."

Lienna slipped away from me, hastening over to a pile of rubble where her Rubik's cube had fallen. Stuffing it back into her satchel, she returned to my side and put her arm around me again as though I might fall over without her. I wasn't complaining.

"Is there a reward for killing us?" she asked Vera.

"Assassins don't do this shit for fun. Most of them, at least."

My partner bit her lip, her expression uneasy. She glanced at me. "Does this all seem familiar to you?"

"Huh?"

"Vigneault's case."

A lightbulb went off in my brain. Holy shit, she was right. Agent Vigneault had lost her mind on Söze because he'd shut down her investigation into a criminal bounty system that sounded an awful lot like these black spots. Was it a coincidence that he'd squashed Agent Vigneault's takedown mere days before the very operation she'd been investigating was weaponized against his personal enemies?

Yeah, that didn't sound like a coincidence.

"Did *he* put hits on us?" I demanded furiously. "He blocked Vigneault so he could *use* the illegal bounty system?"

"Who?" Vera asked.

"Agent Söze," Lienna growled, confirming she and I were on the same page.

I tightened my arm around her shoulders. "He's upped his game. We stole back his new murder toy from Anson's office, and now he's really pissed."

"He must be," Vera said as we came to a halt near the broken-down door where we'd entered the brewery. "He's paying like he is."

"How big a reward are we talking?" I asked, morbidly curious about how much my life was worth to Söze in dollars and cents.

Vera peered outside before glancing back at me. "One hundred each."

I frowned, disappointed. "A hundred bucks? That's it?"

"A hundred *thousand*."

"Oh!" My briefly deflated ego lifted to new heights. There was something awesome about being hated and/or feared so much that Söze was willing to part with a six-figure sum to put me in the ground. But it quickly dawned on me that my and Lienna's deaths were worth a veritable ass-ton of cash, which meant the drone-assassin Daedalus surely wasn't the only murderous slimeball hoping to hit up the Black Spot ATM with our blood on their hands. "Shit."

"Yeah, shit. A lot of shit. Half the criminal underground in Vancouver is watching out for Agent Morris and Agent Shen." Vera crossed her arms. "Which is why I told you two to meet me. You need to get the hell out of the city. I'll drop you off on a cargo ship in the harbor, and it'll take you across the Pacific. Where you go from there is up to you."

I frowned. "Can't you just get us across the border? We can hole up in Seattle until this blows over."

"Blows over?" Vera scoffed. "This shit doesn't blow over, man. It requires permanent relocation."

"Permanent? Isn't there a way to get our names de-spotted?"

"Not that I know of." She glanced between me and Lienna, seeing similar looks of stubbornness. "Look, these sorts of bounties are rare. Not very many people are shelling out six figures for a hit, but when they do, it works. Every time."

"What about the guy who runs it?" I wondered aloud. "What do you know about him?"

Vera shrugged. "Whole lotta nothing. I've heard people call him the Coffer. For all I know, he's a she, or an alien, or whatever."

"But if we can find him," I said, "we can get him to call off the hit. And"—a bolt of nervous excitement hit me, making me vibrate with sudden energy—"we can get evidence that Söze put a hit on us! When Vigneault was yelling at Söze, she said the bounty mastermind keeps records on 'every single user.' We can prove that the bastard tried to off us."

Lienna lit up, her enthusiasm matching mine. "The MPD higher-ups will have a hard time ignoring an Internal Affairs agent taking out a hit on fellow agents."

"Two birds, one iron-clad stone that his friends in high places can't sweep under the rug."

"Or you could *not die*," Vera countered. "My boat's a five-minute drive from here. I can have you free and clear of this shitshow before midnight."

I smiled warmly at her. "I appreciate the offer. Seriously. But I'm not willing to run from this."

Lienna nodded her agreement.

"Your funeral," Vera grumbled. "Which I will not be attending, by the way."

"What else can you tell us about the Coffer?" I asked.

"Did you completely zone out earlier?" she asked sarcastically. "*Nothing.* No one knows anything about him."

"Vigneault does," Lienna reminded me.

"But she's locked up."

"Her files aren't."

I gave her a knowing smirk. "Are you suggesting what I think you're suggesting?"

My partner sighed. "I wish I wasn't."

"If you're planning to break in to the MPD," Vera said, stepping between us, "I want to make it extremely clear that I will not be taking part."

"We don't need to break in," I told her smugly. "We have someone on the inside."

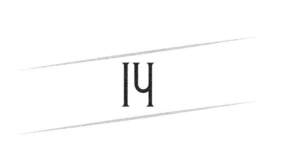

14

LIENNA AND I WALKED side by side along the cracked pavement. The road was quiet and dark, the streetlamps dim and dirty. As I'd gotten steadier, we'd drifted apart until our arms had fallen away from each other, and now we weren't touching, just pacing along in each other's orbits.

That seemed to keep happening. We'd come closer, closer, closer ... then we'd slip away from each other again.

My gaze lingered on her profile as I remembered the panic in her voice while I'd been hanging from the broken catwalk. As I remembered the way she'd hugged me. If I'd been faster to hug her back, would she have let go? Would it have made a difference? What if I'd initiated something last night? Had she been dropping me a giant hint, or was I reading the situation all wrong?

My hand stretched out, fingers hesitantly searching for hers, but before I could touch her, I let my arm fall back to my side.

I was too tired and sore to inflict another sharp rebuff on my equally tired and sore heart.

We'd left Blythe's ice-ploded SUV in the brewery parking lot, and Vera had taken off the moment we'd refused to let her smuggle us out of danger. I didn't blame her. She'd risked enough for us. Daedalus had already been on our tail, and if Vera hadn't been around to help when he'd struck, we'd have died in his first drone attack.

I shivered at the thought.

Lienna glanced at me, but she didn't speak. The silence felt tenuous, fragile, as though words were just waiting to break through.

"Kit …"

I stopped, turning toward her. She looked up at me, her lower lip caught in her teeth. Her mouth opened, bobbed for a second, then closed again. She looked away from my questioning eyes.

A silent, heavy sigh slid past my lips.

Headlights flashed over us. A red pickup truck older than I was rumbled down the dark road, and recognizing Eggsy's ride, I dropped the invisi-warp hiding Lienna and me from any prying eyes. He pulled over beside us and the window cranked down to reveal his glorious mustache quivering in a smile.

"Hey ho," he said. "Hop in."

"You're a lifesaver, man," I replied earnestly, eager to get off my feet. We'd called him for a ride before putting some distance between us and the brewery, and I didn't want to walk another step.

Lienna and I climbed in, my partner squeezing into the middle seat on the long bench. Our hips and thighs were pressed tightly together to leave space for Eggert to drive, but my attention was on a constant swivel, checking everything around us. I couldn't hide us any longer; Lienna's cat's eye spell had run out of juice, plus I couldn't make Eggsy invisible. I'd tried, but I guess there was more to the old-at-heart ex-security guard than just a mustache, because I couldn't make him vanish.

We filled him in on our day, from Anson's murder to the new black spot issue, but there wasn't much we could do about any of it except lie low before Daedalus or his competition figured out where we were. He dropped us off at the condo, and with no sign of assassins or surveillance, we headed up to my old suite.

Inside, I immediately sank my throbbing body into the plush embrace of the sofa. A quiet groan slipped from my throat as I let my head fall back. I needed painkillers and a hot bath.

At a clattering sound, I cracked my eyes open to find Lienna sitting at the computer, leaning intently toward a monitor.

"What are you doing?" I asked.

"Saying hi to our mole."

I shifted against the plush pillows to watch her. "You think they'll answer?"

"Why wouldn't they?"

A quick glance at my phone told me it was almost eight. "Because they're probably off their shift and curled up in their burrow with a nice glass of earthworm merlot. Or whatever moles drink."

Lienna rolled her eyes. "I'm pretty sure our mole isn't using their MPD computer to do their …"

"Mole-ing?"

"Sure."

I shrugged. "Worth a shot."

Lienna followed the same process as last time, starting with the USB key before pitter-pattering on the keyboard. As she sat back to wait, I picked up the TV remote and turned it on. I clicked rapidly through a selection of movies, but not much appealed to me at the moment.

Crazy, I know. Kit Morris, PhD in Everything Film from the prestigious University of Not Enough Other Hobbies, was having difficulty picking his next flick. I passed over *Death at a Funeral*, *Seven Psychopaths*, and *Fargo*, not particularly interested in two hours of darkly giggling at murder, corpses, and bloodshed. Where were the films for when you felt like a popsicle that'd been recently thawed in the most violent tumble-dry cycle ever? Or the films for when you really, really wanted to clothesline your current mortal enemy in the throat? We finally had a plan for taking down Söze, and having to sit around and wait was physically painful.

Or maybe I was just in physical pain. Same, same.

I finally selected the 1973 classic *The Sting*, which didn't really suit my mood, but the idea of watching Paul Newman and Robert Redford team up to get revenge on a violent mob boss sort of appealed to me for some reason. Better than scrolling options for the next hour. I adjusted the throw pillow under my right arm, then stretched out my aching legs with a stifled groan.

Lienna got up from the desk. While Redford was losing a massive chunk of change on a roulette wheel, I listened to her rattle around in the kitchen. The fridge opened and closed. A moment later, she walked in the living area and offered me a glass of cold water and two white pills—painkillers.

"Thanks," I said, surprised but mostly grateful as I tossed the pills in my mouth and downed half the water in a few gulps.

She headed back to the desk. I expected her to reclaim the wheeled chair, but instead, she adjusted the angle of the monitor. With the green "Waiting…" text pointed toward the sofa, she padded over and sat down beside me.

Unlike last night, she sat on the middle cushion—which was a lot closer to me. Another phantom memory of her hugging me in the brewery crept back into my head, and I forced my attention back to the screen, where Redford was getting beat up by the aforementioned mob boss.

I tried to keep half an eye on the monitor, watching for the moment the mole logged on, but aches and exhaustion were wearing me down. My chin nodded forward, eyelids drooping.

"Kit?"

A warm, soft hand patted my cheek. I dragged my chin up off my chest to find Lienna leaning toward me, her brow furrowed in concern.

"You didn't hit your head earlier, did you?"

"Huh?" Oh, she was making sure I didn't have a concussion. "Oh, no. No head bumps. Brain is good."

I could hear my own exhausted words and wasn't sure I'd even convinced myself that my gray matter hadn't been sloshed around inside my cranium.

"Are you sure?" She reached up. Her fingers gently prodded my skull, then swept through my hair, searching for injuries.

My eyes closed of their own accord, a wave of relaxation sweeping over me. Holy hell, that felt nice. I wanted her to run her hands through my hair from now until the heat death of the universe.

"Kit?"

"Hmm?"

"Are you okay?"

"Good," I practically slurred, not opening my eyes. "Just tired."

"Okay."

Her hands slid away from me, but my disappointment was interrupted by her weight settling against my side. She leaned into me, so close I could smell the faint floral scent of her hair.

I didn't open my eyes, unsure if them being closed was a prerequisite for this level of closeness. She wiggled around a little, getting more comfortable, then a soft sigh slid from her. I could try to parse out the exact emotional notes of that sigh, but I'd only be guessing. Whatever she was thinking or feeling, it was all locked behind her mental castle walls.

Maybe because I was too tired to worry about a rejection, or maybe this stuff was just easier with my eyes closed, but I reached out. My searching touch found her arm, and I slid my hand down until I could entwine our fingers together. Hers closed tight around mine, and my own silent sigh escaped me.

Moments later, I drifted off into a light, restless nap.

"They're here!"

Lienna's exclamation and a sudden jostling movement yanked me out of dreamland. My eyes flew open, my left side cold as her warmth vanished. On the TV, a high-stakes poker game was unfolding on an express train. I'd been out of it for a solid half hour.

Lienna plunked down into the desk chair, her fingers already rapid-fire tapping on the keyboard. I hauled my drowsy ass off the sofa and joined her, leaning over her shoulder—our positions reversed since the last time we'd contacted our moley pal. Green text glowed on the black screen.

```
>Beaver has entered the chat.

>Beaver: Who is this?

>You: Rose Petal.
```

"What's with them and rodents?" Lienna said, hands poised to type as she waited for a response.

"They *are* a mole," I answered. "At least it's a patriotic rodent this time."

```
>Beaver: I hope there weren't any more
problems.

>You: I need more info.

>Beaver: I gave you everything.

>You: Different case.

>Beaver: Which one?
```

Lienna hesitated, glancing up at me. "I don't know the case number. How do we describe it?"

I leaned over and typed:

```
>You: Agent Vigneault was the lead
investigator.

>Beaver: Agents work lots of cases. And
Vigneault is in jail.

>You: Do I have to pay for that tidbit?

>Beaver: Call it another freebie.
```

Lienna swatted my hands away from the keyboard with more force than necessary, and because I was leaning across her on my wrists, I damn near face-planted into the keyboard.

I recovered with my face intact, but in the process, I'd inelegantly smeared my fingers across the keyboard.

```
>You: 2q43wesrdyfuvghb;/lm.

>Beaver: What?
```

Lienna shot me a wide-eyed look—a blend of annoyance and oh-shit-ness. "What do I say now?"

"You've got control of the keyboard," I replied, taking a step back. "The conversation is all yours."

Her hands hovered above the keys for a moment before finally tapping out a reply.

```
>You: Sorry. Cat ran across my desk.
```

"Good one," I snorted, eliciting a minor glare from my partner.

```
>Beaver: I don't have time for this. Give
me the details or I'm gone.

>You: Illegal bounties. I need everything
Agent Vigneault had on that case.
```

The cursor blinked as we waited for a response.

"You think the cat scared them off?" I wondered aloud. "Felines are the sworn enemies of rodents everywhere."

She pursed her lips thoughtfully. "Those files have a high security clearance. Maybe the mole isn't sure they can access them."

After a few more seconds, the response came:

```
>Beaver: 3k. Garbage can outside the
computer repair shop at Broadway and
Cypress at 11pm. Send a message when it's
there.

>Beaver has left the chat.
```

With an explosive exhale, Lienna leaned back in her chair.

"At least this one is cheaper than last time," I said. "Does the mole give a discount for closed cases? Or is this a repeat-shopper discount?" I pictured the contents of Blythe's cash stash, trying to mentally tally it. "Still, if we keep spending like this, Eggert will have to switch from fancy pasta to instant ramen cups in a hurry."

Two hours later, I found myself once again dropping wads of cash, hidden in a paper bag, into a public trash can—although I was sans a knockoff Loki wig, opting instead to pull a hood over my head and wrap a scarf around the lower half of my face. It was mildly nippy out, so I wasn't the only late-night pedestrian bundled up.

Again, I created a Split-Kit that walked away from the drop point while I remained invisible, waiting to spot the mole.

And again, Lienna received a reply from the mole that sent me sprinting through the city streets to pick up the package. This time, instead of leaving it in the diligent hands of an upscale hotel's staff, the mole had dumped it on a merry-go-round at a playground two blocks south.

I got there before any hooligans walked off with it, finding not a duffle bag but a slightly crumpled Christmas gift bag. As I picked it up, I noticed a tag attached to the handle.

I flipped it open, and my blood ran cold.

To: Agent Morris
Keep up the good work.
From: your New Friend

15

"WHAT ABOUT VINCENT?" Lienna suggested.

"Vinny's the first person I considered and the first person I dismissed," I replied. "Whoever the mole is, they were feeding Zak info before any of us started at the MPD. We're looking for someone older."

Lienna and I were loitering at the edge of the university hospital's staff parking lot, where we'd been since midmorning. Safely out of the lone security guard's sight, we were watching the back entrance for a glimpse of our target. We'd dressed as incognito as possible, both wearing dark jeans, hoodies, and sunglasses that Eggert had picked up for us.

With nothing to do but wait—and hope we'd avoided any assassin attention on our way out here—we'd been going in conversational circles as we debated how the hell our "new friend" had figured out Agent Kit Morris was Rose Petal. I was tempted to ask Zak—again—if he could provide any clues about the mole, but the notorious druid hadn't replied to my "new number" text. He'd either dropped off the radar again or he'd ditched the phone he'd last used to contact me. He went through phones like Lienna and I went through vehicles.

"I was in disguise," I muttered, not for the first time. "And I was using warps. How did *both* fail?"

"Maybe the mole figured it out some other way," Lienna suggested, also not for the first time.

"But *how?*"

"I don't know, Kit. Can we focus on the Coffer instead? That's a bit more urgent."

She had a point. Who the mole was wouldn't matter if we got offed by an assassin before we could erase our black spots and get the evidence we needed to bring down Söze. Assuming this worked, Söze would have done us a favor; instead of the painstaking process of catching him charging portals at a nexus and figuring out how he'd had two GMs killed, we could nail him for trying to have us killed instead.

A frown tugged at my lips. We'd been so focused on the "how" of Georgia's and Anson's deaths that we hadn't dwelled much on the "why." What reason did Söze have to kill them? As far as GMs went, they'd been quiet ones. In contrast, Darius King was an outspoken and influential GM who alternated between playing the MPD's laws like a chess master and operating outside their laws entirely. If Söze was trying to weaken the city's guilds by removing GMs from the picture, he'd chosen the wrong targets.

"How long is his shift?" Lienna mumbled, checking her watch. "We've been waiting for hours."

Vigneault's case file had directed us to the university hospital, where her inside man in the Coffer's operations worked his regular, non-mythic job. Venturing into the hospital to find the informant was too risky, so we didn't have much choice but to sit tight.

Another twenty minutes passed, the back entrance disgorging two tired, scrubs-clad women before finally swinging open to reveal our man.

"That's him," I said.

Dr. Lloyd Markle: a tall, broad man with sandy blond hair that was starting to show bits of gray, cut short and neatly styled. He was an Arcana healer as well as an emergency room doctor.

"Let's go," Lienna said as we watched the doctor, clad in his navy-blue scrubs and a windbreaker, stroll purposefully toward his car. "*Ori menti defendo.*"

With her cat's eye spell protecting her mind, I dropped an invisi-warp over the entire parking lot, hiding us from the security guard and anyone else nearby. The two women had already driven away, and as far as I could tell, there was no one else in the vicinity. But better safe than sorry.

"Let's do calm cop, chaotic cop," I whispered as we moved to intercept Lloyd.

"As opposed to good cop, bad cop?"

"Exactly. We need him to cooperate, so we can't go in too soft and have him push back." I lifted a hand, showing one side of an imaginary scale, then raised the other, balancing it. "Or too hard and traumatize him."

"You seem to have this all figured out," Lienna murmured, a tentative note in her voice.

I shrugged off that hint of uncertainty. "I'm learning."

As in, I'd recently learned there were some lines I shouldn't cross even though my psycho warps were physically harmless.

Those lines shifted at times, especially when faced with a particularly nasty form of evil, but this wasn't one of those cases.

Lloyd slowed down, approaching his jet-black BMW, and with a bit of extra concentration, I excluded his mind from my halluci-bomb.

"Dr. Markle," Lienna called as he pulled his car keys from his pocket.

Lloyd turned around. If our sudden appearance had startled him, he didn't show it.

"Can I help you?" he asked politely.

"You can," I answered. "And we can help you, too."

He gave me an amused smirk, as though the thought of assistance from Lienna and me in our half-assed incognito getups was somehow funny. "Help me with what?"

"Your boss. The scary one with the even scarier business model."

His face betrayed nothing. "I'm not sure what that means."

"There's no point in lying, Dr. Markle," Lienna said firmly. "We already know about your arrangement with Agent Vigneault."

Ah, there it was: the brief flicker in his eyes. The fear. Almost as good as a confession.

"How long do you think it'll be, doc?" I asked. "Before the Coffer knows you betrayed him?"

Lloyd's poker face broke entirely, his features contorting with dread.

"We might be the only people who can get you out of this alive," Lienna told him in a low voice.

"And who are you?" he demanded. "How do you know all this?"

"Well," I said with a deep sigh, "speaking of scary, shitty bosses, the scrotal wart running our precinct emptied his wallet to pay *your* boss to put an illegal bounty on our heads."

Lloyd frowned. "Precinct? So, you're—"

Lienna interrupted by flashing him her badge from her pocket.

"And he's also the same soggy bag of dicks," I added, not giving Lloyd time to question whether the two early twenties, hood-clad "kids" were *really* MPD agents, "who shut down Agent Vigneault's investigation into the Coffer."

The doctor's eyes widened.

"Which means that he has access to her case files," Lienna spelled out on the off chance he wasn't getting it. "Those files name you as an informant. Since our boss has been talking to your boss, I think we can all agree that you're about to be in deep trouble."

I nodded. "And given his line of work, I imagine the punishment for betrayal is a smidge nastier than giving you detention and taking away your cell phone."

Lloyd's square jaw sagged with fear. "I need to go."

He spun toward his car and fumbled with the door handle.

"Where?" Lienna asked sharply.

He looked over his shoulder at us. "As far away as possible. You kids should do the same."

While still maintaining my overall halluci-bomb to hide Lienna and me from everyone besides Lloyd, I targeted his mind and created a Split-Kit warp. When he faced his car again, fake-Kit was sitting on its roof, glaring down at him. The doctor took a startled step back, cranking his head around to see that real me was now gone; only Lienna was there, a stern, unfazed expression etched into her features.

"That's not your only option, doc," fake-Kit told him as my head throbbed woozily from the complexity of the simultaneous warps.

"We know he has eyes on your son in Nova Scotia," Lienna said, injecting a crumb of sympathy into her voice. "Do you really think you can get all the way to the east coast in time to save him?"

Lloyd Markle's mouth quivered as he stared at her. "What the hell is this?"

According to the files we'd acquired from the mole, the Coffer had pressured Lloyd into acting as his personal doctor—a mob medic, more or less—by threatening the life of his estranged son in Halifax, Nova Scotia. Even though he hadn't seen his son in several years, Lloyd clearly loved the boy.

"We can help you," fake-Kit said. "And your son."

"But you need to help us first," Lienna added.

Fake-Kit's left hand produced a tennis ball–sized fireball and tossed it into the air. The flambe sphere split into three smaller balls. As they fell, my warped doppelganger deftly juggled them, giving him a jester-of-the-underworld vibe.

"That's not a threat," I made my phony self say. "That's just how it has to work. You lead us to the Coffer, and we'll make sure he doesn't hurt you or Lloyd Junior."

"How are you going to do that?" the doctor asked quietly.

Fake-Kit caught all three fireballs and clapped his hands together. The flammable trio erupted, consuming the warp. He and the inferno vanished in a blink.

"We have our ways," the real me said, ending the warp.

Lloyd, who must have been whiplashing himself with all the back and forth, spun around one final time to see Lienna and me giving him a collectively serious look.

My partner held out her hand expectantly. "I'll drive."

Two minutes later, Lienna had her foot firmly on the gas pedal of Lloyd's shiny BMW, and the three of us were speeding down 4th Ave, away from the university campus.

"Are you sure this is a good idea?" Lloyd asked from the back seat. "The Coffer knows my car. If he's put a black spot on me, every assassin in the city will know what we're driving."

"It's the only car we have," Lienna admitted, mostly under her breath.

I sank into the plush front passenger seat of the luxury vehicle. There were very few things in life better than a comfy chair.

"We have a history of destroying our rides, so apologies in advance if your wheels become a write-off in the next few hours." I glanced down at the center console between me and Lienna. "Ooh! Butt warmers!"

I pressed the button and felt the heated cushion caress my tired tush. I might have even moaned with delight. I didn't care if anyone heard me. We were driving straight toward yet another terrifying mastermind in Vancouver's criminal circles, and I would not be shamed for relishing in the coziness of my buttocks on the way there.

"The Coffer is in North Van," Lloyd told us, ignoring my hindquarter hedonism. "You'll need to take the Second Narrows Bridge."

"What kind of HQ does he have?" I asked. "Abandoned warehouse? Underground lair? High-tech skyscraper?"

"A petting zoo."

"Excuse me?"

"Bowman Farms Petting Zoo. That's his front."

"A little too Robert Pickton for my liking," I mumbled. "Is that his name? Bowman?"

"No. He bought the farm a few years back and kept the name." Lloyd sighed. "I don't know his real name. He didn't tell me, and I didn't ask. He launders his money through the zoo, and no one would ever think to look for a lowlife criminal at a family-oriented business overrun by schoolchildren half the time."

"Tell us about the zoo," Lienna ordered. "Does he have guards? Security?"

"Just the workers there. They look friendly, giving kids cute tours of the pigs and chickens, but they're all highly trained killers." He shot a furtive look out the BMW's rear window. "Can you drive faster? We're out in the open here."

"We don't want to draw attention to ourselves," Lienna replied. "How many workers are—"

With a loud bang, the back windshield shattered. Yelling incomprehensibly, Lloyd flattened himself on the back seat, covering his head with his hands. Three more bangs rang out and bullets thudded into the BMW's trunk.

"Guns!" I shouted, slouching in my seat and praying its supple, heated leather was thick enough to stop a bullet. "Somebody's shooting at us!"

Lienna stomped on the gas, rocketing the luxury sedan down the four-lane street and veering around a painfully slow-moving station wagon.

Two more gun blasts were followed by an extended honk from another car. I checked the side mirror and saw two virtually identical white vans swerving around the station wagon to stay on our tail. Hanging out of the passenger side on the lead van was a man in a skull mask pointing a handgun at us.

He fired, shattering my mirror.

I ducked my head lower.

"It's the West Coast Wild Boys!" Lloyd stammered in panic.

They sounded like a goddamn surf brand, and I swore furiously. "Why are they shooting at us?"

"Because they want to kill us!"

"No shit," I snapped. "But aren't they mythics? What kind of magic assassination gang doesn't use *magic*?"

"The kind that doesn't want humans to know about magic! They only use non-mythic weapons in public."

"How considerate," I snarled, turning to Lienna. "Can you outrun them?"

Another bullet flew through the rear window and slammed into the dashboard between us. All three of us jerked instinctively away, as though that would somehow help.

"Can't outrun bullets," my partner said. "Can you warp them?"

"I can get the shooter, but I can't target the rest without a halluci-bomb, and everyone on this street would end up involved."

There was the dilemma: do my best to save our asses and risk harming a street full of humans with whatever warp I directed at the bad guys ... or don't. But if I didn't do something, we would die Sonny Corleone-style without the chance to defend ourselves.

"Kit," Lienna said urgently as more gunfire ricocheted off the car's exterior. "My phone—in my bag."

I grabbed her satchel off the center console and dug her phone out of it. "Who am I calling?"

She gestured ahead of us. "We need help."

I peered through the cracked windshield. On our left, a familiar apartment building rose above its neighbors a few blocks away.

Well, that might do the trick.

I opened Lienna's phone, flinching as another shot exploded the driver's side mirror, and swiped through her contacts. I tapped a number. After two rings, Robin Page picked up.

"Agent Shen, how's the investigation going?" she asked pleasantly.

"It's Kit," I told her. "And not so fantastic. We're in a black BMW being chased by gun-toting psychopaths in two white vans on 4th, and we're headed your way."

A heartbeat of silence. "Are you serious?"

"About-to-die serious," I answered. "We need your demon."

16

A BLOCK AWAY from Robin's building, a bullet took out one of the BMW's rear tires.

Lienna swore as the car jolted and swerved. Metal screeched as the rim ate through the floppy rubber and met the pavement. With a wild glance around, she steered toward a parking garage entrance.

"Not there!" Lloyd yelled from the back seat. "We'll be trapped!"

I gripped the handle on my door like a lifeline, Lienna's phone in my other hand. "I'm inclined to agree with the not-so-good doctor."

Nothing pleasant ever happened in parking garages.

It felt like every time Lienna and I drove into a concrete car structure, we were blitzed by telekinetic douchebags, rogue demon contractors, or shitty mage assassins. This time, it was trigger-happy lunatics in skull masks.

Unfortunately, with a tire disintegrating and the two white vans right on our bumper, we didn't have much choice. As we plowed across the speed bumps at the entrance, I brought the phone back to my ear.

"Change of plans," I told Robin as the BMW shot down the ramp that led to the underground lot, the two vans careening in after us. "We won't make it to your place. We just pulled into a parking garage off—"

Lienna steered around a pillar at top speed, then hit the brakes so hard the phone flew out of my hand. We screeched to a halt inches from a pair of parked Priuses.

The West Coast Wild Boys' vans skidded to stops behind us. Their doors flew open and eight skull-faced gang members emptied out, each one holding a gun. We were a smidge outnumbered. But that didn't make a lick of difference now that we were out of the public eye.

Because now I could halluci-bomb the shit out of them.

"Lienna, Lloyd, stay out of sight," I ordered as I dropped a warp over the parking garage. Lienna had recently used her cat's eye necklace and the spell would be out of commission until it recharged, meaning I couldn't make her invisible. But if she could stay out of sight the old-fashioned way, I wouldn't need to.

With the skull-faced knuckleheads advancing on the BMW, I created a warp of its doors flying open. Fake versions of me, Lienna, and Lloyd jumped out, slammed their doors shut, and sprinted in different directions. My fake Lloyd was shoddy at best, but it didn't really matter when all the assassins could see was his back as he sprinted madly between parked cars.

Gunshots rang out in a deafening, chaotic beat, but my warps kept running. The Wild Boys emptied their magazines into a dozen unfortunate vehicles. Shouting at each other, the eight goons split up and dashed after my fleeing fakes. I sank lower in my seat, ninety-five-percent certain they'd all run right past the car without noticing the real people still hunkered behind the tinted glass.

"Wait!" someone bellowed.

Breath catching, I twisted to peek out the shattered rear window.

Wild Boy #8 was hanging back, a gun in one hand and a phone held aloft in front of his face.

"That was fake!" the guy shouted. "The psychic is tricking us!"

Uh, what?

In terrifying synchrony, the other seven goons pivoted to face the BMW, surrounding it on three sides. Suddenly, being outnumbered made a very large smidge of difference.

Lienna, slouched as low as possible in the driver's seat with her satchel in her lap, shot me a wide-eyed, frantic look as the assassin gang closed in on the car, half of them reloading their guns as they came. My mind buzzed blankly, confusion derailing my ability to think. They knew about my abilities. Söze, that slimy SOB, must have included handy pointers on how best to kill the psycho warper.

A Wild Boy stepped close to Lienna's window, peering through the tint.

She grabbed the handle and flung the door open into the assassin. He staggered back and she leaped out. Her fists flew, pummeling the guy in three swift, violent strikes to his soft spots. As he fell over backward, she whipped a stun marble into the next nearest guy, shouting the incantation.

With no way to get to her quickly, I threw a Funhouse warp into the minds of the Wild Boys on her side of the car before they could riddle her with bullets. They might suspect I was the one responsible for their vision going full Mirror World, but that didn't make it any less distracting.

They stumbled, guns weaving in confusion, and Lienna hurled a second stun marble into the guy she'd punched. He went down.

The window beside me shattered.

My head snapped toward the breaking glass, and I found myself looking down the barrel of a gun. Panic cut through me. I had a split second to stop him from pulling the trigger, and only one trick in my bag o' warps was guaranteed to stop someone in their tracks.

I slammed a Blackout warp over the assassin's mind, then grabbed the barrel of the gun and tried to wrench it from his hand. But another goon was right there, yanking his buddy out of the way to aim a silver artifact at my throat. I switched the Blackout to him as I threw my door open. I was a sitting duck inside the car. I had to get out.

Leaping to the pavement and going straight into a half crouch, I tackled both guys around the middle. They pitched over, but they were still armed, and I didn't want to play chicken with bullets, so I invisified myself.

An earsplitting gunshot rang out—and with a douse of icy horror, I remembered my Funhouse warp, which had gone all soft and ignorable while I'd been focused on the Blackout.

"He's right there!"

Two of the Wild Boys on my side of the car had their phones out and pointed at me—using their cameras to see through my warps. I could defeat that with enough time and concentration, neither of which I had.

Grinning nastily, they raised their other hands. One's palm filled with bladelike shards of ice and the other telekinetically lifted a pair of razor-edged discs.

Oh, fun. They were adding some mythic spice to this gunfight, and I was prepared to defend against neither magic nor bullets.

"Fuck it," I muttered and did the only thing I could think of.

I Blackout-warped everyone.

Pain spliced through my skull and nausea gripped my stomach at the instant, unbearable strain of turning my most encompassing, high-effort warp into a halluci-bomb. Men were whimpering and shouting, collapsing and writhing, but I scarcely noticed, wholly consumed by the mental effort of holding the warp.

I had to hold it. Every second I kept it going was a second longer to live—for me and Lienna.

My knees hit the pavement. My body shook, muscles weakening, head spinning. The shouting had gone quiet. Minds were slipping from my grasp.

Something sharp and ice-cold pressed against my cheek.

My eyes opened. The panting kryomage stood over me, shoulders hunched, his skull mask grinning evilly.

"Fucking psychics," he hissed, his ice blade an inch from my eye socket.

I tensed for the killing blow.

Red light flashed.

I didn't see what happened—what hit the Wild Boy. One moment he was about to put a frozen dagger through my eye, then my vision went crimson and the Wild Boy's skull caved in with a splatter of blood.

As he pitched over sideways, a human-sized blur slammed into the next nearest assassin.

Grizzlies ball cap on his head and his whiplike tail snapping behind him, Zylas hit the man so hard his neck broke on impact. The demon launched off the falling corpse of his victim and straight into the next one. Crimson talons glowed over his fingers as he plunged them into the Wild Boy's chest.

Three dead in six seconds.

The remaining Wild Boys finally reacted to the slaughter, guns and magic firing, but Zylas was a lightning blur. The fourth assassin died under his claws, and as he leaped onto the roof of the BMW, veins of red magic ran up his arms, glowing through his sleeves. He gestured almost casually at his surviving opponents.

Vibrant red circles appeared beneath the Wild Boys. In the time it took them to look down at the magic under their feet, Zylas flicked his fingers. The four spells activated, four sprays of blood drenched the pavement, and four bodies fell.

Silence plunged over the parking garage, and all I could hear was my own harsh breathing.

"Zylas!"

Robin's voice rang out, sharp and urgent. Zylas spun on one foot and hopped off the car, landing on the driver's side.

I shoved to my feet, trembling and gulping back my stomach. My mind was clearing now that I'd stopped warping, and I was relieved to realize I hadn't hit my breaking point. I'd just drained my stamina way faster than normal.

Teeth gritted, I rushed around the BMW, heading for the spot where Zylas had vanished. Rounding the bumper, I came up short.

Lienna was on the ground, Robin kneeling on one side of her and Zylas on the other. Blood drenched Lienna's hoodie, soaking over her shoulder from a gunshot wound in her upper chest.

My heart exploded with horror and rammed itself into my throat.

Lienna had been shot.

She'd been shot and I hadn't known. Not only had I not known, but I'd used *my goddamn Blackout warp* on her while she was bleeding out. Guilt and fear froze me in place.

She was panting, her eyes squeezed shut with pain. Zylas prodded at her wound, then pressed his palm to it. Magic spread from his hand, looping and glowing across Lienna's torso.

"What are you doing?" I demanded loudly, finding my voice.

Zylas ignored me as a demonic array took form on top of Lienna.

"He's healing her."

Robin's quiet response took a moment to penetrate the haze of panic in my brain.

"What?" I croaked.

Zylas's mouth moved as he murmured a guttural incantation. His spell blazed with a fierce light, and Lienna arched up, a pained sound scraping out of her throat. Robin pushed Lienna's shoulders down, holding her in place, and after a few seconds, Lienna sagged against the bloody pavement.

Her chest rose and fell, her features relaxing, the pained tension melting away.

"Healing?" I repeated. "Demons can … heal?"

"Some of them can, yes." Robin looked up at me, her forehead wrinkled with concern. "Are you okay?"

"Me? I'm fine. How's Lienna?"

"A clean wound." Zylas stood up, his tail snapping impatiently. "I fixed it. Be grateful, *hh'ainun.*"

My muscles unlocked, and I rushed to Lienna's side, taking Zylas's place. Leaving me with my partner, Robin shifted back to survey the violent deaths scattered around the garage.

"Lienna?" I whispered, brushing my fingers across her cheek.

Her eyebrows scrunched, and she squinched her eyes open. "Kit?"

I slid my arms under her back and head, lifting her away from the cold pavement. Her breathing was smooth and even. Relief spiraled through my exhausted brain.

"I'm sorry," I whispered. "I didn't mean to hurt you."

She looked up at me, a smile forming weakly on her lips. "You weren't the guy with the gun, were you?"

"No, but I—"

"Then we're good," she said. "You can't save me from everything."

My regret faltered, thrown off-kilter by her words, by her humor amidst the pain and bloodshed. She was right. I couldn't protect her from every assassin, every rogue, every skull-masked asshole with a gun.

But I'd be damned if I didn't try.

17

WITH SOME COMBINATION of the MPD and Vancouver's human cops likely to descend on the parking garage at any moment, we decided to relocate. Lloyd had missed Zylas's gore-tastic victory over the Wild Boys; between the overload of fear and my Blackout warp, he'd passed out in the BMW's back seat. We'd had to shake him back to his senses before grabbing our stuff and abandoning the shot-up car.

Zylas stayed behind to "clean things up" while the rest of us hoofed it toward Robin's apartment, Lienna tucked in the middle of our group to hide her bloodstained outfit. As we hurried along the sidewalk, I couldn't stop my gaze from tracing every splotch of blood on her clothes, or the paleness of her face, or the unsteady wobble in her walk.

If I hadn't been determined to get to the Coffer before, now I was burning with a furious need to shut down that bastard's whole operation.

Zylas caught up to us as we filed into Robin's unit. The petite contractor took Lienna into her bedroom to get her cleaned up and dressed in borrowed clothes. I dropped onto the sofa, elbows braced on my knees and hands clenched into fists. Lloyd locked himself in the bathroom, probably wanting privacy to regain his composure.

The farther away from Zylas he was, the better. No need to let the not-so-good doctor know that he'd been saved by a loosely contracted demon with full control of his magic. Speaking of which, Zylas's demonic death-beams had been a terrifying surprise. As far as I was concerned, demons didn't need automatic murder-rays to be overwhelming whirlwinds of violence, so layering magic on top of his already formidable combat skills made Zylas even scarier than I'd imagined.

My head sank a bit lower between my shoulders. If Zylas hadn't arrived when he did, Lienna and I would be dead. Lloyd, too. I'd assumed it was a coincidence that Daedalus's icy extermination drone had been such a bad matchup for my psycho warps. Then those gun-wielding whackos had used their phone cameras to defeat my magic, and that's all it had taken to critically handicap me.

If this kept up, if we didn't take down the Coffer, we'd be worm food in no time.

Something hard thumped none too gently into the top of my head.

I reared back, gaze snapping up to find Zylas standing in front of me, a deep scowl twisting his lips. "Ow."

"Don't be weak, *hh'ainun*."

My jaw dropped. "Weak?"

"You lost but you didn't die. If you are alive, you can still win."

"That's easy for the super-powered demon to say."

His nose wrinkled with a sneer. "Do I look like a strong demon?"

I blinked. He *was* the smallest, slimmest, least monstrous demon I'd ever seen, and I'd seen a few of them since joining the MPD. "Are you weak by demon standards?"

He leaned closer, his crimson eyes gleaming. "If you are smarter than your enemies, you do not need to be stronger."

The bedroom door opened, interrupting our cozy heart-to-heart, and Robin walked out. Lienna followed her, looking pale but otherwise healthy. She'd replaced her blood-soaked hoodie with a similar forest green one. Not quite meeting my eye, she sat beside me.

"I explained the black spot to Robin," she said quietly, looking down at her hands, fingers twining together restlessly. "And why we were attacked."

Sitting on the coffee table facing us, Robin nodded, her expression grim. "Do you need our help with the Coffer?"

I felt something burning the left side of my face, and when I glanced over, I discovered it was Zylas's warning glare. His expression clearly said, "Don't you dare involve us any further."

"No," I said firmly. "In fact, you two need to get out of town."

Robin blinked. "What do you mean?"

"Söze is going to be all over that parking garage," Lienna jumped in, some liveliness returning to her face in the form of worry. "If he figures out that a demon was involved, it'll be big trouble for you."

Biting her lower lip, Robin glanced at Zylas. "We were planning to go on a trip next month, but I can rebook my ticket for tonight. Zora already has a few teams watching the most likely nexuses. I'll get her to contact you directly if she discovers anything."

I nodded. "Good. You should pack your stuff and head to the airport ASAP."

"Okay. Are you two leaving right away?"

"No time to waste," Lienna said brusquely. "We need to keep moving before another assassin catches up with us."

"We don't want to end up like Anson," I added. "Or Blythe. Or Georgia."

Robin's mouth pressed into a thin line, grief in her eyes. "You need to get justice for them. Especially Georgia. She was such a wonderful person."

My eyebrows rose. We'd told her about the GM murders last time, but she hadn't offered any commentary on the victims. "You knew her?"

"I visit the Arcana Historia library fairly often, and I met her several times. She was always so helpful. I even saw her the day before she …"

"You saw her the day before she died?" Lienna asked sharply, leaning forward. "You didn't mention that yesterday."

"We were talking about portals. I was focused on that and didn't think about the timing until afterward." She shifted uncomfortably. "I only saw her in passing. She'd come back from a lunch meeting, and she mentioned that she'd … oh."

Now I was leaning forward too. "Oh, what?"

"She said she'd just seen my GM. They'd met up for coffee." Her eyes widened slightly. "She and Darius must've been friends. Does he know she was murdered and didn't take her own life?"

"He does." My voice came out flat. "He told us himself that it wasn't a suicide."

That handsome, silver-tongued devil. I knew I'd seen something strange in his demeanor when he'd learned about Georgia's death. Not only had he failed to mention he'd seen her hours before her death, but he'd downplayed his relationship with her. If they'd gone out for coffee, then—

"Coffee!" I blurted.

Lienna jolted upright on the sofa. "The Molly Roger! The barista said Georgia met with *two* men. Anson Goodman and someone else."

"Holy hell. Georgia, Anson, and Darius met for coffee right before Georgia died." I rocked backward, letting this new information percolate like an Indonesian medium roast through my brain. "Someone called Anson before he went all paranoia-mode."

"You think that was Darius too?" Lienna asked.

"Could be." I abruptly pushed to my feet. "We need to go talk to him."

"No." Despite her negatory response, Lienna also stood. "We can't go anywhere near the Crow and Hammer with this much heat on us. We need to take care of the Coffer before we run into any more bounty-hunting crews."

She was more than right. We weren't equipped for this level of assassin attention. Unless we planned to board the same plane as Robin and Zylas, the only way we could avoid a quick trip to six-feet-under was to find the Coffer and force him to call off the hit.

Not that sneaking into a petting zoo full of highly trained mythic bodyguards was a whole lot safer than wandering around, waiting for assassins to find us.

"Time to go, Lloyd," I called in the direction of the bathroom.

Lienna marched toward the door, and as I followed her, worries spinning endlessly in my mind, a sharp blow caught my skull again.

"Zylas!" Robin hissed. "Why are you hitting him?"

I turned as the demon lowered his arm.

"Your enemy is our enemy." His accent thickened, his voice husky, vicious, and heavy with warning. "Don't fail, Kit Morris."

Was he encouraging me or threatening me?

"You got it, Z."

As I hurried to catch up with Lienna, I had to admit there was something reassuring about having an unstoppable, killing-machine demon rooting for you—even if he was only doing it because he wanted Söze eliminated too.

Still, I couldn't complain. It wasn't every day I got a pep talk from a demon.

BOWMAN FARMS PETTING ZOO was nestled in the mountainous forests of North Vancouver on a gravel road a few turns off the main highway. The midafternoon sun was high in the sky, its diffused rays scattering through the cloud cover. Recent rainfall had filled the gravel road's potholes with murky pools that splashed violently as our tires bounced over them.

Having left Lloyd's BMW behind at the parking garage, we'd found ourselves, yet again, in need of a new ride. Robin had been gracious enough to lend us her cousin's blue Mercedes-Benz, though she'd been excessively nervous about handing over the keys, making us *promise* not to damage it with so much as a paint scuff.

Seeing as we were on our fourth car in less than three days, we probably shouldn't have made that promise. It was a good thing the insurance companies didn't know about our history of vehicular violence; my rates would've been through the goddamn roof. It was also a good thing that Robin wasn't fully informed of said history.

"The zoo is surrounded by an electric fence," Lloyd told us as Lienna pulled the blue sedan off the road into a shallow section of the ditch. "The only way in or out is through the front gate, but it's alarmed. The zoo closed to the public about an hour ago, so the gate will be locked."

Lienna killed the engine. "And the staff? When do they leave?"

"They'll be around for a while, finishing up their duties and taking care of the animals."

"What about security cameras?" I asked, thinking of the West Coast Wild Boys and their phones.

"I've never seen any, but that doesn't mean they're not there."

Lienna peered through the trees, trying to see the front gate. "How many workers does he have?"

"Four that I know of. The gate attendant is a young man named Dennis, an aeromage. There are two farmhands, Gracie and Janey—cousins and powerful witches with darkfae familiars. And the Coffer's personal security guard. I don't know his name, but he's a telekinetic and about seven feet tall, all muscle."

"Which means he can toss a whole lot around with his mind," I said. "What about the Coffer himself? What's his class?"

"I have no idea. I've never seen him use magic."

Lienna drummed her fingers on the steering wheel. "According to Agent Vigneault's files, the Coffer is forcing you to help with his diabetes?"

"Yes. He won't go through normal medical channels because that could blow his cover. I do weekly checkups, give him prescriptions, that sort of thing." Lloyd shifted in his seat. "As far as I can tell, he's a shut-in and a bit of a hypochondriac."

"Sounds terrifying," I said snidely.

Lloyd shook his head vehemently. "He may not sound like it, but you've never met him. And his power? His influence? The people around him? That's what you need to worry about."

I settled back in my seat. "So what's the plan, partner?"

The tempo of her drumming fingers increased. She seemed back to her usual self—smart, independent, and with her emotions firmly closed off from the rest of the world—but I was worried. We hadn't had a private moment since the parking garage attack, so I hadn't been able to check up on her. She'd been in a car chase, shot in the chest, infused with demon healing magic, and subjected to my meanest, most mentally punishing warp. And there was still the unspoken *thing*—whatever had been hanging over her head for the last few days.

Then again, if I brought up any of that, she'd just tell me she was "fine."

"Our plan depends on how certain Dr. Markle is about there being no security cameras," she said after a moment.

"Like I told you, I've never seen any cameras, but they could be hidden."

I let my head fall back against the headrest, pushing aside everything but the challenge at hand. "I'd say it's worth the risk. Better than climbing an electric fence, anyway."

Lienna nodded. "Let's do it."

"Do what?" Lloyd demanded nervously. "What's your plan?"

"It's simple." I gave him a roguish grin. "You're going to walk us through the front door."

18

LLOYD AND I APPROACHED the petting zoo's gate on foot—but as far as anyone watching would know, Lloyd was on his own. I had a halluci-bomb hiding me from any spying eyes. Unfortunately, Lienna had to creep along in the bushes, relying on her own stealth instead of my warps. Her cat's eye artifact still hadn't recharged enough to activate again.

Having had the recent and very painful experience of my enemies knowing too much about my abilities, I was feeling a lot less confident than I normally would. But even though Söze had given the Coffer information about me, the hypochondriac supervillain had no reason to suspect two of his bounty victims would show up at his secret property.

"Are you sure about this?" the doctor whispered, approaching the intercom. "Are you here still?"

"Yes and yes," I answered, letting my voice trickle through the warp enough to reassure him.

Beyond the gate, the gravel road led to a small square building with a welcome sign on the front. Beyond that was a large, classically red barn next to an old farmhouse that had been renovated. Around the outside of the property were various animal pens and cages: chickens, pigs, peacocks, goats, and a few ponies roaming in a distant field.

The whole place smelled like shit. Literally.

Lloyd pressed the intercom button. "Hello?"

After a few seconds, a voice crackled back. "*We're closed. We open tomorrow at nine a.m.*"

"That's Dennis, the gate attendant." Lloyd glanced around nervously before pressing the button again. "It's Dr. Markle."

"*You're not supposed to be here today.*"

"I need to see him. It's important."

There was a long pause. Lloyd rubbed his square jaw, trying to quell his obvious anxiety. Finally, the door on the building closest to the gate—the one with a "Welcome to Bowman Farms Petting Zoo" sign painted on it—swung open. A guy a year or two younger than me stepped out. He was of average height, with wide shoulders, stubble, and a brush cut. Jeans, an orange plaid shirt, and a noisy collection of keys dangling from his belt rounded out his friendly rural look.

He ambled down to the gate and eyed Lloyd warily, crossing his thick arms. "What's so important, Dr. Markle?"

"That's between me and him."

Dennis clicked his tongue disapprovingly. "That's not how this—"

"*Ori dormias*," I uttered as I lobbed Lienna's stun marble at the guy from two feet away. It bounced off his chest, and he was crumpled on the ground before I could catch the marble as it rebounded. Dropping my warp, I stuffed my arms between the bars of the gate to grab him and drag him closer, then pulled the key ring off his belt.

Lienna dashed out of the shrubbery to join us and used a zip tie to fasten the farmhand to the gate. Meanwhile, I attempted to match his multitudinous keys to the electronic locking system next to the intercom. After a bit of trial and error, I found the fob that unlocked the gate.

Lloyd stared in bewilderment at Dennis, who'd dropped unconscious for no apparent reason.

"Lead the way, doctor," I told him as I invisified myself again.

He nodded and trudged through the gate. I followed him up the muddy gravel road, past the welcome center and toward the gimmicky red barn. I didn't bother to hide my footprints with my invisi-warp, which would add more stress to my psychic power; my brain was still aching from the super-Blackout. Lienna trailed a dozen paces behind us, flitting from hiding spot to hiding spot.

As Lloyd and I passed the welcome center, two short and wiry women, who I guessed to be in their late thirties, stepped out of the pig pen with empty buckets of feed or slop or dragon souls or whatever criminal farmhands fed to the four-legged pre-bacon they kept cooped up.

Gracie and Janey—the witchy cousins. One had long golden hair in a thick braid that hung down to her waist and swung as she walked. The other's slick black bob seemed oddly manicured amidst the stink and straw.

They gave Lloyd a questioning look.

"Are you lost, doctor?" the blond one asked snarkily.

The black-haired one set down her pail of slop. "Where's Dennis?"

Lloyd faltered, unsure which tale to spin. He was not a gifted improviser.

Looking around sharply, the blond cousin spotted Dennis's unconscious form taking a marble-induced nap against the gate. She pointed and was about to yell a warning when I—being a considerably more experienced improviser—added a large, angry boar to the pig pen. With an earsplitting squeal, it started kicking up mud and shit like a rodeo bull.

The witchy cousins looked over at the pen in confusion.

I made the boar cease its bucking, and in the voice of a cinematic Spaniard, it declared, "My name is Pignigo Montoya. You slaughtered my father. Prepare to die."

Pignigo rushed toward the wooden fence and jumped, soaring impossibly high and clearing it by at least a foot.

The witches scrambled away, desperate to avoid death by vengeful hog. The blond cousin made it two steps before coming face-to-face with Lienna, who'd closed in while I provided a distraction. As Lienna unleashed a stun marble, the dark-haired witch peeled off in the opposite direction—right at me.

Invisible, I caught her around her waist, swept her legs out from under her, and dropped her into the dirt. Lienna was there a second later, slipping a bracelet over the witch's wrist as she muttered an incantation. The thrashing witch went limp and silent.

I popped back to my feet, staring around intently. We'd taken out the witches, but if they had familiars, their fae protectors would show up any second to avenge them. I squinted, waiting as the seconds ticked past.

Nothing? Lloyd had specifically mentioned their scary darkfae familiars, hadn't he?

"What the hell is going on out here?" a bass voice yelled from near the barn.

For a second, I thought a fae had shown up—but although he wasn't the most average-looking human I'd ever seen, the gargantuan, beer-bellied man a few inches short of seven feet with a face that vaguely resembled a pug didn't seem to be a preternatural creature. He was just big and ugly.

The nameless telekinetic bodyguard had arrived.

Since I hadn't yet let go of my warps, not only did the giant see Dr. Markle, Lienna, and two unconscious witches, but also a petulant pig ready to avenge its sire.

Homing in on Lloyd and Lienna, the telekinetic strode toward them, baring his teeth. "What did you do to Gracie and Janey?"

"I didn't—" Lloyd stammered. "I mean, it wasn't—I was just standing here…"

For someone whose literal job description involved reacting quickly in emergency situations, the not-so-good doctor sucked hard at thinking on his feet when interrogated by threatening mythics. I made a mental note to recommend some theater camps when all was said and done.

In the meantime, I had Pignigo Montoya rush forward and plant itself in front of the telekinetic, staring up at him with beady eyes.

"Don't mess with the boar, young man," Pignigo threatened. "You'll get the hooves."

The oversized musclehead frowned dumbly, likely questioning his own sanity, and that pause was all Lienna needed to pull out her third stun marble. As she rapid-chanted the incantation, I incorporated the small orb into my invisi-warp. When she made a throwing motion, he didn't react—he was slightly smarter than a dog, in that regard—but of course, she *had* thrown the marble. He just couldn't see it.

It bopped him in the belly. He keeled over, hitting the ground with a thud that made me wince. It'd been a long fall.

Letting out a tired puff of air, I slumped against the side of the barn and dropped my warps. That hallucinatory adventure normally wouldn't have taken a toll on my mental energy, but I wasn't at full warping capacity. On the plus side, I'd successfully warped my way through all of the Coffer's deadly protectors, and I was feeling pretty damn good about that after our last two encounters with lethal mythics.

"Just the Coffer left, right?" I asked, breathing deeply.

"Yep," Lienna agreed as she zip-tied the unconscious telekinetic's wrists together. "I'm out of stun marbles, though."

The doctor, who'd started badly when I'd appeared next to him, surveyed the scene. "That was …"

"Awesome?"

"Strange."

Taking that as a compliment, I straightened away from the wall and opened my mouth to ask Lloyd where to find the Coffer, when a loud creak stopped me. The barn door three feet to my right swung open.

Framed in the doorway, a short, middle-aged man with a graying goatee plastered onto his sagging round face and a thin, limp ponytail gawked at us. I gawked back.

"That's him!" the doctor yelled. "The Coffer!"

The guy slashed a furious glare at Lloyd and swung the massive barn door closed again. I lunged forward, catching it before it shut. Shoving with all my body weight, I pushed it open enough to dart inside.

The Coffer was sprinting down the wide aisle between empty horse stalls. Resuming my invisi-warp, I ran after him as Lienna squeezed through the barn door behind me. The Coffer reached the end of the aisle and disappeared into an open doorway. I sprinted toward it.

Just as I reached the door, the Coffer reappeared in the threshold—a gun in his hand.

I was getting really goddamn sick of guns.

Near the barn's entrance, Lienna retreated with urgent steps. As the Coffer aimed his weapon at her, she ducked back outside, leaving me alone with our enemy.

Dragging fear deepened in my chest with each rapid breath I took. Gun aside, this man could easily call upon the city's nastiest killers to un-alive a person with the kind of greedy fervor that—as I'd experienced with the Wild Boys—could only be stopped with the firepower of some considerably jacked-up allies. He was a mob boss, shrouded in secret, comfortable in the shadows, hiding in plain sight.

He was damn near a god.

It felt like someone was pouring a steady stream of ice water into my spinal column. My body chilled, and my hands started to tremble. My "flight or freeze" response was hammering at me while my "fight" response had vanished entirely.

The Coffer's beady eyes scanned the seemingly empty corridor, unable to see through the invisi-warp. He smiled tightly.

"You're here, aren't you, Kit Morris?" His voice echoed with malevolence, more chilling than Zylas's menacing growl. "You can't escape. Show yourself and I'll be merciful."

I stared at him, trembling, adrenaline saturating my veins. Only the sheer terror of the Coffer laying eyes on me kept my invisi-warp going.

The Coffer swung his pistol from side to side, as though debating where to shoot first. "I'm not the kind of man you want to anger, Mr. Morris."

I believed him. The dread was overwhelming me, as though the longer I stood in his vicinity, the stronger its hold over me became. The pure, sharp, paralyzing terror threatened to consume me from within.

"You have three seconds to show yourself," the Coffer declared, and the petrifying horror of his threat locked up my chest.

It was so intense, so all-consuming, that it didn't feel real.

And that's when I figured it out. The fear *wasn't* real. And though the realization didn't make my terror vanish, it eased enough that I could think again.

"Time's up!" the Coffer announced. "Show yourself, and I'll consider letting you—"

I didn't let him finish. I dropped my invisi-bomb. His head snapped toward me, triumph lighting his features.

Then I hit him with a Blackout.

He staggered violently. As his sense of touch vanished, he lost his grip on the gun. It fell from his hand as he collapsed sideways, bouncing off the doorway and landing face-first on the dirty concrete. His limbs spasmed as he cried out in terror.

Me, though? I was terror free. Not a drop of fear infected me—just anger.

I released the Blackout. The Coffer sagged against the floor, panting and whimpering. Now that I could see him with a clear head, I could hardly believe he'd scared the shit out of me. If an intern at Madame Tussauds wax museum had made a god-awful attempt at a Steven Seagal look-alike and then left it out in the sun on a hot summer day, you'd end up with the Coffer.

An aged-out, half-melted eighties action star shouldn't inspire abject horror.

Stalking forward, I kicked his dropped gun across the aisle and out of easy reach. As he lifted his head, I crouched in front of him, smiling toothily.

"I consider myself an easygoing guy," I told him, the growl in my voice contrasting with my words. "I think people deserve second chances, and I don't really hold grudges. But for you, I'm going to make an exception."

I poked my finger between his eyebrows. "That was just a taste of my psychic powers, and if you so much as think 'empath' in my direction, I'll show you *exactly* what I can do when I get angry."

This pathetic waste of oxygen had made me shake in my shoes like a little kid, and that *really* pissed me off. I'd dealt with enough of that bullshit at my old guild.

Quentin, my former KCQ coworker and sort-of friend, had been an empath too. His ability to manipulate people's emotions with his mind had far surpassed this joker's abilities, though. Since his death, I'd spent a fair few nights lying awake and wondering how much of our friendship had been real. Quentin's true strength had been in the subtlety with which he'd wielded his dangerous power.

Okay, so I might have some lingering issues with empaths.

My expression must've shown enough of my not-very-nice feelings that the Coffer didn't question either my threat or the implication that I was a stronger, meaner psychic than him.

He glared weakly, anger fizzing in the air around him as he suppressed his empathic emotional leakage.

"What do you want?" he ground out.

"It's pretty straightforward," I said, baring my teeth in another humorless smile. "I want to live."

19

ON THE OTHER SIDE of the door where the Coffer had been standing was a tack room that had been converted into an office. With Lienna's help, I'd dragged him inside and locked his wrists together with a pair of magic-blocking MPD-issue handcuffs from her satchel, leaving him slumped miserably in his chair. I would've threatened him with his own gun just to rub salt in the wound, but it'd turned out to be a bluff. No bullets.

It was the perfect weapon for the all-bark-no-bite nitwit who wielded it.

Lloyd had also joined us inside the barn, and he lingered in the doorway, on edge but also shooting the Coffer confused looks. He was probably seeing the guy clearly for the first time, and I'd bet he also couldn't believe he'd ever feared the jiggly, ponytailed prick.

Standing in front of the Coffer, I crossed my arms. "It's time to end this."

"Nothing can stop what's coming for you. You're a dead man walking." He sneered at Lienna. "You too, darling."

"I think you've underestimated our powers of persuasion," I replied. "I'm sure you've been made aware of my partner's considerable sorcery skills. Rumor is she's got a spell that can swap your kidneys and your ears so all you can hear is the gurgling of your own guts as you slowly die of sepsis."

Unfortunately, he looked more revolted than fearful. "Just tell me what you want from me."

"Call off the black spots," I ordered. "Now."

"It's not that easy."

I lowered my voice to a growl. "Make it that easy."

He shook his head, jiggling his Seagal goatee back and forth. "The system isn't designed like that. Once a bounty is paid for, it stays in place until it's fulfilled. There's no 'undo' button."

Lienna folded her arms, mirroring my aggressive stance. "Fulfill it, then. Check us off as dead."

The Coffer hesitated, a frown pulling at his flabby lips as he thought over the ramifications, namely that if he marked us as dead, none of his assassin pals would know to show up and save his sorry ass.

I leaned closer. "Would you like to spend more time in sensory deprivation before deciding?"

His face paled at the reminder of the Blackout. "Fine. I'll do it."

"Wonderful. Hop to it, bucko."

The Coffer scooted closer to his laptop and awkwardly used his cuffed hands to jab at the keyboard. I shifted around to watch over his shoulder as he went through several password screens and accessed his bounty program. It was surprisingly straightforward. All it took was two clicks and a "confirm" button, and there it was, "DECEASED" blinking next to my and Lienna's names.

"Done," he said, clicking over to another screen. "This is the bounty list that the assassins can access. See? The bounty is marked as fulfilled, and the information on you two is no longer accessible."

Several painful knots of tension in my lower spine released.

"So, that's it," the Coffer concluded. "You're safe now. You can go."

"Nice try, you pathetic lump of shit," I said with a derisive snort. I waved Lloyd over to us. "Hey, doc. You've got some requests for your former boss, right?"

Lloyd took a step toward the Coffer, hands balled into fists, jaw tense. "You're going to leave me alone. Forever. The same goes for my son."

The Coffer withered slightly. "Your son?"

Lloyd's eyes burned with protective intensity. "The people you have in Nova Scotia, you're going to call them off. Give them new orders to never, ever touch my son. And I want to hear you do it."

The goateed dickbag grimaced. "I … I can't really do that."

"Why the hell not?" Lloyd looked at me for support. "Make him do it!"

"No, really," the Coffer said awkwardly. "I can't."

I couldn't help it—a grim laugh slipped past my lips. "He doesn't have any people in Nova Scotia."

The Coffer shrank into his chair, eyes boring a hole into the floor, confirming my suspicion.

"What are you talking about?" Lloyd asked in anxious confusion.

"He barely has people here. I mean, look at this place." I gestured broadly at the shabby tack room with its sad little desk. A quiet horse whinny punctuated my point. "He has a barely legal aeromage and two witches who don't even have familiars. His only real security was a blundering giant who was so confused by a talking pig that he didn't even use his telekinesis. The only reason you or anyone else don't laugh in the Coffer's repugnant face is because he manipulates your emotions with his slightly above-average empath abilities. It's all a goddamn charade. I bet that ugly-ass goatee isn't even real."

I reached across the desk and pinched a few hairs from said goatee.

"Ow," the Coffer squawked, pulling away from me.

I shrugged. "Whatever. My point stands."

"So, my son is safe?" Lloyd asked.

"He's always been safe," Lienna answered. "The bounty system was the real danger, and we're going to take care of that."

She closed the laptop, unplugged it, and shoved it in her satchel. The Coffer moaned pitifully as his reprehensible source of income was removed.

"We know you have a record of all your deals," she told him in her "I will transmute your eyeballs into goldfish" tone. "Where is it?"

The empath pointed at her satchel, now containing his laptop. "It's all in there."

"Bullshit," I snapped. "You were two-finger typing like one of your brainless chickens pecking at feed. I'm betting you're a pen-and-paper type of guy."

STOLEN SORCERY & OTHER MISADVENTURES ♠ 195

"No, I keep it all—"

He broke off as I sent a swirl of numb darkness through his mind.

"It's in my notebook. Bottom desk drawer."

"That's better," I said darkly, stooping to open the drawer. I pulled out a black notebook and flipped it open. "What the hell is this?"

Every page was filled with gibberish—a chaotic grid of letters that appeared to have no meaning whatsoever.

"It's in code," the Coffer told me smugly. "Only I know how to read it, so if you want to know what it says, you'll have to keep me alive. In fact, you can start by removing these handcuffs."

"Who do you think you are?" I asked as Lienna plucked the book from my hand to peer at the first page. "The Zodiac Killer?"

The Coffer's satisfied smirk widened. "I might consider helping you if you—"

"This is a Rot Cipher," Lienna interrupted matter-of-factly. "One of the simplest codes out there."

"And who the hell are *you*?" I asked her. "Alan Turing?"

She showed me the page again, holding her finger against a small notation in the top right corner. "See that? '+6.' It means every letter on this page represents a letter six spots before it in the alphabet. 'G' equals 'A,' and so on."

The Coffer's triumphant expression deflated like an old party balloon, and he looked rightfully ashamed of himself.

"You really suck at this whole villain thing," I told him, disappointed. "I came here expecting Hannibal Lecter, and instead I'm looking at a combination of Harry and Marv from *Home Alone*."

"What are you going to do with him?" Lloyd asked.

"Don't worry. We've got this handled." I gave the Coffer a nasty grin. "We'll take good care of him. Won't we, Lienna?"

"SO, YOU WANT ME to feed him, water him, that sort of thing?" Eggert asked, giving the Coffer, who was now handcuffed to the stove in my former kitchen, a hard look.

I nodded. "Think of him like a houseplant. An evil houseplant. He's about as intelligent as one, too."

Though I wasn't pleased to bring the goateed empath into our hidden HQ, we hadn't had much choice. At least with my MPD-issue handcuffs around his wrists, he couldn't attempt any emotional manipulation during his stay.

While I gave Eggert his new assignment, Lienna remained seated on the sofa, her nose in the Coffer's notebook, decoding his fifth-grade-level cipher onto a pad of paper.

"If he does anything remotely suspicious," I instructed Eggsy, "feel free to shoot him."

The ex-security guard leaned in close to me and whispered, "I don't have a gun anymore."

"He doesn't know that," I whispered back.

"Right." Eggert stood up straight and puffed up his chest. "I will absolutely shoot him. I love shooting people."

I patted him on the shoulder. "Good work, pal."

"Thanks, kid."

Hurrying over to the sofa, I dropped next to Lienna and her translation. Her pen scribbled furiously across her notepad.

"Any luck?" I asked.

She sighed. "It's going to take time. He wrote down *everything*. Transactions, jobs, even a couple of grocery lists."

"A genuine big brain," I said with a half laugh. "Can't have your enemies knowing about the organic broccoli and grass-fed ground beef you eat."

"More seafood and tonic water, actually."

"Gross." I took a peek at the notepad she was scribbling on. "No Söze yet?"

"Not yet, but I'll find him."

And when she did, we would have hard proof that the clammy crap-bucket of an IA agent had paid a shitty crime lord to murder us, which would be the first step in bringing down his corrupt house of cards.

Of course, we still didn't know why he'd killed two GMs and staged their deaths to appear non-murdery.

Or how exactly he and his goons were recharging the stolen portals.

Or how Darius King was involved in this whole mess.

Or who the mole was.

Or how the mole knew who I was.

My foot bounced restlessly. We had so many unanswered questions, and getting evidence against Söze wouldn't instantly fix everything. Without Blythe, I didn't even know what we'd do with the evidence. We couldn't just waltz into the precinct with it.

"We need to talk to Darius," I muttered in a low voice. "He's part of this somehow, and he might have an idea about what we should do with the Coffer's evidence."

Lienna nodded absently, her attention on her work. "We can go see him as soon as I find Söze in here. We have time now that we don't have to worry about the Coffer's assassins."

My intended reply was interrupted by the buzz of Lienna's phone where it sat on the coffee table in front of us.

Reluctantly, she put down the notepad and picked up the phone. "I don't recognize this number."

"Ooh, a mysterious caller," I said. "Put it on speaker."

She rolled her eyes but did as I'd requested. "Hello?"

"Agent Shen," came a perky female voice on the other end. "It's Zora from the Crow and Hammer. Robin told me to call you if we had anything to report on a nexus."

"And do you?" I asked eagerly.

"Yeah, but who are you?"

"Kit—uh, Agent Morris."

"Oh, yeah, the funny guy."

Lienna rolled her eyes again. "Depends on who you ask."

"Anyway, I was staking out the nexus on Burnaby Mountain, and I think I saw one of your guys. He had a stack of little black discs with him."

Lienna and I shared a look; Robin had guessed right. Söze was using a nexus to expedite the recharge times of the portals.

"What did he look like?" I asked. "Like the *Shape of Water* monster but vaguely more human?"

"Uh, no. This guy is buff and bald."

"Kade," Lienna stated. "Where is he now?"

"I'm following him westbound on Hastings, not far from the PNE."

"Stay on him and stay on the line," my partner instructed. "We're on our way to you now."

Lienna stuffed the Coffer's codebook and her translation into her satchel and hopped up from the sofa.

I turned to Eggert. "Keep an eye on him, okay?"

"You got it, boss," Eggsy replied, giving me a set of playful finger guns. He then turned those finger guns on the Coffer and narrowed his eyes. "Any misbehaving, buddy, and these'll turn into a genuine six-shooter here. Because there's nothing I love more than putting bullet holes in bad men."

In an alternate timeline, Trevor Eggert would've given John Wayne a run for his money.

A few minutes later, Lienna and I were on the road. Time dragged painfully by as we drove out of downtown, the lively, lit-up streets giving way to a darker, more sedate residential area. We finally caught up to Zora on a suburban street in Mount Pleasant, across from a condemned skating rink, the building little more than a hulking shadow in the night. Construction signs around the outskirts of the parking lot indicated it was due to be demolished later that month.

Lienna parked behind Zora's black coupe. The Crow and Hammer combat mythic was leaning against the hood of her car, dressed head to toe in black. Like Vera, she was blond and badass, and like Robin, she was a petite terror. I'd once seen her wielding a broadsword almost as tall as she was.

"Where is he?" Lienna asked.

Zora gestured to the rink. "He drove the little MagiPol smart car around the back by the loading dock. I saw him park, but I didn't want to get too close."

"Good call," I said. "Did you see anyone else?"

"Nope. But there are a couple of other cars back there, so who knows?"

I surveyed the dark, empty parking lot alongside the rink. "I can get us back there without being seen easily enough."

"Uh, you guys don't need any help with … whatever this is, do you?" Zora asked, cracking an awkward smile.

I shook my head. Not because she wouldn't be valuable, but because I couldn't incorporate her into my invisi-warp on such short notice. Not to mention I wasn't super eager to get an innocent mythic caught up in this potentially deadly shitstorm.

"Awesome," she breathed, then waved her hands defensively, backtracking her statement. "Not that I don't want to help. It's just that a *massive* bounty was posted like twenty minutes ago, and everyone from the Crow and Hammer is going after it. I don't wanna get left behind."

"No problem," Lienna said with a grateful smile. "We can take it from here."

"Cool!" She opened her car door. "See ya later, MPD."

And with that, she was gone. As soon as her car turned the corner, Lienna activated her poor, overused cat's eye necklace and I dropped a halluci-bomb, rendering us invisible. We made our way across the street and into the parking lot.

"Seeing as this is clearly Söze's supervillain lair," I murmured, "we need to be on the watch for booby traps, henchmen, and high-tech weaponry."

Lienna rolled her eyes. "A supervillain lair? It's a hockey rink, Kit."

"A very Canadian supervillain lair."

"I don't think Söze has a lair."

"Oh, come on. Everything about him screams 'discarded fish-themed comic book bad guy.' Of course he has a supervillain lair."

Around the corner of the building, just where Zora had said it would be, we found a smart car next to a loading dock. A black SUV was parked nearby. The loading dock's rusted rolling metal door was open a few inches, leaking dull orange light into the darkness.

Lienna and I edged toward it. I incorporated the door into my warp, removing any movement or noise it might make from the perception of anyone inside my halluci-bomb. At my nod, Lienna pushed it up.

With a creak, the door lifted enough for me to scramble up and over the concrete lip of the dock and scurry underneath. I held the door up with one hand and helped Lienna inside with the other, lowering the noisy metal gate behind us.

When I turned around to see what we'd walked into, a self-congratulatory grin beamed across my face.

"Oh. My. God."

"Don't say it," Lienna whispered.

I couldn't help myself. "It's a supervillain lair!"

She sighed. "I hate it when you're right."

20

A DARK ROOM.

Eerie burnt-orange lighting, dimly illuminating concrete walls.

One massive, jet-black boardroom table with modernist, monochrome business chairs around it.

Rows of cutting-edge tech carefully arranged along one wall beside a stack of suspicious, hard-sided black cases—the kind that held lethal bioweapons or world-ending technology in spy thrillers.

It was like someone had taken all the Bond villain lairs, shoved them into a blender, and sprayed them into the loading area of an abandoned community hockey rink. On either end were banks of huge machinery with thick pipes and insulated ducts—the chiller plant that kept the rink's ice frozen—which loomed ominously among the shadows at the edge of the light. It was somehow well-planned, utterly chaotic, and woefully tacky all at the same time.

It absolutely reeked of Söze.

"No Kade," I observed. Two of Söze's lackeys—Suarez and a rail-thin Dracula-impersonator, Markovich—stood near the tech station, talking in hushed tones about what I could only guess were nefarious assassination conspiracies. I was used to seeing them in the usual agent attire of a bland suit and tie, but they'd swapped office gear for what I could only describe as "mythic black ops." Armored vests, low-profile helmets, combat belts, and black cargo pants.

The extra scary part was that they both looked a lot more comfortable and competent in their combat gear than they ever had in their blah suits, and that made me very nervous.

Agent Kade, the agent I most wanted eyes on, was nowhere to be seen. He was the one with the all-important portals, and we needed to find him.

"He's got to be around here somewhere," Lienna said, also studying Markovich's and Suarez's "hardcore military" skins. "We need to find the portals before anyone can use them again."

"We should also figure out *who* they're planning to use them on."

My partner nodded grimly, then gestured at Markovich and Suarez. "Let's get closer. Maybe we'll learn something."

Getting closer wasn't all that appealing, and I had to remind myself we were invisible to their minds. As we crept through the crowded lair, carefully avoiding bumping into the furniture and equipment, Lienna took out her Rubik's cube and began twisting it.

"Shield?" I asked.

"Just in case," she confirmed.

Seemed I wasn't the only nervous one. That made me feel better. "Can you stun-marble them? I'd strongly prefer them unconscious."

"I used them all at the petting zoo. They need to recharge."

"Right, I knew that."

She tapped her cat's eye necklace, which was preventing her from falling prey to the invisi-warp that was keeping us safe. "And this only got a partial recharge. I don't know how long it'll last."

"Same goes for my brain," I replied, slipping around a rolling chair by the boardroom table.

As we got closer to the two hench-people, their quiet words grew audible.

"It's not the rain," Suarez said to her co-lackey. "It's the lack of sun."

Markovich nodded sympathetically, his Kevlar vest creaking. "I grew up in San Fran. The instant we're done with all this shit, I'm going home to work on my tan."

Really? He looked like one solid beam of sunlight would turn him to dust. But more importantly, these two goontabulous shit-wigglers complaining about Vancouver's weather wasn't useful intel.

My gaze slid to the table instead. A black case sat open, and inside were four military-grade black gas masks. A chill crept down my spine.

Lienna seized my arm, and my attention whipped to her. I followed her horror-filled stare to a monitor right behind Suarez and Markovich that displayed a security camera feed—a feed with a clearly visible Kit and Lienna glowing in low-def black and white.

"Shit," I hissed.

I spotted the camera on the wall behind the lackeys. Its gaze was focused primarily on the overhead door, but its field of view was wide enough to catch Lienna and me as we snuck around the loading dock.

Fortunately, Suarez and Markovich were too wrapped up in their meteorological grumble-fest to notice our stunned mugs caught live on the screen behind them. I hastily Redecorated the monitor to exclude us, and together, Lienna and I hurried past the boardroom table, finding sanctuary in a corner of the lair between the stack of black, heavy-duty cases and an everyday whiteboard on wheels.

A sticker on the side of the whiteboard caught my eye: "Property of Vancouver MPD."

Was Söze stealing pens from the precinct too? As my focus drifted from the property label up to the contents of the whiteboard, my heart leaped and my stomach dropped in the same shocked moment, leaving me mentally and physically reeling.

"Lienna," I hissed in disbelief, pointing at the board.

Focused on Suarez and Markovich, she glanced distractedly at it—then did a double take worthy of an SNL skit. Her jaw dropped.

If this had been an actual supervillain lair with actual supervillains, the board's contents would've been written in some obscure code. Or it would've been a fancy, wall-sized screen setup instead of a simple whiteboard. But either way, it wouldn't have been easily comprehensible for enemy spies, aka us.

Söze's operation, however, hadn't bothered with any of that clandestine obscurity. Too complicated for the muscle-brain likes of Kade and Suarez, no doubt. Scrawled on the whiteboard in black dry-erase marker was an old-fashioned mind map. It looked like the brainstorming session of a high school English student struggling to concoct an essay on *King Lear*. Lines sprouted off a central nucleus, connecting a maze of names. Most of them were unfamiliar, but I definitely recognized a few.

Georgia Johannesen and *Anson Goodman*, both crossed off.

Aurelia Blythe, a question mark scribbled beside her name.

And there, branching off from Captain Blythe, were the most familiar names of the set: *Kit Morris* and *Lienna Shen*. We'd been crossed off too. The Coffer had marked us as dead, and no one here had realized their bounty broker was compromised.

That wasn't what made my heart race though. My pulse pounded with an exhilarating blend of shock, confusion, mystery, and unsurprised acknowledgment, because the nucleus of the mind map, the name at the very center of it all, was one I knew as well.

Darius King.

"Holy shit," I whispered. "Darius isn't just involved in this. He's right smack in the middle. Every single name branches off his."

"Who are all these other people?" Lienna's lips pursed as she counted names under her breath. "Five, six, seven—"

"Finally!"

Markovich's loud exclamation made me and Lienna jump. He and Suarez had drifted closer to us while talking, but their attention was on the dimly lit darkness that led deeper into the mechanical maze.

Kade strode into view between two monster-sized chillers, a businesslike air giving his movements distinct purpose. He, too, was dressed in full, villainous-black combat gear, but he'd skipped a helmet.

"Are we leaving?" Markovich continued impatiently. "If we take any longer, Söze will have to issue another fake bounty."

Suarez glanced at her phone. "Barrows says there are only a few people left."

"And the target is among them?" Kade inquired, his voice as stony as his usual expression.

"Yeah. Everything is ready."

"Good. Then …"

Kade trailed off. His gaze slid across the room in a careful perusal, slowing noticeably as it passed over me and Lienna. My heart leaped with a fresh dose of adrenaline—but he only hesitated for a moment before turning toward the camera feed on the monitor. He stared at it for several long seconds, his eyes squinted like he was thinking hard. A daily hardship for him, I was betting.

"Head out to the vehicles," he said, dropping his attention back to his fellow hench-folk. "I'll be right there with the portals."

Suarez uncrossed her thick arms, her expression incredulous. "You don't have them? What were you even—"

"If I wanted to be questioned, I would have said so." His steely tone shut Suarez right up. "Go to the car. Now."

She and Markovich made an about-face and strode off toward the loading bay, and I realized with surprise that not only did Kade seem to be in charge of the portals, but he was also in charge of the other lackeys. Interesting.

Kade waited a moment to ensure they were following his orders, then turned and headed back the way he'd come.

I leaned close to Lienna. "Once he leads us to the portals, we'll take him down."

She nodded. "Let's go."

As we hastened around the table, Kade moved deeper into the machinery labyrinth, and with no lights beyond their temporary lair of evil, shadows engulfed his form. He moved at a leisurely amble, giving us plenty of time to catch up—but when we closed within ten paces of him, he increased his pace as though remembering he was on the clock.

Frowning, I wondered why Kade was storing the portals so far away from all their other villainy gear. Why not stick them in one of those fancy, hard-shell black cases?

His silhouette, a dark spot against the dark equipment, wove between two thingamabobs wrapped in shiny, tinfoil-like insulation with fat ducts running off them. Reaching a wall, he turned sharply, my line of sight cut off.

We rushed around the corner, and for a second, all I could see was darkness—but there, a slightly darker rectangle revealed an open doorway. I slid to the threshold and peered in, but it was pitch black.

"Did he go in there?" I whispered to Lienna.

"I'm not sure."

"He was heading this way ..." Afraid to delay any longer and lose him, I stepped through the doorway and dug into my pocket. Lienna gripped my other wrist tightly as I pulled out my phone.

Changing light conditions were a big weakness of my warps, but I didn't have much choice. Forcing my weary brain to concentrate, I turned on my phone's flashlight.

For a second, the flare of light was too much. It cut straight through my warp, but I recovered quickly, more of my attention on the warp than on my newly illuminated surroundings.

Maybe that's why I didn't see him.

"About fucking time."

With Kade's low, coldly amused growl, something hit me between the shoulder blades. Low-volt electricity zapped straight up my spine to my brain. My phone fell from my hand as I pitched toward the floor, body and mind eclipsed by stark, brutal nothingness.

21

PAIN BROUGHT ME BACK to my senses. It was concentrated in my left wrist and burned all the way down my arm to my shoulder. The whole limb was on fire and my shoulder felt seconds from popping out of its socket.

Groaning, I cracked my eyes open. My blurred vision snapped around, trying to make sense of my surroundings. What the hell was all this big, bulky machinery?

Oh right. The defunct ice rink. We'd been following Kade into the dark bowels of the mechanical room when—

Memory returned in a flash, jarring me to full awareness. The hideous pain in my arm and shoulder was the result of all my weight hanging from my left wrist, which was trapped in a handcuff that had been looped behind a two-inch metal pipe bolted to the concrete wall. The other end was cuffed around Lienna's wrist. She was hanging by her arm, slumped in unconsciousness.

My feet scraped across the floor as I got them under me and stood, taking my weight off my abused arm.

"Lienna!" I hissed, scooping her against me with my free arm to remove the pressure from her wrist.

"Finally awake, I see."

My head spun toward the voice, scanning my surroundings for its source. Lienna and I were handcuffed to a pipe in the back corner of the mechanical area, and I couldn't see the evil lair with its boardroom table and tech station, but one of the standing industrial-style lights had been placed nearby.

Agent Kade stood in its harsh orange glow, the light reflecting off his shaved head.

"Good evening, Mr. Morris," he said silkily.

My heart was already racing, but the icy, eager anticipation slicking his tone made my pulse leap even faster. My first instinct was to throw a warp at him, but I couldn't. The handcuff around my wrist was an MPD-issue, abjuration-spelled one, meaning I couldn't access my magic. I couldn't even feel its warm brightness in my head.

Lienna stirred. Her head, propped against my chest, lifted as she looked around. She gasped, the sound thick with dread.

"I'm glad you two woke up before I left." Kade's lips stretched wide in the coldest, most brutal mockery of a smile I'd ever seen. "I wanted to tell you how truly delighted I am that you survived the hits Söze put on you."

For some horrifying reason, he sounded genuinely pleased—but the handcuffs and the terror-smile made me think there wasn't much goodwill in his sincere statement.

He tapped something in his hand: a small stack of dark, disc-shaped portals. "You have no idea how bored I've been. The librarian and the reporter were too easy, too quick. Your captain was a bit more interesting—I got to make her bleed, at least, but it wasn't nearly enough to satisfy me."

He stepped closer, moving in front of the light. Heavy shadows cloaked his face, his eyes gleaming avidly in the darkness.

"But now I have something to look forward to. A reward for finally completing my primary objective."

My breath rushed in and out, and even though I knew it was pointless, I found myself straining against the handcuffs as though I could tear the pipe out of the concrete wall. Lienna's hand had formed a tight fist around the front of my hoodie.

"As far as my superiors are concerned, you're already dead." Kade's fingers drummed across the portals. "So we'll have plenty of uninterrupted time together. No rush. I can take as long as I want with both of you. And while we're at it, we can discuss where your captain disappeared to."

His head tilted slightly, and a sliver of light illuminated his tongue as he licked his lips.

"But first, I have a mission to complete. While you wait …" He stretched his leg out and used the toe of his boot to flip open the heavy-duty case sitting on the floor beside him. "Here's something for you to think about."

I tried not to look. I knew I shouldn't. But I couldn't help glancing down. For once, I wished I wasn't such a movie buff. I wished I hadn't watched *Reservoir Dogs* or *Casino* or *True Romance*. I wished I didn't recognize those shiny, sharp instruments and what they could do to a human body.

"I'll be back soon." Kade's murmur crawled into my ears and nestled in my brain like a terror-spawning disease. "Say your goodbyes while you wait, Mr. Morris and Miss Shen. You won't get a chance later."

His footsteps echoed across the floor, but I was still staring at that case. My eyes picked out details, finding every smear of dried blood or smudged fingerprint. He'd used those tools before.

A door clattered in the distance, reverberating through the space. Then the only sound was the buzzing of the standing light and our harsh, rapid breathing.

"Kit," Lienna whispered.

I sucked in air. "We have to get out of here. Phones—do we have our pho—"

Without thinking, I loosened my arm around her to check my pockets. A pained gasp burst from her lips as she slid down my front and the handcuffs pulled tight, all her weight hanging from her wrist.

I scooped her back up against me, lifting her off her feet. I was half a foot taller than her, and with our wrists trapped above our heads, I could stand but she couldn't. If I released her, she'd be hanging helplessly, toes unable to touch the floor.

"Sorry," I muttered. "Can you check my pockets?"

She slipped her free hand into my jeans pockets, then checked her own. "Nothing. My satchel is gone too, and even my bracelets. He took everything."

"Okay … then we free ourselves some other way."

My statement sounded simple and confident—minus the breathless note in my voice—but it was a pointless bluff. The panic spiraling in my head ratcheted with each passing second as we examined the pipe, the handcuffs, the wall. We tried to pry the pipe free, tried to loosen the bolts, tried to squeeze our hands through the cuffs. Short of pulling a Rose DeWitt Bukater and using a conveniently available axe to chop the cuff chain, we weren't breaking free through force alone.

After fifteen minutes of futile effort, we were back where we'd started: me holding Lienna against my body with one arm, her free arm looped around my neck, just standing there doing absolutely nothing but waiting for Kade to return.

The urge to shout for help until my throat bled was strong, but we were in a concrete tomb in an abandoned building surrounded by an empty field and a parking lot. No one would hear us.

"Maybe … maybe Zora will come looking for us," Lienna suggested, trying hard to keep her voice from shaking. "She knows we came in here. If she doesn't hear from us …"

"But she went off to help with a big bounty. How long until—" I broke off, my eyes widening. "Oh shit. Remember what Markovich said?"

She sucked in a breath. "Something about Söze issuing a fake bounty."

Profanity spilled from me in an explosive exhale. "It's a setup. They're going for him right now."

"For who?"

"Darius." I gritted my teeth. "A fake bounty to get everyone out of his guild. Barrows is watching the guild and reporting back to Suarez. 'Only a few people left,' she said. And Kade said he was going to celebrate completing his *primary objective*. That can only be killing Darius."

Lienna shook her head—not in disagreement but in dismay. "Darius is too smart for them. He's the Mage Assassin. He—"

"He doesn't know about the portals," I interrupted. "One of them is already planted somewhere close to Darius. I'm sure of it. They'll take him by surprise, just like Georgia and Anson. And if the Coffer's shitbag assassins could come up with ways to defeat my warps, I don't doubt Kade has schemed up ways to counter Darius's lumina magic."

A crushing silence fell between us. Kade was on his way to murder Darius. Then he would come back to kill me and Lienna as slowly and horrifically as possible. And we couldn't do a damn thing to stop either.

"When Kade comes back," I said hoarsely, "he'll have to uncuff us to start his horror show. I'll wait for a chance to hit him with a Blackout, and we'll get the keys."

Lienna stared up at me, and I couldn't stand the terror in her eyes.

"It won't work." Her voice was soft, pained. "He'll anticipate that, and even if he doesn't … he already defeated your invisi-warp."

"I messed it up when I turned on my flashlight, but if I—"

"No, Kit." She closed her eyes. "He lured us into the darkness and attacked us from behind. He knew we were here."

I choked on the truth of her conclusion, unwilling to acknowledge it. "Söze was using a 'mental fortitude' potion to see through my warps a week ago. Do you think Kade dosed himself?"

"I don't know. Maybe."

Heavy doubt layered her "maybe." Until we'd shown up, Kade had believed we were dead. Why would he use a valuable potion to guard against a dead psycho warper?

I swore, my head bowing forward. "We need a plan. We need to do *something*."

Lienna's arm tightened around the back of my neck, and she pressed her face against my shoulder. We held on to each other, anchored by the other's warm presence, our only defense against the storm of panic and terror trying to sweep us away.

Seconds crawled into minutes. Holding her against me was tiring my arm and back, but I would tear my muscles from the strain before I let her go. I would chew my hand off before I let Kade hurt her. She was the most important person in the world to me. I had to protect her.

A slow trickle of pain gathered in my chest, gaining in intensity. I'd failed to protect her once already today when the skull-faced assassins had put a bullet in her chest, and to make matters worse, I'd plunged her into a Blackout warp. It wasn't just her body that had been hurt, but also her mind.

Eyes still closed, I dropped my forehead onto her shoulder. "Hey, Lienna?"

"Yes?" she whispered.

"Tell me something good."

"Good?"

"Yeah, like what's the best meal you've ever had? Or the craziest amusement park ride you've been on?" If I couldn't protect her physically, maybe I could distract her from the pain and our inevitable doom. "What's your favorite childhood memory?"

She shifted slightly in my hold and the handcuffs ground against the pipe. I pulled her closer, taking more of her weight so her arm wouldn't have to. My shoulder protested with a deep, throbbing ache that I ignored.

"It's stupid," she said hesitantly, "but there's this movie …"

I nudged her cheek with mine. "You're speaking my language."

"It's called *The Parent Trap.*"

"The Lindsay Lohan remake or the OG with Hayley Mills?"

With our cheeks touching, I felt her smile. "Lindsay Lohan."

"I've never seen it."

"Seriously? Mr. Movie Encyclopedia?" She gave her head a microscopic shake. "It's my favorite—it *was* when I was little. I must've watched it a hundred times. Whenever I was sick or there was a weekend with nothing to do, me and my dad …"

Tension filtered through her, stiffening her limbs as though she'd been Medusa-ed into stone. I couldn't see it, but I could feel it—and it felt like the same tension she'd been carrying around for days and refused to talk about. A tension that was, it now seemed, connected to her father. Was he the one she had called in the middle of the night? Maybe … but probably not. Their relationship was far from amicable. Ever since she'd discovered his less-than-legal side hustle, their father-daughter bond had fallen apart.

"What's going on, Lienna?" I asked softly. "What aren't you telling me?"

She turned her face away from mine. "We don't need to talk about that now."

"Then when the hell are we going to talk about it?" I said, immediately regretting how rough my voice sounded. I inhaled slowly, readjusting my grip around her waist, and quieted my words. "I care about you, Lienna. In the last few hours of my life, I'd like to feel like I matter to you too."

She was silent.

Stupid emotions. That had probably been the wrong approach. "I'm sorry. I—"

"Of course you matter to me," she whispered, and to my utter bafflement, she sounded hurt. "How could you doubt that?"

My mouth snapped shut. I sucked in a breath. "Because you never tell me anything. All I want is to *know* you. I know Agent

Shen really well, but I barely know Lienna because you always push me away."

"I'm not …" She let out a ragged sigh. "I can't just … dump all my worries on you. They're my problems to deal with. Not yours."

"But that's what we do, partner." I grazed her cheek with mine. "We help carry each other's problems. You've done that for me since day one. Let me do it for you."

When she didn't reply, my heart sank like a lead weight plunging to the bottom of the Mariana Trench.

"When I was thirteen …" She swallowed audibly. "When I was thirteen, my dad was diagnosed with cancer. Leukemia."

An ugly, cold feeling drove into my gut. I imagined teenage Lienna learning that her father had cancer and all the fear, anger, and hopelessness she must have felt. I knew those emotions all too well.

"He went through radiation and chemo and couldn't work for almost a year." She pushed her face deeper into my shoulder. "Some days he could barely move, so we would sit on the couch together and watch *The Parent Trap* on a loop. It was the only thing that made him laugh."

"But he got better?" I asked. Papa Shen was still alive and kicking as far as I knew.

"Yeah. But then my mom called me last week to tell me that it … the cancer … it's …"

"It's back."

She nodded, her chin bumping my collarbone. "With everything else going on, it just didn't seem important enough to bring up. I thought it would seem frivolous, especially since me and my dad … our relationship is complicated. I don't even know how I feel about it. Whining about it when Söze was breaking down our precinct and stealing my portals and trying to mass-murder the Crow and Hammer—I didn't want you to think I was distracted by something so … so …"

"So *important?*" I murmured, squeezing her middle. "Just because it's personal doesn't mean it can't be important. He's your dad, Lienna. Complicated relationship or not."

She exhaled, her breath trembling and unsteady. She'd sounded unsteady in the same way during her secret phone call—a brief check-in with her mother, I now assumed.

"You don't have to carry this alone. I never knew my parents, but"—my voice cracked—"cancer took someone very dear to me."

She blinked, her eyelashes skimming my cheek, the moisture of her tears trickling onto my skin. Her fingers curled around the back of my head, sliding through my hair, and she pulled herself up.

Her lips brushed mine, tentative and questioning. Then she kissed me—really kissed me. Soft and gentle, sorrow blending with hope.

She pulled back, her arm quivering with the effort to hold herself against me. My muscles ached too. How much longer could we stand like this? How long until I couldn't hold her anymore, and the handcuff cut into her delicate wrist?

"Kit."

I clenched my jaw.

"Kit, I think there is a way we can escape."

My eyes popped wide, and as painful hope ballooned in my chest, I craned my neck to bring her face into view. Her gaze met mine, somber and determined.

"You can free us," she said. "You need to reality warp."

22

"I'M SORRY," I replied blankly. "I need to what?"

"Reality warp," she repeated in a matter-of-fact tone.

I looked up at the handcuffs locked around our wrists. "Even if I knew how to reality warp on command, which you know I don't, these are *abjuration* handcuffs."

"Abjuration works by blocking specific magical abilities." She twitched her wrist, jangling the cuff chain. "MPD cuffs are designed to block all known types of magic."

I went still. "And my reality warping …?"

"Is completely unknown. I haven't found a single record on it. It might not even be true Psychica."

That bubble of hope attempted to expand again, but I shook my head back and forth with growing intensity. "That logic sounds flimsy even to me, and it doesn't change the fact *I don't know how.*"

"You've done it twice before," she said fiercely. "And you saved my life both times. You can do it again."

My blood was rushing in my veins—not that it'd ever stopped—and I had to control my breathing before I weakened my already tired muscles even more. It wasn't like I hadn't tried reality warping outside of the two successful cases. I'd attempted it in a handful of supremely desperate scenarios, only to fail spectacularly.

Outside of that, though, I hadn't explored the ability for a simple reason: reality warping dried up my magic like water in the Sahara. After the last time, when I'd swapped a grappling hook for a full-sized boat anchor, I'd been magic-less for forty-eight hours.

But losing my magic wouldn't matter if I was dead. I had no reason to hold back.

"Okay." Keeping a tight hold on Lienna, I turned my other hand to wrap my fingers around the handcuff chain. "I'll try."

Letting out a rush of air, I closed my eyes and imagined the metal cuffs turning into plastic. Cheap, brittle plastic like the cuffs in those cops 'n' robbers toy sets from the dollar store. Dull gray. Dumb, sharp little edges where the two halves of the mold met. Flimsy chain links with gaps.

The spot in my head where I could normally feel my magic was muffled and dark, the abjuration magic in the handcuffs most definitely blocking my usual psycho-warping abilities. Maybe Lienna was right and my reality-warping magic was unaffected. I didn't know what it felt like. It might still work.

I filled my mind with every detail of those plastic toy handcuffs as I willed the metal ones to transform—but the cold steel under my fingers didn't change. And why would it? Reality warping was magic on God Mode. Mythics could do some real crazy shit, but I didn't know anyone else who could transform an object on a molecular level with nothing but willpower.

But if I could turn a wand into a snake and a grappling hook into an anchor, I should be able to do this too. With or without the abjuration cuffs. Reality warping already broke the laws of the universe. Why couldn't it break the laws of magic too?

Shoving my doubts aside, I focused as hard as I'd ever focused on a warp. I fueled my desperation with thoughts of that case containing shiny, bloody instruments, of Kade's nightmarish smile, of his insidious voice. I pummeled my brain with feelings of terror and helplessness, imagining myself still trapped when Kade returned, imagining what he would do first—

"Kit," Lienna whispered.

My muscles were rigid with tension, my breath scraping between clenched teeth. The cuff's metal links dug painfully into my palm, and my fingers squeezed as though I could crush them with my bare hand.

"It's not working." The words rushed out and I sagged forward, almost dropping Lienna. She clamped her arm and both legs around me, hanging on as I went partially limp. "I can't do it."

"You can." She put her face right in mine, brown eyes burning with conviction. "You can do this, Kit. You always underestimate yourself and your power, but you're so strong. You're the strongest mythic I know."

I grimaced. "But ..."

"Try again." She released me, pulling back. She grabbed the cuff chain with her free hand, her weight yanking my cuff up against the pipe. She hung there, arms taut with effort. "Keep trying, Kit!"

Sucking in air, I reached up to grip the cuff around my wrist, my other hand clenched into a fist. This time, I didn't close my eyes. I kept my gaze on Lienna, on the stubborn set of her jaw, on the determined glint in her eyes. Her fear had taken a back seat to her faith in me. Her faith that I could do this. That I would save us.

That I would save *her*.

The searing need to protect her rose through my chest and burned at the base of my skull. After she'd been shot, Lienna had told me I couldn't save her from everything. But right now, I *could* save her. I wasn't going to dangle helplessly from a pipe in a dilapidated ice rink while some bald-headed maniac and his bloodstained box of knives cut her open. I wouldn't let Kade hurt her.

I wouldn't let her die.

Again, I focused on the handcuffs. I imagined them morphing from metal to a gray plastic toy, imagined it with exhaustive, ridiculous detail, applying every weird, obsessive cell in my brain to the task.

Heat scorched my hand and wrist.

Snap.

Lienna dropped, landing heavily on her butt. I staggered, balance lost, and as I caught myself, she lifted her arm. The cuff hung from her wrist, and from it dangled two links of the broken chain. With an awed expression, she pushed the small release lever on the toy cuff and it opened. It fell to the floor with the dull sound of plastic.

Her eyes rose to mine, her amazement deepening.

With a rough breath, I unclasped the cuff around my wrist and tossed it to the floor beside hers. Inhale. Exhale. Relief battled with a new flavor of terror as I mentally felt around inside my head where light and warmth used to live. Though the abjuration handcuffs were nothing more than a toy-chest knockoff now, that spot in my brain was still dark and empty, like a cerebral amputation.

"My magic is gone," I said quietly.

Her expression of wonder faltered, and she scrambled to her feet, concern pinching her eyes. Her hand closed around mine, squeezing in comfort.

"It'll come back." She pulled me into motion. "It came back last time, right? The important thing is that we're going to escape."

Yes. Escaping. Priority number one.

We sped through the chiller plant and over to the loading dock. Everything looked exactly as we'd left it—except the case with the gas masks was empty. The stack of heavy-duty black cases had shrunk as well, and not just because Kade had left his toolkit out for us to admire. More than one case was gone.

"We have to warn Darius," I said urgently, scanning the room. "It might already be too late, but—"

"Here!"

Lienna was back in the corner beside the whiteboard. Kade had thrown her satchel on the floor in the shadows. She pulled it onto her shoulder and turned to me. Our phones were in her hands—both smashed.

"Shit," I snarled. "Is there another phone here somewhere?"

We looked around. Reaching the conclusion that there were no phones, we simultaneously faced each other.

Understanding passed between us with a look, and we launched into a sprint toward the loading bay door.

If we couldn't call Darius to warn him, we'd have to do it in person.

Our borrowed Mercedes-Benz waited where we'd parked it, and Lienna pulled the keys from her satchel. We were inside, buckling up, and speeding away within seconds. The dark roads flashed by, the glow of the streetlamps little more than a blur. It was late, the streets nearly empty, and a cold wind had picked up, tumbling leaves and debris across the pavement.

The drive was somehow both too long and too short. Too long because Kade could be ambushing Darius right now, if he hadn't already, and too short because I couldn't think of a way to stop it from happening.

If we drove up to the guild, Kade and his crew of jackbooted jackasses might spot us and launch their attack instantly—and potentially murder me and Lienna as the violent icing on the assassination cake. But if we didn't approach the guild, we couldn't warn Darius.

As Lienna blew through a red light in the empty intersection one block from the Crow and Hammer, I opened my mouth to share my doubts about what we should do—but she spoke first.

"Unbuckle and be ready to jump out," she said, popping her seat belt off.

Well, then. I didn't have a plan, but Agent Shen did.

My seat belt retracted as I pushed it aside, and I almost wished for its safe, snug hold as Lienna sped straight toward the Crow and Hammer's three-story building with reckless abandon. The guild looked quiet and peaceful, all its windows dark except for a single one glowing on the third floor. No sign of Kade and his team, but if they'd been sloppy enough to be spotted, they wouldn't have pulled off two GM murders already.

Lienna slammed the brakes and jerked the wheel. I caught myself on the dash as the car spun in a one-hundred-and-eighty-degree skid and came to a rocking halt with its back bumper two feet from the Crow and Hammer's door, the nose sticking out into the intersection.

As I reeled from that *Transporter*-quality maneuver, she threw her door wide open. I hastily followed suit. We leaped out, ducking low so the open car doors could shield us, and when no one rained magic down on us, we sprinted into the recessed entrance of the guild.

The door offered no resistance, and we spilled into the dimly lit pub. A quick visual sweep confirmed it was empty of both guild members and goons. Not surprising since the fake bounty had lured their combat mythics away, and everyone else was probably at home getting ready for bed.

"Upstairs," I said shortly.

Lienna wheeled toward the staircase and launched up it. As I raced after her, my brain rapidly cataloged the most likely outcomes: one, Kade had already struck and we'd find Darius's body in his office; two, Kade had seen us arrive and would strike at Darius before we could warn him; or three, Kade knew we were about to interfere and would call off the attack for tonight.

Number three didn't mesh with the psycho killer who was eagerly waiting to celebrate tonight's portal murder with the more gruesome, torture-laced murders of me and my partner, which meant we were looking at options one or two.

We flew up the stairs to the third level, blazed down the short hall, and burst through the open doorway at the end without any caution whatsoever.

The large office held four cluttered desks for the guild's officers, one in each corner, leaving an open space in the middle big enough to do a cartwheel or two. Three of the desks were empty, while the fourth was occupied.

A young guy with ginger hair looked up from a stack of paperwork, his blue eyes wide with surprise. Aaron Sinclair, my memory supplied. One of the top combat mythics of the guild. I'd met him recently while busting his ass out of jail.

"Morris?" he said blankly. "What—"

"Where's Darius?" I interrupted, my voice loud and urgent. Not waiting for an answer, I strode toward the closed door across from me—Darius's office. "Is he here?"

"Darius? He's—"

The handle turned, and his office door swung open. For a panicked second, I was afraid Kade would appear in the threshold, a bloody weapon in his hand and that slick, sadistic smile on his face.

But it was Darius, alive and well, his dark brows rising above sharp gray eyes as he stepped out of his office.

"Agent Morris?" he inquired quietly, intensely.

Relief swept over me—but only for a second. "Darius, you need to get out of here before—"

My ears popped as the pressure in the room changed—and with the sound of shredding paper, a swirling oval of cosmic green light tore apart a stack of folders on the desk across from Aaron's. The portal yawned open, scraps of paper flying upward.

From the gaping chasm came not a human but a small orb. Hurled by the exit portal's explosive force, it ejected the orb straight up into the ceiling. Glass shattered and noxious yellow gas billowed out from it, sweeping through the room.

23

THE MOMENT THE PORTAL OPENED, I was moving—leaping toward the nearest desk. As the yellow cloud whooshed through the room, I grabbed the desk's rolling chair, heaved it up, and hurled it into the window.

The chair crashed through the large pane, and blustery wind gusted into the room, sending the thick vapor swirling wildly.

It wasn't enough.

The air seared my throat as I inhaled, and pain splintered down into my lungs. I staggered, spots popping across my vision and my lungs attempting to crawl down into my stomach to escape the toxic air.

In the second it took me to breathe and choke, the portal ejected its next gift: Kade. He flew up out of the green vortex, tucked into a roll, and landed in the middle of the room, a gas mask covering his face. Right behind him, with perfect precision, Markovich and Suarez appeared. Last in line was Yao, looking way more Navy SEAL than the young Paul McCartney lookalike he usually resembled.

The team landed, spread out, and aimed their identical black pistols at Darius in a swift, practiced maneuver that took approximately two-point-three seconds.

"*Ori eradendi torrens!*"

Lienna's voice rang out, thick and hoarse, as though she could barely get the words out, and a wall of watery blue light swept across the room. It crashed into the line of assassins before they could fire, knocking them all backward. Suarez and Markovic fell into a pair of desks.

"Run!" Lienna choked.

Her words were directed at Darius and Aaron, and I realized how much the window I'd broken was helping with the toxic cloud of lung-melting gas. I was standing in the fresh breeze, more or less on my feet, but the farther from the window one was, the less "breathing normally" was an option.

Darius had his sleeve pressed to his nose and mouth, shoulders shuddering as his chest spasmed—and Aaron, farthest from the window, was down on his knees, hacking up his lungs.

Lienna's smash-barrier had stalled Kade and his team, but not for long. Kade was first to recover, his weapon sweeping toward Darius once again—but choking on poison gas or not, the former assassin wasn't going down that easily.

Before Kade's gun could align with his vitals, Darius blinked out of sight.

I took one lurching step toward the doorway, knowing that's where invisible-Darius would head, but the sight of Kade sent dread plunging through my burning innards. Darius's disappearance hadn't stalled the assassin. His gun swung in a steady motion, tracking a moving target.

He fired.

Darius reappeared as he dove clear of the shot. He hit the floor, the potion ball bursting against the desk behind him and spraying a silvery liquid in every direction.

Rolling, Darius flicked a hand at the line of assassins. Startled curses burst from them—since invisibility wasn't working, he must have blinded them. He launched to his feet, listing sideways.

Splatters of silver potion glistened on his left cheek, neck, and shoulder.

I reached him an instant later, steadying him and dragging him toward the exit. We got two steps before a potion ball whooshed past my head, missing me by an inch. I looked back to see Kade aiming at us, his eyes staring sightlessly behind the goggles of his mask.

Yanking on Darius, I bent at the waist and ran for the exit. Just ahead, Lienna had Aaron's arm over her shoulders as she helped the coughing mage to the doorway.

"Go!" she gasped.

Potion balls flew over our heads, scarcely missing as we lunged through the threshold. Behind me and Darius, Aaron twisted, almost flattening Lienna into the wall, and aimed a shaking hand back into the office.

Fire lit up his palm, then exploded outward. The massive inferno of death swept into the office, turning everything into red-hot flames.

I didn't think for a moment that would be enough to stop those overly prepared assholes.

We stumbled down the stairs, Lienna and me supporting the two mages. They were both coughing—wet, tearing coughs that sounded like their lungs were made of Velcro. Lienna was gasping, her airways only marginally healthier, and my throat burned all the way down like I'd inhaled boiling water.

We had to get out of here. If we could get into the car before Kade and his team caught up to us, we might survive this.

We reached the bottom of the stairs. The dim pub, normally cozy and welcoming, felt hollow and foreboding. Every shadow held a potential enemy. I hauled Darius toward the guild's front entrance.

The door swung open.

Decked out in black combat gear, a ponytailed man I recognized as Barrows aimed his potion pistol at Darius's face. The luminamage tossed his hand up, and a flash of light so bright it rivaled the sun flared in front of the assassin's face. He recoiled with a pained shout, blinded by the luminescent attack.

Unfortunately, I was blinded too.

My vision had turned to white spots, and I couldn't see shit. Thudding steps warned me that Kade and his three helpers were on the stairs. One of them bellowed angrily, something collided hard with my shoulder, and I hit the floor. A cacophony of shouts and incantations filled the pub.

I shoved onto my knees, swiping urgently at the tears streaming from my abused eyes to clear my vision. A boom erupted, so close my left eardrum threatened to split.

"Kit!"

Lienna's voice, but I couldn't see her. The pops of potion guns peppered the air, then another thunderous blast of magic.

I leaped up, barely able to make out shapes. There was a long, chest-high barrier in front of me that could only be the bar. Before I got toasted by a spell I couldn't even see, I grabbed at the bar and vaulted over it, landing heavily on the other side.

A few more pained blinks cleared my vision, and I stuck my head above the bar. Kade and his team had joined Barrows. They'd shed their gas masks and potion guns, and they were attacking in earnest.

Three versus six, and it was utter chaos.

Proving yet again that mages are terrifying, Aaron engulfed one of his two opponents in flame. Markovich collapsed to the floor, rolling in a vain attempt to extinguish the flames and screaming in indescribable agony, but the pyromage's second opponent wasn't so easy. As Aaron flung fire at him, Barrows gestured sharply with the long dagger in his hand. A swirl of wind blasted the fire away, and with another twist of his dagger, he sent a honed blade of air slicing toward Aaron.

Aaron dodged, the transparent blade missing his chest but catching his upper arm.

Lienna was fending off Suarez and Yao, both armed with artifacts that they were firing at her. She'd erected her shimmering blue shield, but it wouldn't last much longer, and trapped behind it, she could only defend.

And for the third battle: Darius versus Kade. A luminamage should've had no problem taking out a sorcerer, but Kade was no normal mythic. Darius wasn't even bothering with his lumina magic because it didn't seem to work on Kade—even blind, Kade still knew where to attack.

Or maybe Darius wasn't using his magic because he couldn't. Blood stained his mouth from the internal damage that poison gas had done, and he'd been hit with Kade's silvery potion as well. His movements were uneven and unsteady, utterly lacking his usual smooth, deadly efficiency that I'd glimpsed in the past.

Kade was circling Darius, a dagger held low in his hand. That sadistic, hungry smile stretched his lips as he darted in. They met in a clash of swift blows and blocks, and Kade staggered, tripping on a fallen chair as it blinked back into sight. Recovering, Kade grinned in amusement. Blood ran from a gash in Darius's shoulder.

Even with Kade's unknown abilities, Darius, Aaron, and Lienna were all top-class mythics who should've had this in the bag. But with the mages poisoned and unarmed, and Lienna having used most of her artifacts, we were losing.

We were losing badly.

And me, I couldn't do a damn thing to change that outcome. Inside my head was a dark, hollow pit where my magic used to be. Short of turning myself into a flesh shield for one of my allies, I couldn't do shit.

It was almost ironic. Over the past few weeks, I'd been on a rollercoaster of uncertainty about how powerful I was, how I should use my power, how to compensate when others knew about my abilities, and how to handle it when others defeated my magic. I was either the most powerful guy on the battleground, or the most useless, and there never seemed to be an in-between.

Lienna was fighting for her life in front of me, and the moment I jumped out of my hiding spot, I'd become a target. She'd have to split her attention to protect me. Same with Darius and Aaron. Without my magic, I was unarmed and helpless. Worse than that, I was a liability.

A pang thumped through my chest at the thought.

Was I really nothing without my magic? Was a psycho warper the beginning and end of Kit Morris?

Against Daedalus's drone, I'd been powerless and had to be saved by a smuggler who could see the future.

Against the Wild Boys, I'd overplayed my warps and had to be saved by a supercharged demon and his murder-magic.

Against Kade, I'd been too confident in my invisibility and had walked Lienna and myself headfirst into a near-disastrous ambush.

I hadn't merely been *relying* on my magic. I'd become completely dependent on it. I'd become a psycho warper who couldn't act unless he could flash a fancy hallucination or make himself disappear.

To hell with that.

What had Zylas said? *If you are smarter than your enemies, you do not need to be stronger.*

My gaze whipped across Darius and Kade, Aaron and the aeromage, and Lienna and her two opponents, then jumped to the cupboards around me for something I could fight with. Bottles of liquor, drink glasses, mixers, a keg of west coast IPA. Nothing that screamed "smarter than your enemies." My attention swept up the wall, searching for something I could use.

And *something* was waiting for me.

Hanging above the bar, almost invisible in the shadows, was a silver war hammer. The "Hammer" of the Crow and Hammer. A thick, heavy, symmetrical head at the end of a long, aged wood haft.

Why, hello there.

I didn't need to be stronger *or* smarter than my enemies; I just needed a bigger stick. I was sure Zylas would approve.

I leaped onto the back counter. My hands closed around the smooth haft, and I heaved it up.

The hammer didn't budge.

Shit, was this Mjölnir's cousin or something? Was I not worthy? I might not be as pure-hearted as Captain America, but—

An explosion of magic engulfed Lienna's shield, and it shattered into sparkles. With a victorious whoop, Yao aimed a rune-engraved dagger at her.

Teeth gritted, I hauled on the hammer, and this time, it pulled free, its weight almost throwing me off the counter. As much as I wanted to believe it'd recognized me as worthy, I was pretty sure the real reason it hadn't moved at first was because it was heavier than a goddamn smart car.

The war hammer in my grasp, I stepped from the back counter onto the bar. Raising the weapon above my head, I let out a Leonidas-style roar as I lunged off the counter, hammer swinging down at Yao's unsuspecting head.

The sorcerer lurched backward and the hammer swept past, so close that it grazed his chest. The steel head slammed down between his feet, splitting the floorboards.

But it didn't matter that I'd missed.

Gray sparks flashed off the head and a wave of force erupted from the weapon. The concussive blast hurled Yao, two tables, and six chairs across the pub. They soared twelve feet and crashed into a pile of splintered wood and broken bones.

Holy divine weapon of destruction.

Kade, Suarez, and the aeromage all spun toward me—and aimed their next attacks at the poor magic-less psycho warper with the giant hammer.

Big mistake.

Darius made the slightest movement with his left hand, and light burst in front of Kade's eyes. Aaron sent a fireball whooshing at the aeromage, and Lienna's voice rang out.

"*Ori te formo cuspides!*"

A barrage of black spikes launched from her cube, bombarding Suarez.

I hoisted the hammer into the air, pointed myself at the rectangular goon, and swung it down into the floor again. A second wave of destruction roared out from the weapon, hurling a stunned Suarez off her feet. She tumbled down amidst shattered chairs.

Darius rushed Kade. Blinded but not incapacitated, Kade slashed with his dagger, but Darius caught his wrist. With brutal efficiency, he smashed his fist into Kade's cheek.

Aaron's hands lit up with fire, but before he could finish off Barrows, a coughing fit doubled him over. Barrows raised his dagger toward the pyromage—right as Lienna closed in on his left side. Abandoning her artifacts, she launched at him like a five-foot-five wrecking ball, all fists, feet, and black-belt acrobatics. Avoiding his protective gear, she went for his knees, throat, and groin, then twisted his arm so hard I heard bone pop.

I spun toward Darius, gripping the war hammer, but I wasn't the only one who'd realized the tide of this battle had turned. With a sneer twisting his lips, Kade pulled something from a pouch on his belt and tossed it at the floor.

The small vial shattered, and with a fizzing noise, another cloud of smoke whooshed outward. I recoiled, sucking in my breath to hold it as the pub turned to gray mist. Everyone vanished, and once again, I couldn't see a damn thing.

24

SMOKE FILLED THE AIR. My lungs burned with the need for oxygen, and I couldn't stop myself from gasping in a breath. The air tasted vaguely peppery, but my throat didn't burn any more than before. It was a smoke bomb, not a poisonous cloud.

Kade had just pulled the classic Vegas magician disappearing douchebag trick.

"Lienna?" I shouted.

A shadow appeared in the mist—too tall to be my partner. I hauled the hammer up as a bloodied and burned Barrows charged straight at me, his teeth bared and eyes wild. Jaw clenched with effort, I swung the hammer in a horizontal arc.

The hammer slammed into his upper arm—and lightning burst across his body. He flew sideways and crumpled to the floor, smoke rising from his limp form.

No way. This hammer *was* Mjölnir? I'd just Thor-zapped the shit out of Barrows!

Another shadow appeared in the fog. I half-raised Mjölnir, ready to secure my spot as the newly crowned God of Thunder with a second blast of almighty lightning, but my new challenger wasn't an enemy. It was Kai Yamada, another of the Crow and Hammer's top combat mythics, dressed in black gear and holding a throwing knife that sizzled with electric power.

Damn it. I hadn't been summoning Mjölnir's heavenly high-voltage power. It was just a boring electramage.

"Morris!" he barked as more silhouettes rushed in behind him—an entire group of guild reinforcements. "What's—"

"Kit!"

Lienna's shout cut through my disappointment about not-Mjölnir, and I shoved the hammer's handle at Kai before whirling around and sprinting toward Lienna's voice.

"Lienna?" I called.

"Here!"

I found her beside Darius, who was leaning against a table with his hand pressed to his upper arm, blood trickling over his fingers. Aaron was slumped in the chair next to his GM, breathing shallowly, eyes half-lidded, and blood trickling from multiple slashes.

"Where's Kade?" Lienna asked me.

I looked around wildly at the white mist. "I don't know. He disappeared in the smoke and I got distracted by lightning."

Her face flattened with the same grim realization I'd just arrived at: Kade had escaped.

"He'll go back to his lair," I said. "He can't leave all his stuff there now that we know where it is."

"You're right." Lienna straightened. "If we hurry, we can catch him."

"Wait." Darius's hoarse command brought us up short. The GM peered through the fog. "Kai!"

The electramage zipped out of the fading mist, several mythics that I vaguely recognized following him. His attention snagged on his buddy Aaron, concern pinching his dark eyes.

He swept his gaze to Darius. "Yes, sir?"

"Accompany Agent Shen and Agent Morris."

"Got it." He gestured to the group behind him. "Sanjana, take care of Aaron and Darius."

A woman with a brightly marked medic bag stepped forward, and he turned to us expectantly.

I wouldn't complain about some high-class mage backup. With our new helper right behind us, we raced across the pub, passing more Crow and Hammer members along the way; it appeared their entire team from Söze's fake bounty had returned at once.

Outside in the blustery wind, our car was right where we'd left it, doors open, headlights glaring, engine running, keys in the ignition, and miraculously unstolen. Lienna and I hopped in while Kai jumped in the back, and away we went again, racing the reverse route we'd taken to the Crow and Hammer.

While Lienna concentrated on driving, I gave Kai a swift rundown of the situation. In the rearview mirror, I watched his expression go from wary to grim to coldly murderous by the time I was done. The hair-raising feeling that I was going to suffer the worst static shock of my life the moment I touched something conductive buzzed along my nerves.

A dozen broken traffic laws later, Lienna brought the car to a silent stop on the street near the ice rink. We unloaded without speaking, and Kai ghosted on our heels as Lienna and I slunk alongside the building. Around the corner was the loading bay door where we'd originally entered the lair, and judging by the beam of orange light shining across the parking lot, said door was fully open.

Signaling Kai to wait, I peeked swiftly around the corner—and jerked back again.

We'd not only found Kade, but the mother hen had returned to the coop. Söze had just marched out of the loading dock, and from my brief glimpse, his face had taken on a new shade of sickly salmon pink—likely a side effect of his considerable rage over his lackeys' utter failure at murdering all of us.

Kade had been right behind his boss, calmly carrying one of the lair's large black cases.

"Söze and Kade," I whispered to my compatriots.

"Did they see you?" Lienna asked.

"No, but …"

She nodded tersely. Just because the two dick-headed scab-pickers hadn't laid eyes on me didn't mean they weren't aware of our presence. Kade had a sixth sense for people's whereabouts, which made zero sense whatsoever since he was supposed to be a standard sorcerer.

Well, a standard psychopathic, serial-killing, torture-happy, utterly corrupt sorcerer. But the point still stood.

The steady wind whipped Söze's voice toward us. He was too far away for complete sentences to reach my ears, but I could make out the words "incompetent," "destroy," and for some reason, "insufferable."

"We need to get closer," Kai said in a low voice.

I poked my head around the corner again. Kade and Söze had switched; Kade was in the lead, nonchalantly lugging the black case away from the loading dock, while Söze trailed behind him, yelling obscenities at his back.

"You don't have a ranged attack?" I asked the zap-wizard, momentarily regretting my decision to leave the Crow and Hammer's glorious namesake weapon behind.

"Not at this distance," he answered.

And that distance was only growing. Instead of heading toward the MPD vehicles parked near the loading bay, they were walking across the parking lot. Where the hell were they going?

Staying low and quiet, Lienna, Kai, and I hurried around the corner of the building and rushed toward the two cars. I sincerely hoped that the wind—which was stinging my eyes and doing my hair absolutely no favors—would hide the sound of our footsteps. Maybe Kade's otherworldly skill was clairaudience. That would track. Based on my experience at KCQ, psychics of the super-hearing sort were top-notch crap-monkeys.

The three of us crouched behind the closest MPD-mobile and peered through its windows at the two assholes who had stopped in the middle of the parking lot, illuminated by the light from the open loading bay. Kai craned his neck to gauge the various angles of attack, then shook his head. We were still too far away for the human high-voltage sign to cook up a deadly electrical storm.

But we were close enough to hear them talking.

"I'm struggling," Söze half-shouted at his subordinate, spitting with fury, "to fully comprehend your ineptitude. You had them outgunned and outmanned, and now I have to explain to the Consilium why the only dead bodies in that pathetic guild belong to your 'highly trained' soldiers!"

The Consilium? That was new.

Looking bored by his boss's tireless rant, Kade set down his black case and crossed his bulky arms.

"Never mind your unmitigated mishandling of Morris and Shen," Söze continued. "Not only are they *still alive*, but they could show up any second with half their precinct backing them up."

"I'll know if they get close," Kade replied coolly.

The bald bastard was overestimating his powers of perception.

Kai pulled a pair of small throwing knives from sheaths on his forearms. "If we rush them, I can get close enough."

I shook my head, gesturing at the pistol holstered on Kade's hip. Whether it was the alchemical kind or the faster-than-sound bullet kind, rushing him was too dangerous. We wouldn't make it ten steps before turning this parking lot into Kade's personal shooting range.

The wind was picking up, buffeting my ears and making it harder to hear much of anything.

Courteously, Söze raised the volume of his incessant berating. "The Consilium will get a full report on how you failed to kill Darius King!"

Kade's attention finally turned to his superior. "That was *your* plan, Söze."

The blustery wind grew stronger, and I strained to hear.

"You were ordered to deal with Darius King," Kade continued with a sneer. "Killing him without digging every scrap of knowledge out of his brain first is pure *incompetence*, as you love to say."

Kade put so much mockery in that dig that I would've applauded the burn if I hadn't hated him as much as Söze.

"Which is why," Kade continued, his hand dipping into his pocket, "the Consilium gave me permission to eliminate any liabilities—including you."

Söze's mouth hung open, a black hole in his white face as gusts whipped across the parking lot with increasing violence. The wind sounded almost unnatural, like a rhythmic whumping.

Kai pointed upward. "Look!"

Barely visible against the night sky, a completely black, unmarked helicopter descended toward the parking lot until it hovered thirty feet above Söze and Kade. A rope ladder tumbled down from the deck, the bottom rung bouncing against the pavement a few feet away from the two men.

Söze lurched toward the rope, hands grabbing desperately for it.

Kade flicked the small object in his hand, his mouth moving with words that the wind whipped away. Magenta light flashed off the artifact, and the resulting burst of gore made my stomach roil.

Söze pitched over. His body hit the pavement and his head rolled away, completely severed.

Tucking his artifact back into a pocket, Kade picked up his black case with one hand and seized the rope ladder with the other. His head turned ninety degrees, and from across the parking lot, he looked directly at my hiding spot behind the car.

His gaze met mine, and he smiled—the same smile he'd given me and Lienna when he'd told us he'd be back for us soon.

A chill washed over me as he stepped onto the lower rung of the ladder. The whirlybird ascended, lifting him above the pavement, and all I could do was stare through the car windows as my heart pounded in my throat.

"He's getting away!" Lienna yelled, leaping up.

Before her head could clear the top of the car, Kai yanked her back down. "Stay put," he hissed. "Don't you see the gunman in the chopper?"

My nerves prickled all over again as I peered at the rising helicopter. Dimly lit by lights from within the cockpit, I could make out the open door and a black-clad man hanging half out, positioned beside something long and very machine-gun-esque.

"What do we do?" Lienna demanded urgently.

Hell if I knew. I'd only ever ridden in a helicopter once and I sure as shit had never fought one. One halluci-bomb spread far enough to catch the pilot would've brought the whole chopper down, but unfortunately, that wasn't an option right now.

As the whirlybird ascended into the night sky, I turned toward the lit-up loading bay. We'd lost Kade—and Söze was dead—but we still had the lair. They hadn't had time to clear out the whole thing. Maybe there was evidence inside that would lead us to whoever gave orders to Söze and Kade: the Consilium.

An earsplitting boom put an end to that thought.

I ducked back behind the car, my body reacting to the sound before my brain had processed it. A massive fireball belched out of the loading bay. Heat and orange flames poured from the interior, black smoke roiling skyward.

All three of us huddled behind the car as the fire spread, consuming everything inside the loading bay and mechanical rooms.

I touched Lienna's shoulder. "You okay?"

She nodded.

I glanced over at Kai. "You?"

"I'm fine."

Lienna got to her feet, surveying the destruction, then turned to gaze at Söze's headless body, lying in the middle of the pavement.

"What the hell was that about?" she muttered.

"I'm not sure," I said with gritted teeth, head tipped back to scan the night sky. The helicopter was long gone. "But it was nothing good."

25

HUMMING THE THEME SONG from *The Fresh Prince of Bel Air*, I unlocked the door to my apartment. No, not the one where I rented a single room and shared the bathroom with three other dudes. The *other* apartment.

The door swung open, and I walked into my old condo, which was now my new condo until Blythe kicked me out. I kind of doubted she would. After all, there was no reason I couldn't live in the Batcave and man the computer when Eggsy wasn't here.

Forcefully keeping up my cheerful whistle despite the worries dragging down my mood, I ambled into the kitchen and set my grocery bags on the counter. I'd already brought a backpack full of clothes and toiletries to put in my bedroom and bathroom, and now I was stocking the kitchen. Eggsy seemed happy to eat takeout each and every day, but I was ready for a change of pace.

I unloaded my shopping onto the counter, put most of it into the fridge and pantry, then started washing the leafy green lettuce. Chicken and avocado salad with green goddess dressing, here we come.

Twenty minutes later, I was cutting two baked chicken breasts into slices to throw on top of my big serving bowl of green things when the front door clattered open. Lienna stepped inside, her jacket dotted with raindrops.

"Sorry I'm late," she said breathlessly as she toed off her shoes. "That smells great."

I managed a smile as she shed her jacket and hastened to join me. Pulling out a pair of large bowls, I split the salad into two servings and stuck a fork in each. She chose one and sat across from me.

Shoveling a forkful of greens into my mouth, I pretended not to notice her intent gaze lasering into my face and dissecting my blandly positive expression. Wordlessly, she reached into her satchel, withdrew a soda bottle, and set it in front of me.

I blinked at the Dr. Pepper. My favorite.

"You always drink these when you're stressed," she murmured. "Still nothing?"

I didn't need to ask what her question meant. Pulling the drink closer, I twisted the cap off. "Nothing."

Her lips pressed thin. "It'll come back."

I didn't point out that it had been over seventy-two hours since I'd warped reality. It had only taken forty-eight hours for my magic to return last time. Not a good sign.

"Reality warping must use an insane amount of magical power and effort," she continued in a knowing tone that made me want to believe every word she said. "It makes sense that it would burn out your abilities for a short time. Like overworking a muscle. You just need time to recover."

I nodded, hope battling with the pessimistic fear that my magic was gone forever.

She ate a few mouthfuls of salad. "I have good news, at least."

"Oh?"

"Captain Blythe is back at the precinct, and she submitted all our evidence on Söze's crimes and all of the Crow and Hammer's testimonies to the Judiciary Council. A bunch of other agents also put together reports on Söze's abuses of power."

Yesterday, our intrepid captain had returned home from wherever Darius had hidden her to recover. I hadn't seen her yet, but Lienna had visited to drop off our reports and evidence on Söze's and Kade's craptacular crimes.

"Excellent." I sipped my fizzy drink, and the bubbly sweetness chased away a little of my gloom, like always. "Though I already knew that."

She frowned. "How?"

I tilted my head toward the computer setup. "I asked my rodent pal."

"You mean the mole? You've been chatting with the *mole*?"

"I figured why not. They know who I am, and talking to them gives me an opportunity to suss out their real intentions."

"Their intentions of making money off you by trading MPD secrets, you mean."

I waved my fork. "But remember the note? 'Keep up the good work.' What good work did they mean? They could've been referring to solving Georgia's murder or taking down the Coffer or even working against Söze. We can all agree those are positive things."

She studied her salad, a crease between her brows. I waited for her to berate me for trusting a crooked agent, but she surprised me by dipping her chin in a nod.

"I have my doubts about the mole being anything more than a self-serving information dealer who's abusing their position with the MPD," she said, "but you could be right that there's more to their motivations."

"I'm glad to hear you say that, but I'm also worried."

"Worried?"

"You've been steadfast about ethics since the day we met," I reminded her.

She quirked an eyebrow. "And you've been trying to sway me to the dark side this whole time."

"True."

"I've swayed you toward the side of a law-abiding agent, haven't I?"

"Swayed? More like dragged."

She rolled her eyes. "Well, I still have lines I won't cross. Whether the mole is completely corrupt or only halfway corrupt doesn't matter. But if they're pretending to have morals, we can use that against them to bring them down."

A laugh burst from me. "That's the cutthroat agent of justice I know and love."

Her eyes widened, and she was suddenly very focused on eating. I blinked at her flushed cheeks, then belatedly realized what I'd said. A dozen options whirled through my head—pretend I hadn't said that, change the subject, crack a joke—but I didn't want to avoid the topic now that I'd unintentionally brought it up. I'd halfway confessed while we were handcuffed together, waiting for Kade to murder us. Why not finish the job?

I opened my mouth, but before I could speak, Lienna looked up.

"I talked to my parents."

That derailed my intended and likely embarrassing confession. "How's your dad doing?"

"Not very well." She bit her lip, teeth digging in hard enough to make me wince. "Kit, you were right. This is important to me, even though I have mixed feelings about my dad, and I can't just ignore it."

I set my half-eaten salad aside and braced my elbows on the kitchen island. "Of course not."

She puffed out a breath. "My parents asked me to come home for a while."

I froze in place.

Staring distractedly at her salad, she didn't see my reaction. "The doctors are talking about him needing palliative care, and my mom is struggling to cope. They need me. But ..." She looked up. "But you need me too. We need each other."

I stared into her anxious brown eyes, my brain stuck in a useless "I should have seen that coming" loop.

"I'll go with you," I blurted—but that was the wrong answer. I couldn't run off to LA—not with Kade on the loose, the "Consilium" lurking in the MPD's shadow, a target on Darius's back, and his inexplicable connection to all of this unsolved.

"Kit ..." she whispered.

I rolled my shoulders and tried again. "Do what you need to do, Lienna, and I'll be right here when you get back."

"I should stay. There's too much going on here. It's too dangerous to leave you alone with everything."

I reached across the counter and wrapped my hand around hers. "If you don't go, you might regret it for the rest of your life. Vancouver and LA are only one flight apart. I'll keep you posted on everything, and if you need to come back, you can be here in a day."

She bit down on her lip again, punishing the soft skin. "You aren't upset?"

"No." I withdrew my hand, stared at my salad for a minute, then resumed eating, my thoughts miles away from my taste buds. "I'm not. I promise."

We finished our dinners, our conversation turning to lighter, inconsequential topics. Together, we cleaned the kitchen and loaded our dishes into the dishwasher. Silence fell between us, but it was a comfortable quiet, each of us lost in our thoughts.

As I finished wiping the counter, Lienna hovered nearby, an oddly shy expression on her face. I was highly aware of her nearness as I tossed the dishcloth into the sink and faced her.

"Kit, uh … we could both use some downtime, and … um … the TV setup here is nice."

I nodded at her not-quite-a-suggestion. "Do you want to watch a movie?"

"Sure."

Suppressing a smile, I led the way into the living room and dropped onto the sofa. This was now our fourth movie-watching experience in this spot. As she sat beside me, I couldn't help a grin.

"Remember our first movie here? You were hauling my sorry ass back to lockup and I convinced you to stop for my stuff."

Her smile was soft. "Then you somehow convinced me to watch *Casablanca* with you."

"I think you just felt sorry for me. I remember feeling pretty pathetic, moping about losing my comfortable condo and movie collection."

A movie collection she'd saved for me. Even though we'd barely known each other, she'd gone back for it before my landlord had pitched out all my stuff and put the unit up for sale.

"You were scared to lose your freedom," she murmured. "That's not pathetic. That would scare anyone."

I slouched back into the cushions, pointing the remote at the large flatscreen TV while watching her from the corner of my eye. "I thought you were such a hard-ass back then."

"I am a hard-ass."

"No." I scrolled through streaming apps. "I just hadn't seen your compassion yet. What do you want to watch?"

Pressing her lips together, she pushed to her feet. I half rose, no idea how I'd upset her and ready to beg her not to leave, but she didn't go far. Reaching into her satchel, she pulled out a DVD case, marched right back to me, and held out the movie.

I dropped my gaze from her pink-tinged cheeks to the movie case. Staring up at me was a pair of adolescent Lindsay Lohans with the title splashed between them: *The Parent Trap*.

She didn't need to say anything.

Two minutes later, the opening credits had begun and we were sitting on the sofa side by side, several conspicuous inches between us. But as the compressed love story between Dennis Quaid and Natasha Richardson rolled across the screen, my partner scooted a little closer. Without a word, she tucked herself against my side, her head resting on my shoulder, and I wrapped my arm around her waist, holding her snugly against me.

"Kit," she murmured as we were introduced to a gold-digging Meredith Blake lounging by the pool. "Can I ask … who did you lose to cancer?"

"My foster mom, Gillian. She was the best foster parent I'd ever had. Losing her was …" The sentence caught in my throat and I couldn't finish it. "I was with her for two years, and it ended way too soon."

Too soon to override any of my horrible relationships with foster parents, siblings, authority figures, and human beings in general that had turned me cold and indifferent to the point where working for Rigel hadn't bothered me all that much.

"Tell me about her?" Lienna asked quietly.

I almost refused, but it felt right to tell her. Even though it hurt. Even though it made me miss her, the first person to ever love me, so much that my voice broke. It was worth it because Gillian would've wanted to know Lienna, the second person in the world I'd ever loved.

When I finally fell silent, Lienna was curled up against me, her head on my chest now, ear against my heartbeat. The movie was still playing, but we weren't watching anymore.

"Thank you," she whispered. "I can't … I can't right now, but when I come back, I'll tell you about my childhood too."

I played with the end of her ponytail, running my fingers across the silky strands. "When do you plan to leave?"

She was quiet for a moment. "My mom bought a plane ticket for me. The flight is tomorrow morning."

Her words cut through me. That soon?

"But I'll have them switch it to a later flight. I can't leave until your magic is back."

I tugged her ponytail lightly. "My magic won't show up again any faster or slower with or without company. You don't need to wait around."

"But—"

"Don't waste any time, Lienna. You don't know how much you have left." I brushed my thumb over her cheek. "I'll drive you to the airport in the morning."

"Okay," she whispered.

I pulled her closer, wishing I could keep her beside me all night—and not have to let go in the morning. The prospect of her leaving made me feel like I was standing in an earthquake simulator. From the moment my life had been upheaved— going from Rigel's conman to the MPD's prisoner to a bona fide agent—Lienna had been there.

But family was family, and I'd learned from Gillian that you had to treasure the time you had. Lienna needed to go, and I'd have to deal with whatever happened until she returned.

THE SUN POKING through the blinds woke me the next morning. After a moment of bleary-eyed disorientation, I realized where I was: on the sofa in my condo. Or Blythe's condo. Or whatever. I had a blanket pulled up to my chin and my t-shirt and jeans still on.

We must have fallen asleep after the movie.

We …?

Where was Lienna? I sat up and looked around. No sign of her. The shower wasn't running, and I couldn't hear anything except for the low hum of the fridge in the kitchen.

I checked my watch. It was a little past eight. We should have left an hour ago to get her to the airport in time for her flight to LA.

As soon as I swung my feet off the sofa, I saw the piece of printer paper sitting on the coffee table. I'd read enough of Lienna's reports to instantly recognize her handwriting scrawled across it.

Kit,

Sorry I didn't say goodbye. I'll text you when I arrive in LA. Stay safe.

Lienna

I flipped the note over as though there might be a postscript on the back. Seeing nothing else, my heart sank to the soles of my feet. Even if she hadn't wanted a ride to the airport, she could have woken me long enough to say farewell. We had no idea how long it would be before she returned.

If she returned.

I crushed that thought right out of my brain as I re-read her brief note. My whole relationship with Lienna had been an extended, vacillating game of tug o' war. She would let me draw her close, then pull away with the strength of a hundred Lou Ferrignos. She would kiss me, then ram the "coworkers" label down my throat. She would confide in me about her complicated relationship with her father, then refuse to tell me about his cancer recurrence. She'd shared her favorite movie with me, promised to open up to me about her childhood, fallen asleep in my arms ... then vanished the next morning without a word.

Some days I was so damn certain she was in love with me. Other days I wasn't sure if she even thought about me.

My hands were calloused, and my heart was tired.

I groaned, rubbed my dry eyes, and headed for the kitchen. Some coffee might clear my head. Maybe there was some espresso somewhere and I could whip up a "Sleepy Kit Special," as Lienna had called it.

After I put a pot of joe on, I opened up the fridge to peruse the breakfast options I'd bought yesterday—but my bacon, eggs, fruit, and yogurt weren't front and center on the top shelf like I'd expected. Instead, five Dr. Pepper bottles were lined up in a neat row as though saluting me.

A stupid grin spread across my face. Had Lienna been hauling all of those around in her satchel? And did she think that imbibing gallons of syrupy liquid paradise would restore my psycho-warping abilities?

Of course not. I'd known from the moment she'd handed me the drink last night that it had nothing to do with magic. She'd brought it because she knew I liked it, and she'd thought it might make me feel better.

Just like she knew my "Sleepy Kit Special" order.

And my favorite burger.

Just like she'd photocopied an old MPD file on Lon Chaney for me for no other reason than she'd known I would love it.

Just like she'd rescued my beloved movie collection from my shitty ex-landlord.

I sighed and leaned back against the kitchen island as the light bulb illuminated inside my early morning brain.

Oh, Kit, you emotionally stunted nincompoop.

Lienna might not be prone to grand gestures of romance, bold declarations of love, or late-night deep dives into her personal history, but she had shown me all the time in a hundred little ways that she thought about me, that she paid attention, that she knew me at a level that no one else alive did, and that she cared about me.

Why had I waited until after she was gone to figure this out?

Shaking my head, I closed the fridge. The coffee carafe was half full, and if I hopped in the shower now, it would be done by the time I was toweled off. I stripped out of my shirt and jeans, balling them up and tossing them across the living room toward my bedroom, and I was just about to do the full monty when a knock at the door stopped me.

Did Lienna have a change of heart and come back? Was it Eggert and his bushy mustache, eager to start the day? Had Captain Blythe stopped by to pay me a visit? Oh god, I hoped it wasn't Blythe. I wasn't ready to explain why I was half naked in her kitchen.

Wait. Lienna, Eggsy, and Blythe all had keys. So who the hell was knocking?

Only one way to find out. As another rap sounded against the wood, I eschewed redressing in favor of answering the eager ratta-tatting in nothing but my boxers and socks.

I immediately regretted that choice when I opened the door to find none other than Darius King, fully dressed in an immaculate blue vest/jacket ensemble, on the other side.

"Darius?" I blurted, crossing my arms awkwardly over my chest.

He arched an eyebrow at my partial nudity. "Agent Morris. Am I interrupting?"

"No, no, no." I held the door open for him. "Come on in."

"Thank you."

As he stepped inside, I rushed into the kitchen, nearly skidding into the island on my tractionless socked feet.

"Do you want coffee?" I babbled. "I've got a fresh pot almost ready. Medium roast. Nice and hot."

When I turned around, he was still giving me that amused eyebrow quirk.

"You know what?" I said, forcing a poor approximation of nonchalance into my voice. "I'm gonna grab some pants. Coffee's all yours if you want some."

I scurried toward my balled-up outfit and pulled it on. By the time I returned to the kitchen, Darius had poured each of us a cup of java.

Selecting a mug, I nodded in thanks. "How did you know where to find me?"

"You used to live here, didn't you?"

"Yeah. 'Used to' being the operative words there."

He took a slow sip of his coffee, his expression imbued with flawless silver-fox mystery. "You've had an interesting few days."

"Understatement."

He set his mug down, all traces of amusement leaving his face. "As unpleasant as the reality is, I wouldn't be alive today if not for you and Agent Shen. I was thoroughly unprepared, and that needs to change."

I gave him a questioning look.

Bracing his elbows on the counter, he steepled his fingers together. "Tell me everything."

"Everything?"

"Söze, Kade, Aurelia, the precinct, the murders, the portals, the mole. Everything."

Holy shit, he knew about the mole too?

I studied the man across from me. Darius King. The troublesome GM of a troublesome guild. A former MPD-contracted assassin suspected of murdering half the Supreme Judiciary Court. A master manipulator with a dozen hidden agendas I could guess at and a dozen more I couldn't imagine.

Darius could be helpful or extremely unhelpful depending on the situation. I'd put my faith in his quality of character before, but this was different. He was asking me to divulge information and secrets Blythe had entrusted to me and Lienna alone.

On the other hand, Darius was a key player in all this—and I had no idea how or why. He knew things I didn't. A hell of a lot of important things, I was betting, including the reason Kade had murdered Georgia and Anson.

"If I tell you everything," I said slowly, "you need to do the same. Starting with why you're *numero uno* on the Consilium's hit list."

A breath-stealing chill crystallized in Darius's gray eyes at the word "Consilium." The former assassin smiled, and I had the sudden urge to crawl under the counter and hide.

"That is exactly my plan, Agent Morris. It will take more than either of us can do alone to uproot the Consilium."

"We won't be going at it alone, though," I pointed out. "Lienna and I didn't get all the evidence we wanted, but we pulled together enough of a case that the MPD will launch a big ol' investigation into Söze's actions and whoever was pulling his strings."

"That won't happen. The evidence will disappear. Your witnesses will suffer mysterious deaths. The case will die before it gets anywhere, and no one will ever suspect the depths of the corruption."

A fresh shiver rippled down my spine at the steely certainty in his declaration. "What makes you think that?"

"Because that's what happened last time."

My breath caught in my throat. "Last time?"

"Our goals align, Agent Morris. Together, we might stand a chance."

I leaned forward. "Are you suggesting what I think you're suggesting? As in a full team-up, Tango and Cash style?"

A cool smile curved his lips. "Are you in?"

Tamping down my reflexive excitement, I put my mug to my lips and took the longest sip I could, trying to emulate the mysteriousness with which the GM drank his coffee as I considered all the ramifications of his three-word question. Judging by the steady intensity of his patient gaze, no matter what I answered, it would change my life.

I set my mug down. Braced my hands on the countertop. Released a long, slow exhalation.

"Hell yeah, I'm in."

KIT'S ADVENTURES CONTINUE IN

MAGE ASSASSINS & OTHER MISFITS
THE GUILD CODEX: WARPED / FIVE

The weirdness level of my life has reached an all-time high. Which is saying something, considering I started out as a psychic conman and somehow ended up as a MagiPol agent. And not just any agent. Lately, I've been Captain Blythe's right-hand man and most trusted confidant.

Yeah, I know. Super weird.

It's also kind of awkward, because unbeknownst to her, I've also teamed up with her most loathed nemesis, Darius King, guild master of the Crow and Hammer and the number one guy on the Consilium's "To Be Eliminated" list.

Oh, and the Consilium? It's just a secret organization embedded deep in the upper echelons of the MPD that's using its nefarious influence to take over the world. Or destroy it. We're still figuring that part out.

"We" being me and Blythe. And me and Darius. But not Blythe and Darius. Like I said, it's awkward.

Unfortunately, the Consilium knows we're on to them. It's only a matter of time before they reveal how much power they truly wield— and eliminate all three of us for good.

www.guildcodex.ca

ABOUT THE AUTHORS

ANNETTE MARIE is the best-selling author of The Guild Codex, an expansive collection of interwoven urban fantasy series ranging from thrilling adventure to hilarious hijinks to heartrending romance. Her other works include YA urban fantasy series Steel & Stone, its prequel trilogy Spell Weaver, and romantic fantasy trilogy Red Winter.

Her first love is fantasy, but fast-paced adventures, bold heroines, and tantalizing forbidden romances are her guilty pleasures. She proudly admits she has a thing for dragons and aspires to include them in every book.

Annette lives in the frozen winter wasteland of Alberta, Canada (okay, it's not quite that bad) and shares her life with her husband and their furry minion of darkness—sorry, cat—Caesar. When not writing, she can be found elbow-deep in one art project or another while blissfully ignoring all adult responsibilities.

www.annettemarie.ca

ROB JACOBSEN is a Canadian writer, actor, and director, who has been in a few TV shows you might watch, had a few films in festivals you might have attended, and authored some stories you might have come across. He's hoping to accomplish plenty more by the time he inevitably dies surrounded by cats while watching reruns of Mr. Robot.

Currently, he is the Creative Director of Cave Puppet Films, as well as the co-author of the Guild Codex: Warped series with Annette Marie.

www.robjacobsen.ca

SPECIAL THANKS

Our thanks to Erich Merkel for sharing your exceptional expertise in Latin and Ancient Greek.

Any errors are the authors'.

THE
GUILD CODEX
WARPED

The MPD has three roles: keep magic hidden, keep mythics under control, and don't screw up the first two.

Kit Morris is the wrong guy for the job on all counts—but for better or worse, this mind-warping psychic is the MPD's newest and most unlikely agent.

DISCOVER MORE BOOKS AT
www.guildcodex.ca

THE
GUILD CODEX
SPELLBOUND

Meet Tori. She's feisty. She's broke. She has a bit of an issue with running her mouth off. And she just landed a job at the local magic guild. Problem is, she's also 100% human. Oops.

Welcome to the Crow and Hammer.

DISCOVER MORE BOOKS AT
www.guildcodex.ca

THE
GUILD CODEX
DEMONIZED

Robin Page: outcast sorceress, mythic history buff, unapologetic bookworm, and the last person you'd expect to command the rarest demon in the long history of summoning. Though she holds his leash, this demon can't be controlled.

But can he be tamed?

DISCOVER MORE BOOKS AT
www.guildcodex.ca

THE
GUILD CODEX
UNVEILED

A vigilante witch with a murder conviction, a switchblade for a best friend, and a dangerous lack of restraint. A notorious druid mired in secrets, shadowed by deadly fae, and haunted by his past.

They might be exactly what the other needs—if they don't destroy each other first.

DISCOVER MORE BOOKS AT
www.guildcodex.ca

STEEL & STONE

When everyone wants you dead, good help is hard to find.

The first rule for an apprentice Consul is *don't trust daemons*. But when Piper is framed for the theft of the deadly Sahar Stone, she ends up with two troublesome daemons as her only allies: Lyre, a hotter-than-hell incubus who isn't as harmless as he seems, and Ash, a draconian mercenary with a seriously bad reputation. Trusting them might be her biggest mistake yet.

GET THE COMPLETE SERIES
www.annettemarie.ca/steelandstone

SPELL WEAVER

The only thing more dangerous than the denizens of the Underworld … is stealing from them.

As a daemon living in exile among humans, Clio has picked up some unique skills. But pilfering magic from the Underworld's deadliest spell weavers? Not so much. Unfortunately, that's exactly what she has to do to earn a ticket home.

GET THE COMPLETE TRILOGY
www.annettemarie.ca/spellweaver

A destiny written by the gods. A fate forged by lies.

If Emi is sure of anything, it's that *kami*—the gods—are good, and *yokai*—the earth spirits—are evil. But when she saves the life of a fox shapeshifter, the truths of her world start to crumble. And the treachery of the gods runs deep.

This stunning trilogy features 30 full-page illustrations.

GET THE COMPLETE TRILOGY

www.annettemarie.ca/redwinter

Made in United States
North Haven, CT
31 August 2023

40976426R10178